The Stranger Within

A NOVEL BY

Nanette M. Buchanan

Copyright 2014 by Nanette M. Buchanan

Type of Work: Fiction
Published Date: March 2014
13: 978-0-979-3883-8-5
10: 0-9793883-8-4
Cover Design: I Pen Books/Fideli Publishing

I Pen Books

www.NanetteMBuchanan.com

PRINTED IN THE UNITED STATES OF AMERICA.

Acknowledgements

I am humbled that my writing has not become a fly-by-night adventure, or a temporary fix; the prelude to a fantasy. God has seen fit to bless and fulfill my fantasy and it is to Him; I give the praise and honor.

To my family, there is nothing more important for an author than support. There is nothing more important to me than your love. I can feel your spirit, your smile, and your touch each time I write. I don't have much to give and what I have given has come from my heart…thank you for allowing me to share with you my intimate thoughts and writing.

To my readers, reviewers, book clubs, stores and distributors… Thank you. Thank you for walking the walk with me no matter what the beat or tune. You are an intricate part of this path of freedom in this walk through literacy that I have chosen. My journey will always be worth the travel because you all have made my dream come true.

To my son-in-law Dekese, I can't tell you how this story tore at my soul as I developed each character. The basis that you gave, the problem that you wanted to be in the spotlight brought so many other issues to the forefront. I welcomed the challenge. Thank you for the opportunity to pen your vision, your thoughts. This is a story that needs to be told.

Thank you all for your support…
It is because of you all that I Pen.

Forward

The Stranger Within… *tells of the internal struggles of two victims of abuse. Brenda and Dominique Preston represent many mothers and daughters who become strangers to themselves and others. When fears are internalized eventually they will erupt. The ripple effect of abuse goes beyond the interior walls of any home and often cripples the support from others as well. The Stranger Within answers the call of the victim, a desperate need to survive.*

One

The rain drops upon her bedroom window were no longer soothing. The comforting sound she once welcomed during a storm was now an annoyance. Dominique Preston was beginning to think her workload was now becoming a serious problem. She couldn't remember the last night she slept peacefully.

It was the pre-holiday season and her trips to the city left her more than fatigued. As a Merchandiser for Macy's it was a part of her daily routine. The red neon light on her alarm clock read two o'clock. The tunes from WBLS would be bouncing off her bedroom walls in four hours.

Reluctantly, she sat up repositioning the pillows and comforter. The dim glow from the street light peered through the sheer curtains and shades. Dominique allowed herself to fall into the newly fluffed cushions. She knew immediately that the prepared surface would soon become uncomfortable. She had been tossing and turning since the eleven o'clock news. She was kidding herself thinking it was her days that caused this insomnia. She refused to get up as she had the past two nights. She thought about the remedies her mother suggested whenever she couldn't sleep while living at home.

Brenda Preston thought her daughter should have stayed home, although her paycheck was more than enough to support her independent living expenses. Dominique inherited the home her mother was raised in after the death of her aunt, Moreen Carter. Her great aunt died after an aneurysm leaving what she had to Brenda and Dominique. She had no children of her own and Dominique's mother refused to live at the home with mixed memories. Moreen's great niece finally moved, got settled, and now two months later couldn't sleep.

During her teenage years, Dominique suffered from recurring nightmares. She had been through "night fright" episodes as a child and periodically took medication for relief. She didn't dream as much as she had in the past, but she now was finding it hard to sleep through the night. She knew the dreams would be returning. In college during her junior year, she suffered for two months resorting to sleep aids and wine.

Sleep wasn't her only problem, and it was nights like this that her mind drifted to self-evaluation. Dominique Preston was twenty-four, single, and her mother's only child. She grew up in East Orange, New Jersey before it began to look like an urban suburb. She went to East Orange High School, graduated, and staying local, went to Montclair State College for business. There wasn't much more. There was no lover, no boyfriend, and she wasn't gay. Her social life held no fantastic moments, but she was satisfied.

Love never was a priority. Her friends were few in numbers, and no one, including Claudia her coworker, would be claimed as a close friend. Lawrence Boatright, the perfect picture of a man, was mistakenly identified as her boyfriend, fiancé, and her man over the years. Neither of them bothered to correct the rumors. Boat, his nickname since their high school days, wished the 5'6" beauty would give him a chance. Dominique, who he affectionately called Dommi, enjoyed his company but didn't allow their friendship to be spoiled with the talk of a serious relationship.

He understood her need for space as well as he understood her late-night calls. They were completely honest with each other, which made him the only man she trusted. They were intimate frequently over the years, but she never thought of it being much more than physical satisfaction. She didn't require his commitment, but he gave it freely as he did his love.

Now starring at the ceiling, she regretted telling him she didn't want company for the evening. He would have held her. The warmth from his body would have lulled her into a few hours of needed sleep. She would definitely invite him to stay until Saturday. He could bring his clothes, as he often did, one of the reasons she enjoyed living in her own place. This weekend she would tell him her sleepless nights were returning.

Her mother wouldn't be consoling. The topic of her sleep habits, and other insecurities, were camouflaged with hugs and reassurance that God would make a way. Dominique didn't understand the miracles that allowed her mother to sleep. After the death of her father, there had been no male in their home. Dominique couldn't remember the last male guest Brenda had. Her father's brothers, maybe Randall and Kendall Stevenson, and of course, Pastor Turner; none of them counted as guests. The Stevenson brothers were the sons of Estelle Stevenson.

Though both men vied for Brenda's affection, Brenda chose Randall to date years after her husband passed. It didn't stop Kendall from trying to be more than a friend. Ms. Stevenson thought the widow was a little too lonely. Brenda and Randall's relationship ended soon after it started. Kendall didn't visit as often, and their friendship became distant. They were treated as extended family members, visiting more during the day.

The schedule set by her mother was rigid, and most men weren't free to come and go as they wanted. Brenda kept the gossip down in the church by following the advice of Estelle, who had no prospects for a husband. Dominique couldn't recall anyone staying much past dinner and never was there a guest for breakfast.

Brenda Preston was pretty and petite. Her nickname for years was "Tiny". The softness of her voice attracted the men to her. Although she avoided being the center of attention, it didn't stop the Deacons and men from the church from openly complimenting her appearance, fragrance, and beautiful smile. She took on the position as Church Secretary at Faith Temple, and no one questioned her reasons for spending so much time at the church. She was a widow, but she wasn't looking for a husband. When Dominique was young, all of them would offer to fill in the position of father or uncle reminding Brenda that she was depriving her child the privilege of having a male figure in her life. None of them knew Pastor Jacob Turner spent many days at their East Orange home.

Dominique began to nod. She couldn't remember when her thoughts ended and when sleep began. When the music blasted, she hit the snooze button and pulled the comforter over her head.

Two

Lawrence snatched his jacket from the back of his kitchen chair. He glanced at the clock on the wall realizing if he didn't leave at that very minute he would be stuck in the traffic on Route 280 leading to Newark. His office was located in the Outpatient Mental Health Clinic on William Street. As a Counselor, his morning began at seven thirty. His clients usually were there waiting when he arrived. He pulled out of his parking space at seven and prayed he would beat the morning rush.

It wasn't long before the cars began to slow down on the crowded highway. He looked at his console and took a deep breath. If he made his usual stop at Dunkin Donuts, he would be late. He heard the familiar muffled tone of his cell phone. Reaching in his pocket for his Bluetooth and turning down the radio, he answered trying to disguise his frustration.

"Yeah, what's up?"

"Nothing, are you on your way?" The question brought a grin to his grimaced face. Eric Flanders worked at the office with him and drove through the city to avoid the traffic Lawrence met daily. Although his distance was longer, coming from Hillside into Newark, he often got to work sooner.

"Listen, don't talk smack this morning. I got a late start. I'm on my way."

"Well I'm almost there. Listen coffee on me. I stopped to get bagels for that meeting at eight. How's Dominique?"

"I guess she's alright. Why?"

"Just asking, listen, don't forget to ask her about Saturday. I've got to get tickets for you if you're going."

"I didn't even mention it when I saw her."

"Are you sure you and her… aren't an item?"

"I told you we weren't, you and Stacy keep insisting we are."

"Stacy believes you are or will be. Female intuition I guess, anyway, the show should be nice. Stacy and Dominique get along. Pam and a few others from the office are going. Besides, it's the last cruise up the Hudson for the season. It'll be cold soon."

"Yeah, what are you guys doing for the weekend?"

"No plans yet; is the traffic moving?"

"By inches; I can see the exit though. I should be there in a few."

"Alright man, I'll see you then. I'll have your coffee."

"Thanks man."

Eric and Lawrence met when they started their jobs as interns. They both were new in the field. They looked forward to assisting with the evaluations of the clients sent to them through Social Services. They were friends since their first day at the job. It seemed Eric always knew when to step in offering options for the clients. Lawrence was the realist, and Eric needed him to add stability to his sporadic moments of anger both on and off the job. He was the ear for many of his friends, including Dominique. He noticed how close he was to the exit and put on his indicator. The rhythmic ticking reminded him his radio was near inaudible. He turned up the volume and sped up to catch the light at the next corner.

Arriving at the office ten minutes late, he nodded good morning to Pam, the receptionist who smiled while handing him his list of clients. He could have recited the list since he made the appointments himself. As promised, the coffee was on his desk and a note reminding him to ask Dominique about Saturday. Eric's question regarding the status of their relationship was haunting him. He couldn't help but think how many of the other co-workers who saw him and Dominique together thought he was wasting his time. He often wondered, maybe it was time to move on. He was scared to lose a good friend. It was a risk he wasn't willing to take.

Asking himself questions, he tucked away the thoughts again. He'd give her another hint after the show on Saturday.

A few of his other friends, including Pam, openly said he was a good catch and needed to leave the sistah with the "issues" alone. He knew Pam's comments came after she realized he was the new prospect for the women in their Division. Although she took a step back, he knew she was waiting in the wings for a sign that he was open to a relationship. Pam was no comparison to Dominique in personality or looks. She was a professional on the job, but Lawrence had seen her alter ego at a few of the office outings. After a few drinks, she was more carefree than he liked a woman to be. His discussion about mixing dating with working went around the office, and soon after she refrained from mentioning the things she could teach the new intern.

Lawrence took a sip of his coffee and went to the door nodding to Pam for the first client of the day. She stood smoothing her "A" line dress slowly and deliberately. He was sure her hand motion was meant to be enticing. Her hourglass shape gained his approval, but he didn't grin until her back was turned. She summoned the first client on the list. It was near eleven before he came to confirm there were empty chairs in the waiting area.

"Pam, I'm out for an hour."

"Lunch?"

"Yeah. Any calls?"

"No. Oh wait, Claudia called. She said for you to call her."

"Thanks."

Pam cut her eyes letting him know she wasn't found of giving him the message. She watched him as he went back in his office. The man was a gem. His features would never be the cover of any model magazine, but his personality and clean appearance taunted the females who worked there. None were a part of his world beyond the four o'clock hour. He did take them to lunch, usually with Eric and other counselors. He was always the gentleman, but Pam couldn't put her finger on what made him tick. She knew he wasn't gay, unless he was down lower than the group that the office rumors spoke about. Pam was determined to change his mixing business with pleasure rules.

She was perfect for the job she held. She ran the unit and dispersed the work fairly to the counselors. She was a perfectionist and more than confident about her skills on and off the job. She just wasn't the type of woman he was attracted to, or so he said. This became a challenge for her, and she made an attempt daily.

"Boat?"

He stopped as he was passing her desk.

"Yeah, oh I'm sorry. Did you want anything?"

She wanted to answer him emphatically, *"You on whole wheat."* Instead, she continued with her question. "No, thanks, are you going to Eric's party Saturday?"

"I thought it was just a thing up the Hudson?"

"No, I think he's asking Stacy to marry him. So I guess if she says yes it will be a celebration."

"Yeah, I guess I'll have to now. Wow, Eric married. Strange huh, wow, be back; see you after lunch."

Pam watched him open the glass office door and stand waiting at the elevator. She really wanted to ask if he was coming to the party alone.

The lunch crowd hadn't joined the traffic of shoppers on Washington Street. Lawrence dialed Claudia's number as he turned the corner heading for the deli on Branford Place. He heard her familiar Beyonce' tune indicating she was unavailable. He closed his phone not leaving a message. The thought crossed his mind to call Dominique, but as he approached the entrance of deli, the aroma of the food took over his senses.

He placed his order and took his seat. He ordered the same sandwich he ate at least once a week, pastrami on rye with mustard and melted cheese. Looking at his watch, he decided he had more than enough time to take a seat in the booth near the window. Pam did him a favor ending his morning appointments earlier than usual.

The deli buzzed with chatter and laughter as the booths filled quickly with customers. Eric walked toward the podium pointing to the seat across from Lawrence. Lawrence waved him on, and the waitress nodded as he proceeded to his seat.

"I thought you had a client at eleven thirty?"

"I waited fifteen minutes; she didn't show. She'll be there when I get back ruining my afternoon schedule."

The waitress brought over a menu. She stood waiting as Eric eyed the selections.

"Corn beef and pastrami on whole wheat, mustard, and add Swiss cheese please."

"What do you want to drink?"

"Coke."

"Yours will be out soon." The waitress said to Lawrence. She paused waiting for him to notice her. He watched as she sashayed with Eric's order in hand. He knew she was smiling with each step.

"Boat, man she tries you every week. Tap that and get it over with."

"Ain't nothing to her man, we leave and the next brotha that sits here will get the same show. I'm good."

"So you called Dommi?"

"No, she's probably at lunch with a buyer or something. I spoke to her yesterday, but you know how that ended."

"Explain that shit. You take her out and get sent home for the night. Man, I still think you're wasting your time."

"Maybe, maybe not; she's a good woman. They're hard to find."

"No, a good man is hard to find, and you're wasting your good man time on her. Do you know how many women I've watched you turn away?"

"Alright enough about my love life; what's up with you? Marriage bells ringing; when were you going to tell me?"

"Pam right, she can't keep her mouth shut. I wanted it to be a surprise."

"To who, me?"

"Everybody, man I might change my mind. This isn't the first time I thought about it."

"So you're not ready then."

"Oh I'm ready. She's the one."

"So you ask her and then what?"

"She'll know I'm serious."

"Does she want to get married?"

"I hope so. I mean she says it's what she wants. Man, I don't know what she really wants."

"Don't do it."

"Don't do what?"

"Man, wait until you're sure."

"Shit then I'll be like you."

Three

Claudia waited until three o'clock to call Dominique. It was the third time in two weeks that she had called and said; she just wasn't feeling well. Her friend was going through something, and she didn't know how to help her. The phone rang three times and went into her recorded response. Boat hadn't left a message when he called. She wasn't able to reach either of them. She wondered if they had taken the day off. She would be off in an hour and as the minutes ticked away, she could feel her anxiety building.

Claudia worked with Dominique at Macy's. As a buyer, she worked closely with the Merchandisers but Dominique was special to her and the department. She had an eye for hot buys and a personable demeanor with the clients. They all noticed when Ms. Preston wasn't around. The calls had been few, and the fall previews were due to display before the end of the month. Not being able to wait any longer for her phone to ring; Claudia left her office at three forty five. Dominique would have to get mad. She was definitely going to pay her a visit.

The ride on the subway was uneventful. Claudia would have to tell Dominique they should leave a little early every day to avoid the new sideshows. Her feet throbbed, indicating it was past the time of needed release. In her haste, she forgot her "traveling slides" she would put on at four before leaving the office. Most of the women who traveled by public transportation carried a second pair of shoes. Dominique and Claudia carried their "traveling slides" unless they dressed down and wore their sneakers.

The travel took the usual time with no rush hour delay. Claudia walked toward her car that was at Penn Station in Newark. She was glad she could beat the downtown traffic. She decided to call Lawrence again before going to Dominique's house. She didn't want to be an annoyance, but the feeling that something was wrong wouldn't leave her spirit.

"Boat, its Claudia." She could hear the sound of traffic. She put her ear close to the phone instead of using the Bluetooth.

"Hey Lady, I'm sorry I didn't get back to you. My day was filled. What's up?" A horn honked, causing Lawrence to come to a sudden stop. The driver gave him a mumbled curse as he allowed the car to pass.

"You still near the job?"

"I made a stop," he replied wondering why she asked.

"Have you heard from Dommi? I tried calling her all day. Boat, there's something wrong, or maybe I'm just paranoid. She's been overly tired."

Lawrence was unsure what Claudia was trying to say. Dominique spoke often about her friendship with Claudia. Lawrence wasn't sure he should mention his concerns about Dominique's lack of sleep.

"Hello?"

"Yeah, yeah, I hear you. Listen, it's hard to hear you in this traffic. Let me get in my car. Are you headed home?"

"I was going to check on her if you hadn't heard from her."

Lawrence didn't think dropping in on her unannounced would bring a friendly welcome. "I'll go. I'm closer to her house or are you on your way already."

Claudia paused before answering wondering what he was hiding.

"Well call me please, and let me know."

"No problem. Give me an hour or so with her."

"Boat, please don't forget."

It was his turn to hesitate. He refrained from making a sarcastic comment. "Yes ma'am."

"Seriously, she may be coming down with something or worse."

"I'm not gonna ask what would be worse," Lawrence said as he opened his car door. He was glad to get out of the wind that made it hard to hear. He was now more interested in the conversation. The sound of Claudia's car engine in the background interrupted his questions.

Claudia spoke first. "Go ahead I'll wait for your call." The phone went dead. Lawrence decided he would prepare himself for the worse. He scanned the satellite stations, deciding he didn't need the afternoon talk on WBLS or KISS FM. The thirty-minute ride would be filled with a mixture of Classic Soul, as the red light on the radio indicated.

Pulling into her driveway, parking behind her Honda, Lawrence noticed the wind had blown the trashcans around. They no longer lined the side of her house. He got out of the car and did her the favor of putting them in their place and locking the wheels. It was a definite sign she hadn't left her home. Lawrence often stayed overnight on days of trash removal. When he didn't Dominique would lock the wheels, keeping her cans from rolling down the driveway.

The side door opened quickly, causing him to look up from his task. "Hey Lady."

Dominique stood in the partially opened door and gave him a nod of acknowledgement. "What brings you here?"

"Your trashcans, they were about to roll away."

"Yeah right, your way home is not on this side of town."

"Who said I was on my way home?"

Dominique sighed, too tired to continue the game. She left the door opened allowing her guest to follow her into the house. "Put the lock on the door please."

He entered, doing as she requested. The kitchen was huge with the counter bordering it entirely. The oak cabinets and granite countertop was accented by the flooring. The house was renovated prior to Dominique's occupying the moderate living quarters. The home had three bedrooms. She used one as what she called her dressing room. A beautiful vanity, full-length mirrors, and all of her facial and hair care necessities filled the room. The shoe racks and shelves for her matching handbags adorned one wall. Throughout the house was black art, chosen by her and her mother.

The furnishings were modern contemporary, but it spoke volumes as a match with the accessories she purchased from Macy's. She was grateful for their discounts.

She sat at the kitchen table where it became obvious to Lawrence, she had been working most of the day. He pulled out a chair and joined her.

"So, what's up? No work today?"

"I overslept again. Boat, I actually slept until two o'clock this afternoon."

"Well you've been saying you were tired. So you made up for it."

"You know better than that. I won't be able to sleep tonight, and this mess will still be on my back tomorrow. I've got to get my sleep pattern in line. I can't keep missing work to sleep and then go for two or three days waiting for it to happen again."

"Dommi, did you talk to your doctor? Did you try the p.m.'s?"

"I don't want to get hooked on those damn things again, and I don't want to sleep drunk every night." She softened her tone. "I didn't call the doctor."

"Why?" Lawrence asked remembering Claudia warned him it could be worse.

"Boat, suppose something is wrong with me. I mean I've had this for years. Maybe I'm suffering from some type of serious disorder."

"You won't know until you visit a doctor. Did you ask your mother about what they said it was when you were younger?"

"That's the other thing. She doesn't like to talk about it for some reason. What that's about, I'll never understand. It's like I'm making too much about it. She doesn't know what I'm going through. She gets her sleep on, believe me."

"So how long has it been this time?"

"I took off two days this week, and I used 'No Doz' during the day all last week. It seems like my clock is backwards. I can sleep during the day. It's just at night things bother me."

"Maybe you need to see a doctor. Maybe a Psych or …."

"So you think I'm crazy?"

"No, not at all, you're cranky, tired, beautiful…"

"Boat, be serious."

"I am serious. You're beautiful with bags under your eyes, your hair all over your head, and girl I'm loving that outfit."

His comment brought laughter for them. Her baggy lounge wear was an old tee shirt with faded letters and a pair of sweat pants. She had on thick socks that fell loosely around her ankles. She hadn't thought about her outfit. It was too late to care.

"Just think about it. Maybe seeing a doctor or a therapist could have the answer you need. But you don't need to keep on going this way, eventually you'll get sick."

"And lose my job." Dominique let out the tension of the last few days. She was exhausted.

"Did you call off this morning?"

"I called. I'm taking off the rest of the week to get myself together. Boat, I've got to get it together. I feel like I'm losing it."

Tears began to roll down her face. It was then, that Lawrence realized; this was the worse.

Four

Brenda checked over the dates on the calendar. She was right when she told Deacon Pratt that they booked the wedding for Sister Smith's daughter and the speaking engagement for Pastor Turner on the same day. Now she would have to call and make apologies for the mistake. The Pastor wouldn't mind changing the date for his sermon during the recital for Chapel Hill Church in Philadelphia. There would be a problem if the Ministerial Staff couldn't make the change.

The recital was more than three months away. She was sure they would accommodate Pastor Turner's schedule. She would remind Deacon Pratt again that before any scheduling, he should check the calendar kept in the main office. She made herself a note, a reminder to speak with him in the morning.

She left the main office and pulled the door close, careful to leave it partially open, so she could hear the phone if it rang. Brenda continued with her end of the day ritual. There was mail that hadn't been picked up scattered on the table in the foyer. She took a moment to sort it again into neat piles. It would soon be time to leave; she knew the mail would still be there in the morning.

Brenda checked the other offices ensuring the lights and computers were off. The sound of Pastor Turner's voice caused her to pause waiting to hear a second voice answer his questions.

"Not a problem, I'll give the information to Sister Preston. Yes, yes I understand totally. Thank you so much and I'm sorry about the confusion."

Brenda could tell from the conversation, Pastor had made contact with Chapel Hill. She shook her head, aggravated that he would have to make the call to reschedule his sermon. As quickly as she thought about it, she dismissed it. Pastor handled it. She learned over the years not to dwell long on the problems others created. Pastor Turner helped her through those years when she worried about every problem, both large and small.

There was no way to define her relationship with Jacob Turner. They were friends for most of her adult years. She met him at a party given by a mutual friend. Brenda and Dominique's father, Zeke were introduced to the man who was leaving at the end of the summer for theological studies in Philadelphia.

Brenda walked into the next room. She checked the magazines, putting them back on the tables and paused in deep thought gazing out of the large bay window. The visitor's sitting room was where she often fell into her memories from a time that was.

The party was a surprise for a friend. Neither Brenda nor Jacob could recall her by name. They both were guests of other people. Zeke, as usual, became argumentative and loud. Brenda was ready to leave. His accusations about her and the men who were in attendance had become vulgar. The nods and smiles, as she tried to explain, were all cordial. Jacob's smile from across the room was the only gesture she wasn't sure of. She prayed Zeke hadn't seen it. The young couple had been together off and on since high school, and she knew his jealousy would cause a fight.

Zeke snapped. He pushed Brenda back on the couch when she tried to leave with him. His harsh words let the young crowd know he thought she, and Jacob had been sleeping together behind his back. Brenda was paralyzed by his words hoping she could disappear without anyone noticing. The silence brought on by Zeke's outburst broke when the whispers and laughter around the room increased. It was a matter of minutes, but it seemed like eternity.

Brenda waited until she was no longer under an imaginary spotlight to attempt to leave the room. Jacob noticed her as she eased through the crowd heading toward the apartment door. He followed her, and as he often told her later in their friendship, he thought Zeke might have been waiting for her outside. Their friendship started from that night and lasted longer than her marriage to Zeke. Jacob went on to become a minister and never married. Brenda often thought what it would be like to be the minister's wife. After Zeke's death, his murder, she couldn't bring herself to marry or date again. Their friendship would have to be enough.

"Tiny, are you ready to leave?" Jacob called from his office. She didn't answer, and his entrance into the room startled her. "Are you okay? You're not worrying about that mistake with the schedule are you?"

"Oh no, I was just reminiscing." She turned and smiled at her friend. "Good memories."

"Must be, you're smiling. Are you done in here?" He scanned the room looking for items she would deem out of place.

"Jacob, Dominique is having trouble sleeping again."

"Is that what you were thinking about?"

"No, but I guess my thoughts would have led to it. I thought she got over her father's death. You know those dreams, and her sleepless nights began after the murder."

"Is she remembering anything?"

"No, but what am I going to say when she does?"

Five

Boat ordered the next round of drinks. Eric's proposal was a complete surprise to Stacy. Everyone teased the couple saying she gave him an ultimatum. Stacy and Dominique left the men at the table to walk to the ladies' room and mingle through the crowd. The weather was more than perfect for an early fall night.

The temperature and humidity allowed the women to feel free to comb their wisps of hair without the threat of a deflated hairdo. Reapplying their lipstick and checking themselves in the mirror, they nodded their approvals and left the bathroom. Periodically, they paused to speak to the other guests who wanted to congratulate Stacy. Eric was sitting at the table alone when they returned.

"Everything okay ladies? Boat went to speak to some friends he spotted."

"This is really nice Eric. I didn't know you could throw parties on these boats." Dominique loved his initiative, impressed she looked around taking it all in.

"Eric knows someone; I'm sure of it." Stacy smiled hoping Eric would admit he didn't make the arrangements by himself. She didn't want to gloat only to find out someone else made the arrangements for the beautiful evening.

"Listen, it doesn't matter. Stacy, are you enjoying yourself, you Dommi?" Their comments made him feel uneasy, a mood he didn't want to cloud the evening. The women, sipping their drinks could only smile. Stacy stood and put out her hand for Eric to join her on the dance floor. The D.J. started his session with "All I Do" by Stevie Wonder. The two got up and their bodies blended with the other dancers on the floor. Dominique looked through the couples hoping Boat would make it to the table before the end of the song. She picked up her glass and leaned back in her seat taking in the moment.

Boat smiled, pleased Eric's invitation was accepted by Westlene, and that she had made it to the party. They picked up their conversation where they dropped it earlier in the day. She patted his hand softly before she answered his question.

"She has to want my help my friend. I can't just give my opinion by sight; I must sit with her. Learn more about her. These things you may not know about her. They may be things the lady does not want you to know."

Her Haitian accent gave her words a sexy overtone, a tone he was now accustomed to after working with her for more than a year. Westlene worked with clients that suffered from clinical depression. Most of her clients found they had deep-rooted problems that they needed to face as a first step to recovery. She and Eric shared offices at the clinic. Boat often talked with her about Dominique's sleepless nights unbeknownst to Dominique.

"I don't want her to know I spoke with you."

"Dis' cannot be easy on her. Introduce me and we'll see what the spirit says to me."

"I don't want you reading her palm."

"I'm aware of what you want my friend, but it is not in your power to stop what her spirit may want. Boat, I am a professional, no?"

"Yes, you are."

"Thank you and leave this to me. You go back to your seat. I will stop at your table, and we'll talk later about dis' thing you call a problem."

"Westlene, she's not a client."

Westlene leaned forward waiting for Boat's ear to meet her lips. Her locs fell upon her face adding cover for her words. "She's a dreamer and that makes her interesting to me."

Boat leaned back puzzled at her words. Her eyes closed as though she drifted into a trance. She opened her hazel eyes and smiled. Her dark skin and full lips didn't match the eyes that most would say was the stolen beauty from a woman of a lighter hue. Her eyes reminded him of a black cat's, beautiful and full of mystery.

"I don't want her to be a project Westlene. She's my friend, a good friend."

"You love her Boat, I know. I will do my best. Go now, I will come to your table before the night is over."

The D.J. kept the floor filled with couples. They showed their appreciation to the pumping of the rhythmic mixtures and beats. It was nearing ten o'clock when the band returned to the makeshift stage. As the lead singer took the microphone, the couples returned to their seats and the crowded bar. Boat guided Dominique to her seat. Pam brushed past him before he could sit down.

"Save me a dance pretty boy." He turned to give her a bit of sarcasm but she turned quickly leaving only the scent of her perfume. The odor caused his body to react. He couldn't help but think they should get together at least once. He immediately shook the thought realizing the Grey Goose was affecting his judgment. He took his seat and noticed Dominique's questionable look.

"What?"

"You tell me. I see Pam is at it again."

"Baby Pam is Pam, you know that." Boat answered confused by Dominique wanting to play the jealous girlfriend. He had been staying at her place since Wednesday but they hadn't been intimate. She did catch up on her sleep during the day while he was working, but the nights were more than she could handle. After tossing and turning or waking up screaming they both agreed she needed professional help.

The vessel made its turn in the middle of the Hudson River and began the return trip to the dock. Westlene approached the table of friends when she noticed the seat next to Dominique was available. Eric and Pam were in a heated discussion about relationships, one that held no interest for Boat, Stacy or Dominique. Pam's escort for the evening found it more entertaining to mingle with the other guests leaving her and her friends for most of the evening.

Pam paused mid-sentence after she spotted the tall slender beauty approaching. Westlene's mystic personality demanded an instant reaction from the men around, one Pam loathed. She excused herself walking past Westlene without speaking.

"The two of you still at it?" Eric asked, making light of the obvious conflict between the women.

Westlene ignored the question giving him a glowing smile instead. "Eric congratulations to you and Ms. Stacy. How are you?"

Stacy, who met Westlene during the summer, greeted her with a smile and thank you. "Won't you sit down? Westlene have you met Dominique? She's a friend of ours, more so Boat's."

Boat was grateful, Westlene had perfect timing. Stacy's introduction helped explain her presence. Dominique wouldn't suspect he led Westlene her way.

"Dominique, what a beautiful name, I'm pleased to meet you. May I?"

"Please, certainly." Dominique moved her seat over giving enough room for Westlene to sit in the chair next to hers.

"Well this looks like a ladies moment, Eric let's grab another drink. Are you ladies good, can we get you anything?"

"No thanks", chimed the women.

Six

The next few weeks went by quickly, although the nights seemed longer than the days. Dominique became annoyed when she stayed home. She would toss and turn in her bed during the day. She thought about going back to the doctor her mother and Pastor Turner suggested for sleeping aids. She had begun to dream more often.

The shadowed figures, their actions and her fears were the same each night. Boat stayed with her whenever she requested. He even suggested that she considered staying with him a few nights out of the week. Nothing helped; she still had the nightmares. Now, close to midnight, she was scared to close her eyes.

The phone rang causing her to jump. She couldn't imagine who the unidentified caller would be. She used the remote to turn the volume down on the television.

"Hello?"

"Hey, you're still up?" It was Claudia. Dominique took a deep breath before answering. She had avoided Claudia's concern at the job. She really didn't want her co-worker to be so involved in her personal problems. She needed to vent though, Claudia must have known she needed a friend.

"What's up with you calling so late?"

"I'm sorry, but Dommi, you're scaring me. I've known you for more than five years and we work well together but you don't look like you usually do and…"

"I know, and I'm sorry. Claudia, I don't know what to say. I don't know what's happening with me. I'm having a break down or something, I just don't know." Tears began to flow; she wiped her face and continued. "I know I should have treated you better. You've been a friend and I've been trying to stay away from our friendship. A friendship I need. Claudia I'm sorry."

"Why, for what? Girl you're just private. I'm okay with that. But there's more to it than that Dommi. Have you been to the doctor? You said you haven't been sleeping much. You need to check that out. Maybe it's your diet or…"

"It's nightmares. I've been having them for years. I was on medication when I was younger, then they went away. Claudia, the same thing keeps happening in my dreams, but it feels so real. Like I'm right there or I was there. I just can't see what it is, and I wake up screaming, crying, and sweating."

"Talk to a doctor Dommi. You're driving yourself crazy. You can't keep going on like this."

"I know." Her eyes caught a glimpse of the brochure she picked up on the cruise up the Hudson. She lifted it, remembering Westlene. Her business card fell to the table. She flipped the card through her fingers as she listened to Claudia.

"Try to get some sleep. Are you coming to work tomorrow?"

"Yeah, life goes on. I'll take your words as advice. I've got some p.m. medication that works sometime. I'll pop them tonight. I'll be okay."

"Talk to your mom, maybe she knows something that you don't. Maybe something that happened when you were little that scared you."

The card read *"Westlene Adashay Dream Interpreter"*. Dominique tapped the card on the table. "Claudia, you're right. It's something that happened and it's happening again in my dreams. I've got someone to call tomorrow and then I'll talk with my mom."

Seven

Brenda checked the oven and then the clock. Her dinner was almost prepared; it was close to six. She told Pastor to come by at six thirty. Dominique called that morning repeating the torment she suffered over the past month. Her sleepless nights were worse than ever. Boat had begun staying with her more often. Brenda didn't condone her daughter's choice to have a man in her bed at night, but she understood her fear.

Dominique mentioned the shadows, she couldn't quite make out any familiar faces or places in the dream. It was just as it had been in the past. Her mother remembered the endless appointments with therapists, psychiatrists, and out-patient care. The options for Dominique ranged from her being heavily sedated at night, to commitment in an institution. There was no option that satisfied Brenda. She did as she believed. Prayer worked, her daughter would get over it; they would be just fine.

When the news of Zeke's murder gave rise to questions and rumors, Jacob and the church members helped the widow and her daughter find a new home. Neither would live peacefully with Zeke's spirit in the house where he was killed. The dreams seemed to occur less.

During Dominique's college years she didn't have many complaints about her sleeping, unless it was related to late night study. Brenda thought college life had filled her daughter's hours with better memories to reflect on when she became an adult. After her call, Brenda panicked. She didn't know what else to do but call Jacob. He would be able to calm her nerves with his comforting words. He had been there in the past and promised he would see her through her troubles. Trouble was stirring again.

Pastor Turner was sitting at his desk hesitant about leaving. Brenda sounded as she had years ago when Zeke's murder was haunting her conscious. There wasn't much he could do to comfort her. He would listen and be a shoulder for her to cry on. It took months before she would stop blaming herself. Zeke wasn't a loving husband and he definitely was not a doting father. After their initial meeting Jacob became a close friend of Brenda's. He was convinced she would leave Zeke and they would become an item, but Zeke's charm was more than Jacob was willing to offer. As a man destined to become a minister, he didn't lead a flashy life. He continued to offer her a sincere friendship. Jacob was in love, but his love for the ministry meant so much more.

Jacob left, went to college, and lost the girl he loved to an abuser. He returned after his freshman year hoping to pick up their relationship and convince her to leave Zeke. He was sure after their conversations Brenda would leave him and his abusive ways. Brenda said she was in love, and was willing to marry Zeke. Jacob couldn't convince her that the abuse she suffered would continue. They stayed in touch throughout his college years without Zeke knowing. Through letters, phone calls, and periodic visits, they remained friends.

It was Jacob's senior year when Brenda called crying that she was pregnant and feared Zeke was cheating on her. After one of his violent rages Brenda begged Jacob to come home. It was two months before his graduation. They admitted they loved each other, but the dilemma of her pregnancy was a topic of concern. Brenda, due to deliver in July of that year, broke the news to her love stricken friend that she had no choice; she would marry Zeke. It was the only thing she could do if she expected him to support her financially. Jacob wanted to stop the marriage but without a job or a solution he sat in the church audience and witnessed Brenda King become Brenda Preston.

Zeke moved his family to the border of Bloomfield and East Orange, away from Brenda's family and friends. The distance discouraged drop in visits. Jacob continued checking on Brenda and her new born. His love never died and Zeke never trusted him. Over the years Jacob kept watch from a distance so not to cause problems within the Preston home. He invited Brenda, and her family to church functions. Zeke would remind him that he, not any God Jacob served, was the head of his household. She would need his permission to be a part of any church. Brenda was not allowed to visit Calvary Christian as long as Jacob Turner was the Pastor. She joined the church the day after Zeke was killed. Brenda would want to talk about it all again. She always did when Dominique couldn't sleep.

The doors of Calvary Christian were locked and checked carefully. Pastor Turner could only smile to himself as he realized he was purposely delaying his visit with Brenda. The truth was he was a faithful servant of God, but he was a man. Sister Brenda Preston, Tiny, the woman he always loved stirred his emotions. He was able to contain himself around others, and at the church, but lately he wanted to tell her the truth. He loved her more and more each day. Zeke and Brenda should have never married.

Then when she thought she would venture out and date, the Stevenson brothers stepped into the picture. Jacob had been too proud to vie for her affection. In fact, the thought of it angered him. Neither Randall nor Kendall, were looking to love her the way she needed to be loved. They dated woman who were easy; those who allowed men to undress them with their eyes in the bar; those who teased and taunted men for the fun of it. Brenda wasn't that type.

The amber light at the corner of South Clinton and Main caused him to speed through the intersection. He didn't want to wait at one of the slowest lights in the city. Darkness was beginning to fall on the streets and the streetlights began to light up block by block. He found a parking space as close as he could to Brenda's front door.

His phone vibrated in his pant pocket. He saw it was a text message from Randall. Jacob laughed at the text, which read, *"Tell Sistah Preston hello. My brother is coming into town this week. He's completed the rehab program. He was questioning what we offered at the church in support of his release. I told him about the outreach program we're working on.*

Maybe we could meet with him. He may be good to work with others struggling with addiction. Let me know what you think."

The deacon never hid the fact that he thought he knew why his relationship with Brenda never went to the next level. He didn't believe that Pastor Jacob Turner and Sistah Brenda Preston were just friends. He knew they had spent many times together alone. In the past he blamed Jacob for his failed relationship with her. After getting involved in the church and spending time with Jacob, he knew it was Brenda's choice to end the relationship.

Jacob took a moment to text him back. He told him to set a day and time after his brother's arrival for them to meet. Kendall had been sent to a rehab facility in Florida. His family felt he needed the program and the distance to break his alcohol and drug addiction. He was known to be a top connection for any drug on the street. After close calls with crimes, violence and women, his mother Estelle asked for the church's help. Jacob made the arrangements.

He looked at his watch. It read six forty five. Brenda would be peering through her living room window for his vehicle. He got out of the car and headed for her front door. The fence gave off its squeaky signal. He secured the latch, making a mental note to oil it over the weekend. Brenda was opening the door as he ascended the stairs.

"I thought you got hung up in the office. It's not like you not to call when you're running late."

She stepped inside the foyer reaching for his trench coat. He knew she would be wondering why he didn't call. It didn't bother him at all that she was indirectly scolding him as she often made a habit of doing. Jacob loved her concern regardless of the tone.

"Everything's done I hope you're hungry."

"Let me just use the restroom and I'll meet you in the dining room."

"Was everything okay?" Brenda raised her voice so he could hear her through the closed bathroom door.

The house looked small on the outside but all the rooms including the two bathrooms were large. The three-bedroom home was perfect for Brenda and Dominique. Brenda's touch was felt in each room, a touch Jacob was careful not to give in to. She never pushed herself on him, nor did she hint toward a deeper relationship. She was just what a minister needed, a settled woman, a woman who was faithful to herself and the word of God.

Jacob returned to the dining room hoping they would eat before talking about Dominique's problem. He would also have to tell her that Kendall was returning. She and Kendall were distant in comparison to his brother Randall. He would start the conversation with the plans to help Kendall.

"Kendall's coming home soon."

Her silence, though understood, didn't help to move the conversation along.

"I guess that means you haven't forgiven him?"

"Jacob, I just don't believe there's rehabilitation for everyone. Kendall is just, well he's evil."

"When he's under the influence; I think we owe it to him to help him if we can. Randall wanted him to get involved with our work with the recovery efforts. Maybe he would be a catalyst to other addicts."

"Hmm, believe what you want. I think Kendall uses drugs and alcohol as an excuse to do what he wants. All that robbing and thieving, he did before he left here, Lord knows. He stole from his own Mama. Did I tell you he tried to push his way in here? He claimed he loved me too much not to try at least once. I don't believe that was drugs or alcohol, it was Kendall Stevenson. I told Randall about his late night visit. That's what caused a problem between me and Estelle. She thought I was such a grieving widow that I wanted both of her sons. Randall was sweet, a little too sweet for me…."

Jacob gave her a perplexed look. Brenda reached across the table for a paper towel she didn't really need. Twirling it between her fingers she continued.

"No, I don't believe he's funny or anything, but he's not enough of a man for me. I don't know, he just…well forget him. Kendall was too aggressive."

"Nothing could satisfy Mama Bear huh?"

"Seriously, neither of them," she grinned allowing him to read her mind, "They're a lot different than you think. So you're considering letting him work around the church?"

"Unless you have an objection."

Pastor Turner ran most of the church business by Sister Preston before presenting it to any of the board members.

"You'll have to watch him and the program he works with. We don't need any problems from our sponsors. Randall will keep his eye on him, he always has. That's another problem he'll take to the grave with him."

"What's that?"

"He can't keep a woman, always checking on Kendall. Estelle leaves him with that responsibility, too much for me to deal with. When you get to be my age you want a nice relationship without the mess."

Jacob listened imagining the relationship they could have. Brenda got up to prepare their plates.

"Dominique is beginning to see shadows. Jacob, I don't know how this will work out this time, she's older. I can't brush her hair back and soothe her with soft words. I don't know what to tell her. What if she begins to see Zeke again, lying on the floor? How will I explain that night? I don't know if I can tell her that story again? There may be other questions. I don't want her to question me about the things I didn't tell her."

"So you explain she was young, too young to tell her about her father's murder. How much does she really remember?"

"I don't know. I wouldn't allow them to hypnotize her or push her into talking about it at the time. It was too much. Jacob, was I wrong?"

"Brenda, how would you know this would happen? Has she decided to see a doctor again?"

"She'll have to Jacob she can't go on like this."

They ate until they were full, enjoying the food and talking about church matters. Brenda got up from her seat and reached for his empty plate. He stood helping her clear the table. He followed her into the kitchen as thoughts of Dominique crossed his mind.

"Unfortunately, I think you'll have to wait for her to remember, or recognize the shadows. That might be best. Let her ask you the questions. I don't think you need to give her information until she's ready to confront it."

"Oh Jacob," Brenda turned to face him at the kitchen sink, "I don't think she'll be able to confront those shadows, that night, it was horrid."

Brenda turned her back and held on to the sink with both hands. Jacob walked up behind her. He knew it was another moment for tears. She had been silent off and on throughout the dinner trying to refrain from shedding any. He wanted to close the space between them, hold her in his arms. She turned into his chest and broke down. He felt her pain as he led her into the living room. He sat her on the couch with his arms around her.

"Brenda, if it will make you fill better, tell her everything. I'll be here with you."

"I can't. I won't. You're right it may be better for me to wait until she asks. She said she was going to call a therapist."

"Well maybe she's got it under control."

Eight

Dominique finished the dishes while talking to Boat on the phone. She assured him she was tired and after the eleven o'clock news she would be taking her nightly dose of medicine. His concern was genuine, but she felt their relationship was going too fast. Another night of cuddling would be enough to take her emotions over the edge. She didn't understand her mixed feelings.

At times she wanted to embrace the love Boat offered. She wasn't ready for a committed relationship. She knew she wasn't being fair to him, she knew she was leading him on. She didn't want him spending time with the women waiting in the wings either. Pam, and the others from his office, would be more than appreciative if she released her hold on him.

Dominique thought about Boat's words of comfort, he had a hold on her too, she hadn't been in any serious relationships. There were those she dated and hung out with in college but her feelings for them didn't equal the love she had for Boat. She knew she loved him, but there was the unexplainable fear she had about openly loving any man.

She cut off the kitchen light yawning, and that was a plus. She took a shower earlier thinking she would be in the bed before ten. Westlene's card was sitting on the table where she left it while talking to Claudia. After speaking with her mother she was determined to follow through with her call to Westlene's office. The thought of talking with a "dream chaser" seemed odd, but if it would help she was all for it. Taking sleep aids wouldn't be a permanent solution. After she checked the locks, she cut off the lights and proceeded to her bedroom.

The eleven o'clock news held no more information than the reports that aired earlier. The voices were beginning to fade as she drifted in and out of a sleep state. The dim light in her bedroom came from the television. She reached for the remote and pushed the button while mumbling, "thank God", her silent prayer for a good night's sleep.

Dominique opened her eyes awakened by voices coming from outside the bedroom door. She lay still looking around the room. Her surroundings were unfamiliar. The curtains were pink and white in color and the juvenile furniture was white oak with pick floral trimming. There were stuffed animals and dolls on a hutch with children books and other games. The voices were muffled but fear kept her pinned in her bed. An argument was brewing as the voices increased in volume.

There was a sound of glass or dishes breaking, a scream and silence. Dominique began to sweat. Her eyes widened as she looked at the bedroom door's entrance, watching for the shadow to approach. She closed her eyes tight fearing what held her captive night after night. She felt the heat from his body as he loomed over her. The female's voice screamed outside the door, "Please, please don't."

Dominique wanted to scream, she held her breath as she felt smothered under the weight of the shadowed figure that entered the room. She felt his breath on her neck as his raspy voice whispered, "I love you baby girl." She felt his rough hands rubbing her across her face and down her neck, his failed attempt at being gentle. The thought of what would happen next caused her to scream. She sat up in the bed.

Frantically she looked around. She was in her own room. Quickly, she cut on the light as she focused on the door where the intruder entered. There was no sign of a disturbance. She listened closely for the voices to speak. She eased on her slippers, careful not to make any noise. She paused at the top of the staircase. She crept downstairs only to find everything in place as she left it. She cut on the kitchen light. It was two thirty; she wouldn't be able to get back to sleep. For the first time, she could remember the dream. It would be the beginning of piecing together her fear. She pulled out a pad and wrote down what she remembered.

Fifteen minutes passed, she had calmed down. She poured herself a glass of juice and took refuge on the couch with a blanket. Dreaming didn't come as easy on the couch and she often thought about it becoming her alternate resting spot. Sleep came instantly once she stretched out. She didn't need the space her bed would give her as badly as she needed the rest.

Nine

The train arrived as scheduled and Randall was glad to see the schedule chart flip showing its arrival. He had been waiting in Penn Station for over an hour unsure when his brother said he would arrive. The passengers were filling the lobby scurrying to connecting buses and taxis. Kendall Stephenson waved from the newsstand that sat in the middle of the station.

"Randall, hey Randall." The younger brother waved feverishly attracting the attention of those who were walking by. Randall shook his head wondering why his brother always drew attention to himself. He walked to the stand where Kendall was in line waiting to pay for a soda and chips.

"You want something?"

"Nah, I'm good. Are these your only bags?" Kendall looked down at the two duffle bags and smiled.

"They don't let you keep much." Randall looked his brother over. He looked healthy. His skin was no longer withered. When he left New Jersey, he looked as though he was strung out and homeless. He was strung out. Cocaine was his drug of choice but, it soon became the gateway to a little of everything. His biggest problem was his craving for women who avoided him like the plague. It didn't seem to bother him. He would annoy them until they'd call Randall or the police. He was saved the embarrassment of charges being filed. The rehabilitation center in Florida seemed to be a solution. He had been there for more than eighteen months.

The program lasted nine months. Kendall took on a job as an intake counselor for the remainder of the time. The program lost a grant and his job was cut, he wanted to come home. Randall extended his home with the agreement that Kendall would continue his work at the church. The church had a drug program that helped those who had been through rehab or needed intervention. He could only pray that Kendall was ready to move on with his life.

The brothers walked to Randall's car in silence. Kendall was taking in by the renaissance that swept through downtown Newark.

Randall pointed to some of the places he wrote about in their letters.

"A new Newark, huh? It's nice. I wouldn't believe this if I didn't see it. Do you know the last time I was in Newark? Believe it or not, it had to be more than five years ago. You know I spent most of my time in New York. I never came down this way much."

"I thought you had a girlfriend that lived in Newark?"

Kendall paused as though he was thinking. He didn't answer the question and his brother let it go. They rode the next few blocks with the music from the radio filling the void.

"She lived in Hillside, near that park over on Elizabeth Ave," Kendall finally responded.

"Weequahic Park, yeah I remember now. I'm sorry. I forgot she passed away."

"How's your girl, Tiny?"

"You mean Brenda. She doesn't go by Tiny these days. We've gotten past the nicknames."

"So you still see her or what?" Kendall finished the chips, crumbling the bag.

"Yes, but she's not my girl. You and mom saw to that, remember." Randall hoped they wouldn't argue before they got to the apartment.

"No, I don't. Listen man, I hope you're not gonna throw my past in my face. I know I did some shit but I've atoned for it. You know, I can't change what was done. As I remember Mama didn't like Brenda and you stopped seeing her. I don't remember me being in that equation."

Randall turned into his complex. He was glad the ride wasn't longer. He would have to avoid certain topics. The men got out of the car and headed toward his apartment door. Kendall put his bags down checking out the area.

"This complex is new too, huh? What was here before?"

"It was projects and I guess some homes. It's still North Newark. Nothing has changed much other than the houses. If you go around the neighborhood you see the same thing, just like when you were home. Kendall, I said that to say, don't fall victim to the same things. You're headed on the right path, stay there."

Randall opened the door and grabbed one of the bags. "You can have the guest room. I've stripped the closet and the dresser so feel free to make it your room. There's more than enough room here. It's a two bedroom; we've got separate baths. You can use the one in the hall. I've got one in my room. I didn't go shopping yet. We can do that later. There's a phone in your room as well. Anything else you think you may need, ask me, I may have it. Mom wants you to call her."

"Does she still work at the church?"

"No, she's working out of the hospital. I'm not sure what she does, something with the nursing homes."

"Not mom, Brenda?"

"Yeah she works there."

"With you? And you mean to tell me, you're not seeing her?"

"No, I'm not."

Kendall walked over to the curio, which held plaques and framed certificates from the church. "You never told me you were a Deacon. Wow, how's that working for you?"

"Working for me? I don't know. If you want to eat there's enough in the fridge." Randall was beginning to feel uneasy.

"Nah, I'm good. Really, is it different being a Deacon?"

"Is what different?"

"C'mon man. Sex, love, dating. Do you get out much, socialize? What do you do for fun?"

"I socialize, there's a lot of activities with the members of the church. I don't date much, so, the rest is as it comes."

"Shit, you ain't doing much cuming, if you ain't dating." Kendall laughed and looked to his brother to share in his humor. "C'mon Randall you've stopped having sex?"

"I've had sex," he answered annoyed at the question.

"Brenda was your last?"

"No, she wasn't. Listen check out the room, I promised Mom I would bring you over her house."

"I want to check out the church." He placed the plaque back on the shelf. He walked around the room nodded his head in approval. "This is a nice place. Maybe I'll have one of my own shortly. How much is the church program paying?"

Randall didn't have an answer. He hadn't discussed a paid position. Pastor Turner thought Kendall would be a volunteer.

"We'll have to check with Pastor about that. We'll see how you work with the program. Our program may not be on the level of the program you worked for."

"Pay is pay. If that program's not paying than I'm sure your church can find something for me to do."

"True, that shouldn't be a problem. I really wanted you to work with that program."

"Well we'll see. I'm looking forward to getting reacquainted with the church. Who knows maybe I'll follow my big brother, become a Deacon. I've got some things I need to handle. Does Mom still have that old car sitting in the garage?"

"No, she got rid of it. She doesn't use hers much."

"So let's go see Ms. Stephenson. I'm sure she misses yelling at me."

"She don't yell much these days. People change over time."

"I hope you're right. That was a part of my rehab — change. I hope people see it in me. You know, accept me as who I am now, even your girl."

"My girl?"

"Tiny, I mean Brenda."

"Brenda?" Randall got up from his seat and waved his brother toward the front door.

"Yeah, I want to start over, with her. I owe her an apology. I miss her friendship."

Randall allowed Kendall to go out the door before him. His brother's statement left him numb. He had no idea they had a friendship.

Ten

Pam tried to hide her disdain for Westlene's drop in visit to Lawrence's office. She tapped her desk with her manicured nails while waiting for him to answer her call over the intercom. She tried to explain he was out of the office; Westlene smiled and simply said she'd wait. After watching the admiration shown by the clients who recognized the uninvited therapist in the waiting room, Pam was more than disgusted.

"Yeah Pam, what's up?" Boat couldn't imagine there was a serious reason for her interruption.

Pam spoke loud enough for her conversation to be heard. "Mr. Boatwright, Ms. Adashay is here to see you. I told her you were out of the office but…"

"It's okay I'll only be a minute."

Westlene pretended not to see at the receptionist's frown. She knew from the grunts of displeasure Lawrence would be returning shortly. Adjusting herself in the waiting room chair she picked up a magazine and casually flipped through the pages. Reluctantly, Pam called the name of the next client on the list and gave them directions for their paperwork. It wasn't more than ten minutes later that Lawrence rushed through the door and greeted the therapist with a warm hello.

"Pam, hold my calls. I'll only be a few minutes."

"Your next client is in fifteen minutes." She replied; rolling her eyes, as Westlene dropped the magazine on her desk.

"Thanks." He closed the office door giving her comment little attention.

"One would think you and the little woman have a serious affair going on. Are you sure you are not, what do you say, feeling her?"

"No, I can't say that." He smiled and shook his head, if she only knew. Westlene's appearance spoke confidence, something Boat always admired about her. She wore a beautiful Adielle wrap dress and matching shoes. A lab coat was never a part of her attire like many of her colleagues that walked through the building. Even when her choice was to wear her native garb her beauty drew attention. He offered her the seat that many of his clients took. She chose the couch and tapped the space next to her for him to join her.

"There's nothing between Pam and I. She's a friend and a co-worker. I'll admit though, she tries to make it more."

"And you don't respond at all?"

"Westlene, stop analyzing me please, I'm good. Did you speak with Dominique?"

"Yes, she wants to meet with me this day. I came to ask you a few questions. Has she told you anything about these dreams, or what she thinks they may be stemming from?"

"No, well sort of, but I'd prefer not to give you my interpretation before you speak with her."

"If you know anything that would help, please…."

"Are you unsure of your ability to chase her dream? I mean you're not like Cleo with the fake ass crystal ball are you?" His humor didn't go over well. He wanted to retract his questions immediately.

"This is no game Boat. I've seen people so wrapped into their dreams that they kill themselves or others. Some have made attempts while asleep. Your friend, she is in pain. I could tell that by her conversation. You do want her to get help, eh?"

He understood the serious tone she took with him. Westlene had conferred with him often about clients who were suicidal or emotionally unbalanced. Their discussions would determine what treatment would or should be provided to them. He didn't want to think of Dominique in that manner.

"Yes, and I want you to help her." He reached for her hand. "I want you to work your magic and get to the root of her problem. I'm scared for her. Her father was murdered and her mother raised her afterwards. I don't think there was anything more traumatic in her life than his death."

"Yes, the loss of a parent during childhood is enough to cause emotional scars."

"No, she was there when he was murdered. He was killed in the house where they lived. That's about all I know. She doesn't really talk about it much. I think she was close to seven or eight. Maybe she saw more than she told me. I never thought to question that."

The ring of the phone interrupted Westlene's response. She stood to her feet and waved to him. He held up his finger causing her to pause with the door cracked. Pam was talking into her phone and never noticed Westlene was watching her and Boat simultaneously.

"I don't think you should be spending your client's time talking with the Voodoo doctor. Boat, it don't look good."

Westlene turned and faced Boat with a questioning stare.

"Pam, hang up the phone." He hung up the phone on his desk and returned to the couch waiting for Westlene to return to her seat. She closed the door, allowing it to sound off. Pam looked in the direction of the closed door as she made another call.

"I need to get going. Dominique will be in this day, and I will talk with you this night."

"I don't know why, but I love your English conversions. This day, this night, it's today and tonight."

"Whatever. Did I say that right?" She turned ready to leave. Boat was glad she understood he was teasing her.

"If you can't reach me here, call me on my cell."

Eleven

"I think it's strange that every dream starts the same. I wake up the same way, and Ma, I keep having this feeling that I know these people."

Dominique stopped by the church before her appointment with Ms. Adashay. Brenda listened to her daughter trying to hide her own fears about the dreams.

"So this dream interpreter, Ms. what did you say her name was?"

"Adashay, her first name is Westlene."

"Is she a licensed doctor? She sounds foreign."

"She's from Haiti or Ghana, I don't remember. She's not a doctor; she's a therapist. She works in the same facility as Lawrence."

"With addicts, why do you think she'll be able to help you?"

Dominique got up from her seat. She could feel desperation building in her chest. She didn't want to cry.

"Someone has to. I can't keep on like this. Last night I felt his breath, I heard his voice. And the woman's cries too, I don't know where I was. Does any of this make sense to you? The room, was it my room Mama, did Daddy's murder happen in my room?"

Dominique turned from the bookcase to face her mother. Brenda answered softly, her voice barely above a whisper.

"No, he was killed in the kitchen."

Dominique turned back to the bookcase; her mother closed her eyes in prayer.

"I've got to piece this together. Okay, was it my room? Did my room have pick and white curtains, the furniture I described to you? It was so vivid. I could feel him on me. I was pinned to my bed. It was like I was about to be—"

"Dominique, talk with the doctor. Don't push yourself like this. Your room wasn't decorated like that; maybe it means something else. If you believe this woman will help you, go to her. I pray she'll help you."

"You've been praying, maybe God sent her my way. I pray about it too and if she can help, it's about time my prayers were answered."

Brenda looked at the Grandfather clock in the corner of her office. Her daughter stood in front of it admiring its workings, just as she did as a child. She didn't want the conversation to go any further. The memories were too painful.

"Dominique, I don't know what to say. His murder took a toll on both of us. I don't want you to be hurt when this, this, therapist can't find any answers. We've been to doctors, therapists…"

"Yes and now years later, I'm still swallowing pills to sleep. I'm still hearing those voices Mama. Something happened. Maybe it happened to me, and I was too shocked to tell you or anyone at the time. I don't understand why I'm being tormented with the past."

"Dommi baby, why do you have to dig up the past? It's gone; your father's gone. Find out about your sleeping problem and be done with it."

Dominique couldn't answer. She remembered her mother saying the same thing to the doctors who wanted to hypnotize her at the age of nine. She never explained her objection, but she remembered she didn't want them digging up the past. She later mentioned it would be too much for her child to handle. Maybe her mother didn't want to handle it. There was no need to push the matter any further. Brenda would only repeat her opposition to doctors, hypnosis, and discussion. If she were to begin to find answers, she would start with Ms. Adashay, the dream interpreter.

"How do you know if this woman isn't just a psychic, she may be practicing some kind of native rituals?"

Dominique smiled, "You don't really believe that and you know I don't. I'll call you when I get home. I'm going to dinner with Boat later, so it'll be after eight when I call."

"I can't believe he lets you call him Boat. Well tell Lawrence hello for me. Hmmm…Boat, what is his last name?"

"Boatright." Brenda walked behind her daughter and gave her a hug. Dominique kissed her and yelled goodbye to Pastor Turner as she headed for the door that led to the side entrance of the church.

The offices, recreation room, nursery and resource center was open during the week from nine to five. The entrance separated the church from the offices and was monitored with cameras. Pastor Turner watched from his office, as the door closed behind Brenda's daughter as she left.

He leaned back in his chair hoping the brief talk Brenda had with Dominique would answer a few of her questions. She had been nervous after receiving the call that Dominique wanted to discuss the dream she had the night before. She got to the office late and had been unusually quiet. Jacob returned to the papers before him ignoring the buzz of the bell. The voice of Randall Stephenson alerted him that the Deacon and his brother had arrived.

"Brenda, you sure look well. How have you been?"

"Fine, just fine, how about yourself?" Brenda answered the door watching Randall's expression as his brother made himself comfortable on the couch in the waiting lounge.

"Is Pastor expecting you this morning Deacon?"

"I called him last night. We just stopped by after visiting my mother. I saw Dominique pulling off, is she okay?"

"Yes, why'd you ask?"

Kendall interjected as though he was tired of the small talk.

"You know how she does Randall, she ain't never liked me. She didn't wave back to him Brenda, just pulled off. I believe if we were out of the car she may have run over us, she pulled off so quickly."

"Well, uh, let me get Pastor. Deacon have you had your coffee?"

"You got a pot brewing? I missed out on it this morning not being here and all. Can I bother you for a cup?"

"No bother." Brenda's voice became faint as she continued down the hall. Randall took a seat in the winged chair near the entrance. He fiddled with his Fedora hat keeping his thoughts to himself.

"Got to get my wardrobe up if I'm gonna be working here. This is a lot nicer than I remember. How many offices in here?"

"Three, maybe four, the resource center is where all the programs are held, the nursery and this up front. It was renovated about six months after you left. Big project but it only took a few months. Men of the church helped out."

"So you and Brenda formal now I see."

"Naw, just here at the church. You know respect for where we are. We all abide by it. That way no one gets offended and ain't no gossip to start." He knew that was a lie. There had been rumors for months about Brenda and the Pastor. Even he had his suspicions about the pair.

"She sure looks good. You know she's really a good woman. I mean mama don't know her like we do."

"Yeah, you're right." Randall didn't want to continue the conversation they had with his mother that morning. She gave her speech about wayward women and included Brenda Preston.

"So, I mean you really don't talk to her after y'all finish your church duties." Randall didn't answer. He could hear Sister Preston and the Pastor heading their way. He sat up straight fixing his appearance. Kendall watched from across the room not sure who was entering.

"Gentlemen, good afternoon, good to see you Kendall. You looking healthy. Morning Deacon Stephenson."

Kendall was confused with the formal pleasantries and didn't know how to respond. He stood accepting Pastor Turner's extended hand. Randall and the pastor shared an embrace. The three men parted allowing Brenda to place the tray with coffee and cups on the table.

"I'd invite you into my office but I've got papers spread all over. You know the 'Open House Open Homes' project is receiving a lot of response. Maybe you'll be interested working with Deacon Matthews on that project Kendall. A lot of the people seeking shelter are in need of direction or should I say re-direction."

"Is that a part of the drug program you have here." Kendall responded watching Brenda set the cups up to pour the coffee. Jacob noticed his glance and looked at Randall for his reaction. Randall quickly stepped in back of Brenda as she bent over to assist the men with stirrers.

"Anyone need anything else?" She asked confused about Randall's positioning. "What do you need Deacon, I'll get it for you."

"Not a thing Sistah Preston. I think we all have what we need. Pastor, are you straight?"

Kendall smiled, stepping around his brother, "Sistah Brenda?" he said sarcastically. "Do you think I could have a word with you before we leave?"

"Uh, uh, I don't see why not. Deacon show him my office will you, on your way out?"

"I'll remind him." Kendall turned to fix his coffee ignoring his brother's eye of disgust.

Twelve

Dominique couldn't understand why she felt so relieved waiting for the receptionist to call her name. There were two other ladies in the waiting area but no other name was on the list. She explained to the young girl taking the information behind the window, marked intake, that she was not a client or a patient. The girl nodded her head and handed her the clipboard with a questionnaire. Dominique still had the clipboard and questionnaire on her lap. She had no intention on completing the form.

She looked in her purse and pulled out her paper with the notes from the dream. She secured it on the clipboard and sat back. It was close to two o'clock and as it did each day, sleep was trying to creep upon her. The receptionist opened the window and called for Ms. Smith, the woman who was sitting across the room. Dominique closed her eyes.

"Ms. Preston, have you completed your form?"

Dominique, caught off guard, rushed to the window. "I tried to explain, I'm not a patient. I mean client. Ms. Adashay told me to stop by. I spoke to her this weekend."

"Forgive me," the girl replied. She turned and spoke in the native tongue Dominique had heard periodically while waiting. The women, who sat in the cubicle behind the window, were diverse in culture. The girl was talking with an older woman whose lab smock was a beautiful African print. Her hair was braided in tiny cornrows, which gave her an astounding crown. A sense of pride tickled Dominique's nature. The office was clean with an Afro-centric flare. She felt comforted, as the women seemed to have come to an agreement regarding her blank form. The older woman approached the window smiling pleasantly as she began to speak.

"Miss, if you would please take the form in with you?"

"Sure."

The window closed. Confused, Dominique returned to her seat. The scent of oils, a pleasant aroma, filled the air. Unlike most therapeutic offices, it was hard to believe one may be visiting as a patient. She closed her eyes again and began to drift.

The sheets fell across her face. She opened her eyes. The sight caused instant tension in her body. She felt herself tremble. She listened in the darkened room to a pleading voice that increased in volume. "Don't. Please, don't."

"Ms. Preston, Ms. Preston?"

The accented voice brought her back to the present time. The other woman who shared the waiting area was standing near her. The look on her face told Dominique they had been calling her for more than a minute.

"Are you okay dear," she asked. The receptionist politely helped her from further embarrassment. "Ms. Adashay will see you now Ms. Preston."

Dominique pulled herself together. The ten minutes seemed more like an hour. She knew from the sweat on her brow that a little longer, she may have shouted out in fear. She thanked the woman for her concern and entered the door that buzzed as she made her approach.

She was led to an office that reminded her of a living room or lounge. If the room didn't have a desk and other office equipment in a far corner, she would have thought she was in someone's home. The vertical blinds were a fair shade of blue and the grey furniture gave it all a professional touch. The Afro-centric mode was continued through the halls. The plaques and certifications were on a mantel that bordered the wall. Westlene stood to greet her newest client, although Dominique would deny that she had come to be evaluated.

"I must apologize for the delay. Sometimes the sessions last longer than the scheduled appointment. I have a habit of giving more time when I feel it is necessary. I hope you were comfortable."

The sincerity of her apology and her softness in her voice was the bedside manner that Dominique needed after her nap in the waiting room. Her anxiety began to diminish. She tried to smile as she handed Westlene the empty questionnaire and clipboard. She held on to her notes waiting for the right time to refer to it.

"I told them I wasn't a client. They said to give it to you."

"That is fine. If we need your information for anything, I'm sure we can get it later. It is merely for our records."

"I love your office, the waiting area too." Dominique's nerves were still on edge. It was as though she could feel the therapist looking through her.

"So tell me about Dominique Preston. You have not filled out the questionnaire, so I will have to ask about you."

Dominique was clearly embarrassed; she hadn't read any of the questions on the form. She assumed it was basic health questions for insurance purposes. Westlene didn't have a pen or pad in hand leaving her to wonder how she would remember any of her information. She started with her age, her education, where she worked and lived, her mother and father's names and her medical history.

"No sisters, brothers, friends, lovers?"

"Lovers? I've had dates, nothing serious, I wouldn't call them lovers."

"What about now?"

Dominique hesitated unsure about the reason for the question.

"Dominique, we have a lot of questions before revealing the source of your problem. If you're embarrassed, or feel the need to hide information, your fears will continue to haunt you."

"No, I don't I mean, I'm not hiding anything. It's just there is no one; I guess for my age that does sound strange."

"It only is strange to you. You are careful about who you love. This should be looked at as a good thing. We will be looking into your relationships and I just needed to know where to start. Are you comfortable with me?"

Dominique didn't want to rush to any judgment. She had her share of the probing questions from doctors, clergy and family friends. She wanted it to be on a different level this time.

Westlene pretended not to notice the pause before Dominique's answer of "yes". She could tell the woman who sat before her had deep rooted issues, issues that may have never been talked about before. Her experience taught her that her sessions would sometimes need to be personable if possible. Dominique would respond better away from the walls of the office.

"What do you do in your spare time?"

"I, uh, I …I really don't know. I guess, read, and watch a little t.v. I don't get out much. I work after work, if you know what I mean. It's become a bad habit. I think I work to keep from falling to sleep. If I'm busy I won't nod off."

"Dis is not good. I guess you would say, 'I know, that's why I'm here,' right?"

Dominique forced a smile afraid of the next question.

"What type of work do you do? I mean at your home. You are a buyer of clothing right? How does one do that after hours?"

Relieved Dominique explained her position; details that could have gone on forever. She gave examples of problems that needed to be sorted out with e-mails and faxed correspondence. Westlene seemed to be absorbed in her answers when she cut her off mid-sentence.

"Does your mother agree to your visit here today?"

Baffled, Dominique repeated the question in her mind. "My mother wasn't sure what you could do for me. She believes in praying and waiting for the Lord to send me a good night sleep."

She giggled in spite of herself as Westlene picked up a pen and pad from her desk. She watched as the pen moved quickly across the page.

"Today, I want you to go to this address. You are to go there before you go home to retire. The woman there, Imani, will see you and give you a full body massage. She will give you a box of herbal tea that will last you until we meet again. It is nothing special, but it is soothing. The taste is bland but it is not for your liking it is for your spirit to rest peacefully. I would like to see you for lunch on the following Tuesday. Your instructions for the weeks will be with Imani. You will see her three times during the week and finish your tea each night before retiring. There is no doubt you will sleep peacefully while we find why this shadow lurks over you."

"Westlene, if I sleep well with the tea, why do I need anything else."

"Closure my dear that is what has not been done for you. There is an opening, a gap, undone sorrow, or pain in your life. It must be closed. If you should have a problem, call me.

Thirteen

Claudia waited for Dominique to come out of the spa. The two were to have a girl's night complete with comforters, videos and small talk. There was a runway show in Cherry Hill, New Jersey they would be attending Saturday afternoon. It was Claudia's first time sleeping over in Dominique's home. She was enjoying their new level of friendship.

The radio's broadcast of the weather reported there was the threat of showers overnight continuing into the morning. Claudia hoped they were wrong. She turned the station hoping for a few of her favorites to play back to back. It was slated to be a great outing and a chance to ask Dominique how her therapy was coming along. She hadn't mentioned anything to her after the initial visit. The two of them discussed the concept of the massages and daily "spots" of tea. After their laughter they agreed anyone would love massage therapy and a good night's sleep. Claudia wanted an answer to the important question, was she still having the dreams.

Dominique opened the passenger door, smiling as Claudia belted out her off key vocals of "I want a freak in the evening, just like me."

"You won't find him at my house, that's for sure. What's up girl?"

"Are you relaxed? Damn you look relaxed, maybe I need to complain about my sleep."

"No you don't. It's a temporary fix. What you want to eat? I didn't cook last night."

"We can go anywhere you want."

"Let's not splurge tonight. I hear there's a fierce seafood buffet after the show tomorrow, but the drinks aren't included. I need a little money for those expensive ass drinks."

"You think they'll be that expensive?"

"Believe me they'll get their money back one way or another. Seafood buffet, yeah, the drinks are gonna cost."

Their reimbursement requests were never denied but their pockets usually set a limit. They rode to Applebee's hoping to beat the Friday night crowd. Their orders arrived just as the conversation became personal.

"Claudia, where's the man in your life?"

"Wow where did that come from?"

"If I'm overstepping my boundary say so. I just never heard you speak of anyone special. I told you, I've been taking you and our friendship for granted. I don't know much about you."

"Well, there is no special someone. Not because I don't want to have a relationship, but my time is consumed with the industry. I really want my own someday. You know, a shop, maybe a boutique with new or upcoming designers. Affordable though, not like New York. That's why I love the runway shows."

"Really, you see yourself in that position? That's great, I mean if you really want it. I don't think I've ever really looked that far in the future."

"I've got my money saved and invested. If the right spot comes along I'm grabbing it. I've networked with enough designers and suppliers so if the opportunity presents itself, I'm good."

Claudia took a sip of her water and patted her mouth with her napkin. Dominique took a good look at her co-worker. She had dreams, a vision and no nightmares. There was no limit to her seeing herself in a future position. Jealousy tried to peek into her emotions. The woman who showed her more concern than her mother was stable. Claudia's revelation made her appear different. Dominique understood her silence in the office when others spoke of their weekends. Most of them splurged either shopping, or some form of entertainment. Neither Claudia nor Dominique would chime in.

"So, you see Mr. Right has not come calling." Dominique hadn't heard the rest of her explanation.

"Maybe it's better if you wait. Everyone who comes calling; is not Mr. Right."

"Well you and Boat make a nice couple."

"Claudia, we're not a couple, we're just friends."

"I could use one like him, does he have brothers?"

They laughed. Dominique refilled their glasses with water.

"Understood, but I don't know, sometimes he's not Mr. Right either."

"Whenever he is, that's what counts. None of them are Mr. Right all the time. He understands you and that helps. Dommi, how's the dreams since the therapy started?"

"I don't know. I'm scared to death. I've woke up in the middle of the night but no dreams, no sweating, a pause in sleep I guess. But girl, I don't know what will happen after I stop drinking this tea."

"Is it a drug?"

"No, she said it was herbal. She gave me enough for two weeks. I sleep peaceful. After the last few dreams I needed it."

"Did your mother have a clue about the room, or the voices you heard?"

"No, but Claudia, I think she knows. I didn't think like that before sitting with Westlene, but she knows something."

"So what's next?"

"I've got three more days. My appointment is Tuesday. I really don't see what she'll ask since I won't be drinking the tea…"

Her voice drifted as she ended the sentence.

"What's wrong Dommi?"

"Fourteen days ends on Monday. I went there on Monday. The tea will only last until Sunday night. Claudia what about Monday night?"

"You'll be fine."

Dominque wanted to take Claudia's confidence and keep it for Monday night. She felt she would need it. The night movies kept the young women entertained for the evening and there was no more talk of Dominique's condition. It was close to midnight when they said goodnight and retired. Boat called just as Dominique laid her head on the pillow.

"Hey Sweetness, how's the girl's night thing working out?"

"We had a great night. Movies, popcorn, conversation and you know what, Claudia's pretty cool."

"Good, you had a friend all the time. How are you feeling?"

"Okay, was that a Westlene question?"

"Listen, I'm not asking questions for Westlene. I care about you girl, you know that."

"I'm good. I'm still able to sleep at night so it's all good."

"Yeah, I guess that leaves a brother in the dark."

"Why?"

"Seems like when you sleep I can't get an invitation. Now, you got a therapist and a girlfriend. I'm left in the dark."

"Stop, you know how we do, don't pretend you don't, things haven't changed. I still…"

"Need to have safe sex."

Dominique was shocked. He hit a nerve, but he told the truth. He was safe and he was just security, in and out of bed. She felt an argument brewing. Listening to his breathing, her emotions took over; tears fell from her eyes.

"I'm sorry Boat, I'm really tired. Can I get with you tomorrow?"

"No, call me like you always do, after the dream."

"What the f…"

Dominique's angered response was cut off by the sound of the dial tone.

Fourteen

Boat and Eric stood in the hall watching clients entering the building for appointments. The morning coffee was Boat's treat. The two men sipped between greetings and nods of approvals as they spoke to the female coworkers that passed by. They positioned themselves so the flow of traffic moved in all directions, the main entrance, elevator and stairwells. Some of their male counterparts replaced them in the afternoon.

Both men agreed the morning was when the women looked their best. Even the clients who thought they were above an "evaluation", dressed to impress. Eric refrained from commenting but his groans and facial expressions said enough to keep what appeared to be a one sided dialogue going.

"Hey look, haven't seen her in at least two weeks. You know they say Maurice is with her now."

"Lucky man. Eric, when did you know Stacy was the one?"

"I don't know exactly. I just knew I didn't want to be without her. She became more than that Friday night date, or a lover, you know what I mean?"

"Yeah." Boat and Eric's attention followed a five foot eleven beauty that turned the heads of every man she passed. There were whispers and polite "Good Morning," greetings as she opened the office that sat opposite the security podium. The guard smiled at Boat and Eric as they shook their head, an affirmation that Ms. Colter was a walking fantasy.

Eric looked at his watched and put his hand out for his friend to give him a handshake and a manly embrace. After their exchange they bid each other a good morning, promising to talk at lunch. Boat waved at the security guard, who shouted, "Have a good day", as he entered his office. He counted the clients he recognized as returns and picked up the sign in sheet. Pam hadn't marked any of the names, which would have indicated how many people he had to see for the morning session. He would have to wait for her to return to her desk.

The thought of asking her out crossed his mind again. He was beginning to think Eric was right when he told him Dominique was stringing him along. She hadn't called since their talk Friday night. He would have explained his comment, his emotions, his fears and again, his love. The intercom rang and the red button flickered. Pam's voice fueled him each morning when she asked, "Mr. Boatright, are you ready?" While his mind was confused with physical desires, he wanted to tell her he could show her better than he could tell her. He didn't want the clinging relationship that would follow, so he kept the words to himself.

"Good morning Ms. Stubbs." They started each morning with professional formalities only to lose them as the day progressed. "Could you tell me my total for the morning?"

There was the usual pause. Boat couldn't understand why they went through this each morning. Pam knew he would ask, but she insisted on breathing softly into the phone while counting the names on the sheet. "Eight for the day," she paused certain she had his attention, "Four and four."

"You pushing me girl."

The phone rang. "I would pull you if you relaxed. Mr. Dexter is your first client."

Boat knew answering the phone would mean she had a smart comment. He smiled feeling the response in his pants. If Dominique didn't call, he would be relaxing with Pam at least once.

It was close to lunch before Boat took a break from his notes between clients. He called Pam and told her to hold the last appointment for the morning another five minutes while he made a call.

The phone rang and after there was no answer Boat dialed Dominique's cell phone. He felt like a love struck fool for calling, but he wanted to have a reason to turn his attention elsewhere. He did as he had done the call before and disconnected the line before the answer machine could pick up. Westlene's office was his next choice.

"New Jersey Therapeutic Counseling, good day."

"Good Morning, this is Lawrence Boatright, is Ms. Adashay in?"

"She is sir, please hold the line."

Boat smiled, hearing the woman's accent pleased him. It was something about her effort to pronounce each word that seemed to give him a chill.

"Good day, Boat. How are you?"

"Good day to you Westlene. I have clients waiting, but I wanted to ask you about Dominique? How is she holding up?"

"She hasn't called you?"

"No, I spoke with her Friday. A friend of hers spent the night, I haven't reached her since."

"No news, how does one say? Is good news, right?"

"Hmmm. I don't know, I think I created a gap."

"That will past, I am certain."

"You know more than me. Have you spoken with her since the last appointment?"

"I needed her to relax so, no, I haven't seen her. She'll be waiting for me Tuesday. I believe that's the day of her next appointment."

"Well are you making progress?"

"I haven't done much more than allow her to talk about herself. Even that seemed to be a challenge. I don't know Boat, how do you say, the woman has issues. I want to tell you more but you have not waited until the evaluation is over. That tells me something about you."

"What?"

"You are hooked my friend, no? More than you want to admit. One thing, though. If I find a major issue I need to tell you, her information is confidential. She will have to let you know, I won't."

"I understand. I just want her to be at peace with herself. The dreams are rough on her. She never talks about them, maybe she doesn't remember. At least that's what she says."

"Well, as long as you understand I won't tell you more than she wants you to know. You are working now, you said?"

"Yes, I have another client this morning."

"Well you won't get paid by me, so tend to yours."

"Westlene?"

"Yes, no need to thank me."

She hung up the phone before he could ask would Dominique be able to handle a major issue.

Fifteen

The day ended early for Dominique. She stopped by her mother's on the way home only to find their visit would be cut short. Brenda reminded her daughter she had to be at the church for the youth choir rehearsal. The group was practicing the entire week for Youth Sunday that would be held in a week.

Dominique declined the invitation to sit through the two-hour rehearsal. She spoke to Claudia briefly letting her know there was a change of plans and she would be home earlier than expected. After spending the weekend together she felt a true friendship brewing. The thought of calling Stacey crossed her mind, but she was sure she would be either with Eric, or engrossed in wedding arrangements. She didn't really want to hear about their perfect relationship.

Dominique stopped at the store and picked up a few items to fill her snack jars. It was a habit she developed after finding a midnight snack seemed to help ease her into sleep. The tea and massage had helped over the past two weeks. Today was the first day that she would be without the tea. The massage was comforting, but with each passing hour she could feel the tension building. She wanted to call Westlene and beg for the herbal mixture that had become her liquid lullaby. She gave in to what she hoped would work, Twinkies and Funny Bones.

She checked her phone; there were no messages. Boat hadn't called; she felt a twinge of disappointment. She knew he spoke in anger but he usually came around in a few days. She picked up the cordless phone not sure if she should break the ice. Deciding against it she laid the phone on the end table and cut on the television. Dinner would be a salad and baked chicken. It would be done in the minutes it would take for her to shower and check her computer for any incoming e-mails.

It was close to ten before she thought of calling Boat again. She found herself busy after dinner, preparing contracts and sending messages to prospective clients. Dominique glanced at the clock realizing she was doing exactly what Boat accused her of. She wanted to call him because she needed him to help her sleep. Ten o'clock was teatime. She hadn't called him during that hour in the past two weeks as she sipped her tea minus the herbal blend and watched television.

The papers were spread across the table, another sign of anxiety. She hadn't worked late either during the past two weeks. She was causing herself to panic. There was no reason for her fears to be mounting. She tried to convince herself of this fact as she flipped through the channels on her television. She decided against watching the repeats or searching for a movie. She grabbed her tray with the dinner dishes she used and made herself busy in the kitchen for thirty minutes.

The phone rang, startling her, she was glad to have any conversation. "Hello?"

"Hi, I uh, I was wondering how you were?"

"Hey, I'm good. What about you?" Dominique answered; glad to hear Boat's voice.

"I'm okay. Listen, I want to say I'm sorry about the other night. I—"

"No need, I understand. Claudia and I had a great weekend. She's really cool. How was your weekend?"

The conversation went on for forty-five minutes. They didn't mention her appointment with Westlene or how she was progressing. Dominique hoped he would ask so she could tell him she was scared to close her eyes.

"Listen call me, tomorrow I'd like to take you out to dinner. I still feel I owe you an apology."

"How about just dinner, you really don't owe me anything. Boat I needed to hear what you said. I needed to hear what Claudia said as well. Sometimes it takes those moments to make one realize how they're treating others. I'm the one who should apologize. It's not fair to you."

"So does that mean that we can stop playing this game? I mean neither of us is seeing someone else, why not a relationship?"

"Boat, what if this treatment reveals something horrible?"

"What could be so horrible that I wouldn't want to be with you?"

Dominique closed her eyes. She didn't want to say what she thought.

"Dommi, are you okay?"

"I don't know Boat. I guess I'll know before the night is over."

Sixteen

ominique's bladder was full, but the fear of going to the bathroom entered her mind. She was holding herself captive in her bed. She opened her eyes and looked at the red neon numbers on the clock that indicated it was 2:30. There was no doubt it was either go and relieve herself or wet the bed. She leaped out of the bed running for the toilet. An eerie feeling came over her. She listened closely as muffled voices could be heard coming from the room below.

"Please, don't I'll do it for you, leave her be."

She could hear the heavy footsteps approaching the stairs. Dominique's fears heightened, it was then she noticed the hall; she was no longer in her home. The earth tone colors of her stairway were replaced with a soft shade of green. She didn't see the picture of her mother and Pastor Turner on the wall near the guest room. There was a vase on a table near the bathroom, an accent to the area she didn't recognize. The stairs began to creek. He was coming for her again. The warmth of the urine running down her legs made her cry. Her pajamas became heavy around her ankles. The woman pleaded again.

"I'll call the police. I will. I'll call them."

A second voice spoke. Another man was with them. She couldn't make out what the baritone voice was saying. She couldn't remember where she had heard their voices before. The footsteps stopped. She ran back to her bed never making it to the bathroom. She covered her head.

She tightened her eyes fighting the tears and praying he wouldn't enter her room. Laughter came from the men as the woman tried to reason with them.

"She's a child. Why do you always tease her?"

The stairs creaked, once again. Dominique knew he wouldn't be stopped by the woman's pleas or threats. Her bedroom door opened slowly. The light from the hall fell upon the yellow sheets. Dominique opened her eyes hoping to see his face through the cotton cover. His odor made her gag as he leaned over looking for any opening to peek through. She held the sheets tightly in her hands.

"She won't be here to protect you one night and that's when I'll show you my love. You're a pretty little girl. Your daddy and mama must be proud."

Dominique held her breath in fear until the light was cut off by the closed door. Her cramped fingers released the sheet as she began to cry. There were no voices to be heard but the air held his smell that left her nauseated. She waited before removing the sheet from her face scared he would return. When she opened her eyes again it was morning.

She sat up slowly, remembering her urgent need to urinate. The sheets were no longer yellow. It was her favorite patterned sheet set with a matching comforter. She flipped back the covers looking for the stain or sign of moisture. She was sure there would be a sign of the bed being wet. Dominique sat trying to remember the details.

She stepped into the hall recalling the unfamiliar décor. It wasn't a home she remembered from her childhood. Quickly, she returned to her bedroom hoping she hadn't overslept. The clock read six. The alarm would be ringing in thirty minutes. There was no need she wouldn't be returning to bed. She pushed the button on the clock and sat on the edge of the bed. Flashes of the dream kept her from moving.

She couldn't stop the tears. She reluctantly picked up the phone and dialed Claudia's number. Glancing at the clock again she realized the call would have to be returned. Claudia would probably be in the shower, if she kept to her daily schedule. Leaving a message would only send a signal of distress. Dominique felt disrobed and violated by the shadow that taunted her each night. She couldn't quite explain it in a two-minute message. She curled into the fetal position; phone in hand, waiting for Claudia to return her call.

Ten minutes passed. Dominique closed her tear filled eyes mumbling silent prayers. The phone rang causing her hand to vibrate. Her head was heavy, the beginning of a headache she was sure would be with her all day. She looked in the drawer next to her bed for relief. She answered the call as she headed for the medicine cabinet.

"What's up girl?"

"Claudia, I can't go to work today. I want to see Westlene earlier than my scheduled appointment. I can't wait all day to see her."

"You don't sound good, are you okay? Do you need me to come over?"

"No, I wanted to let you know I won't be meeting you this morning." Her tone said it all. She turned on the faucet running the water into a cup. She put the two pills into her mouth and swallowed.

"Headache again, huh, listen I'll bring you something to eat later and we'll talk. What time are you going to see her?"

"As early as possible, I'll call you and let you know."

"Try to relax."

"Shit I feel like, what was that movie Freddie Kruger was in?"

Claudia controlled her laughter, "Nightmare on Elm Street?" She asked glad her friend was able to joke about her overnight experience.

"Well he's on a new street and one of us has to move."

"Girl later, call me if you need me."

The levity of the conversation gave her a moment of relaxation. She cradled the phone wishing the moment could last. She would work on her laptop filling in the hours until Westlene's office opened.

Seventeen

Kendall got to the church early. He had been trying to break the wall of silence between himself and Brenda. Her schedule didn't require her to be there every day. She avoided him as though he was a plague. His flirtatious comments didn't help the situation. He hoped she had forgiven him for his actions that he attributed to his addiction.

Brenda had all but forgiven him for being Zeke's get high partner, but his forwardness reignited her disgust for his uncontrollable behavior. Kendall wanted to show her he had matured. That man she once knew was gone, he was well aware of the pain he caused.

He thought of dropping in one evening during choir rehearsal or a bible study session. It would look odd if he was there in the evening. He didn't want to bring attention to himself. Kendall had no intention on being a member or participating in any of the after hour activities.

His job at the church was exactly as his brother described it, voluntary. He mentioned his need for a real job, but his troubled past wouldn't guarantee him instant employment. His mother and brother were happy with his determination to change his ways. They had no problem giving him financial assistance as they had before he left.

Randall explained their understanding, something he never questioned. He knew they couldn't understand. They had no idea of the internal demons he fought day after day. The demons that were calmed with the drugs, alcohol, anger and finally the rehabilitation. The demons could finally be put to rest now that he returned home. The job at the church was the first step.

The solace of the church office was something that would take time for him to get accustomed to. It gave him time for deep thought. An atmosphere he hadn't been a part of while in the rehabilitation center in Florida. There was always someone talking, the sound of a radio or television, some activity to remind him of the residents chaotic lives. It was those sounds that kept him from revisiting the past.

Randall and Pastor Turner gave him an overview of the program they wanted for the church. Kendall would have the responsibility of linking the program with other community resources. The program would start with fifteen identified members. People who had been addicts and needed a support group filled in the questionnaires he prepared. They would be returned to Kendall's mail slot after the Sunday services. He was well aware of the hours he would spend in the community promoting the program. He spent the early hours reviewing the answers on the questionnaires while making notes for their first formal meeting.

He shared Randall's desk promising not to rummage through his meticulously arranged files. His side of the office would be worked on once the program funding was received. He found it ironic that he would be once again sharing a room with his brother. The pictures on the desk told a story of Randall's ministry in the church. Kendall lifted the pictures to get a closer view of the people in the background. The faces were familiar but he couldn't name the eyes that seemed to give him an accusing stare. He wondered how many of them would remember him.

His departure was like a thief in the night. He begged his brother to help him. Randall asked only one question, *"Where did he want to go?"* He said he didn't want to know what happened. The memories were fragmented, the pain still pierced his emotions; he needed forgiveness. It took more than a month for the arrangements to be made. Now that his mind was clear of drugs and alcohol, he would apologize.

Zeke had been drinking and getting high with him most of the day. They agreed to meet later, pick up a few of their female friends and finish the night off. Brenda was no longer naïve about Zeke's cheating ways.

She was preparing to leave her husband and his abuse. Kendall often wondered why Zeke treated her the way he did, but after a few pulls on a joint she was just another woman.

After Zeke was murdered he made his move hoping she would welcome his advances. Brenda's voice broke his trance and he pretended to be busy with paperwork when she entered the room.

"Mornin' Kendall."

"Hey Brenda, I mean Sister Preston." He answered; aware she would be annoyed with his informality.

"Kendall, are you here because you're serious about this ministry?"

"I believe I am, yes. I'm serious about…."

"Watch yourself, just like you changed so did I. Things ain't what they were when you left here."

"I realize that. I…" Brenda moved closer to the desk looking around as though someone would enter before she finished her statement.

"Sssh. This is your chance to redeem yourself with your family and the Lord. Don't mess it up. I don't know Kendall. Zeke and you were close. That tells me you had a lot in common. Zeke didn't care for anyone that was different. Behind closed doors he was an evil man. What does that say about you?"

"Brenda, what would make you…" Brenda's stare spoke for her. "Sister Preston, I've been trying to set things straight with you since his death. I'll admit that while my brother loved you, I interfered, but that was jealousy. I had just lost my friend, your husband. I thought I should be your protection. I wanted to take care of you and your daughter."

"Why? Tell me why? You ruined my marriage Kendall. Zeke would get drunk with you and beat me. You knew it. You wanted to take care of me? There's something about you Kendall. I know I'm not wrong. I get this gut feeling every time you're around. You're here on the pretense of doing good for those who have addictions. I won't interfere with that. Walk in God's light Kendall. Zeke walked in a different light and well, you know he died as violently as he lived. It should haunt you since you were such good friends. It still haunts me."

She left him sitting at the desk. He was without words. She was a different woman. She spoke with a voice of strength she never had before. There was nothing weak about her. He sighed. Kendall wanted to repent, a part of his twelve-step program. He knew why his friend had died. She was right. Their addiction altered their behavior. Zeke became abusive. Kendall felt the need to appease his sexual appetite. Together, their disrespect for women had hurt many. He wondered if she had the strength to handle the truth that really haunted him.

Eighteen

Randall walked in talking, not noticing his brother's somber mood. "You had a few calls last evening. I guess questions about the program's start date. I left the note on the computer screen at home. I didn't know you would be here working this early. Did you stop by Mama's?" He paused, "That note was there too. What's up man? You alright?"

"Yeah," Kendall replied letting out the air he had been holding. "Randall, was there anything strange to you about Zeke's death?"

"Yeah, he got shot in his own home. I never believed that story about a robbery." Randall closed the office door. "Zeke had enemies though, you know that. But you know why I say I never bought it? Nothing was stolen; nothing was even touched. There was no broken window, and I don't remember a busted up door. I think it was something else to it. But you know the cops didn't like Zeke."

"What? I never knew that. I mean we all had our bouts with those punk ass cops, but I don't think they would look over a murder. C'mon you've got to be joking. They had to investigate something. I mean Brenda didn't request one?"

"And that was strange too. Then you know months later, when we started dating, she never mentioned anything about the shooting or what they found."

"Yeah, you're right. So did your boy the Pastor mention it?"

"No, what would make her talk to him?" Randall could tell his brother was upset about Brenda confiding more in Pastor Turner.

"Man, c'mon, I ain't stupid. That's how their relationship started. She only talked to me until she found out Zeke was with me earlier that night. She never said much though. The usual, you know, talk about him being abusive. Man, we were drinking buddies that's all."

"What was up with you and Zeke though? The two of you had problems right before his death, I remember, something about that girl. Viola, that chick from the bar across town, was he really seeing her?"

"Randall, I've got so much to confess. That's why I wanted to come back. Somebody needs to know the truth."

"What, she had Zeke killed?"

"I don't think so, but you're right he was dealing with her. So was I."

"You both dealt with her?" Randall sat on the edge of the desk. "The two of you were dealing with her at the same time?"

"Yeah, literally, it was a weekly thing for us to get together. She was a friend of Brenda's back then. I was dealing with her for a while. Man when you're drunk. No, I won't blame it on the drinks. It was wrong, that's all."

"Brenda found out?"

Kendall leaned back in the chair. "I don't know, I found out about Zeke two weeks after the funeral remember. I was locked up. Never saw Viola again. She could have had him done I guess. But I just don't see her sending someone to his house. That ain't how it's done. I mean she knew about Dommi, you know.

"Viola and Brenda were close friends?"

"I guess, yeah, she was her babysitter when Brenda worked that night gig. She didn't trust Zeke."

"Why, he was Dommi's father?"

Kendall didn't answer. A knock at the door ended the conversation. Randall excused himself following the man who didn't have to say what he needed. Kendall held his head in his hands. Randall stirred the past. He hadn't thought about it. *Did Viola know how Zeke died?* She didn't hang around the bar or the neighborhood spots once the news of Zeke's death got around.

Things were so twisted then. Brenda was fed up with her home life and determined to finally fight back. Zeke didn't care one way or the other. Between the coke and the alcohol, he just wanted to get high and get laid. Brenda didn't fit in the end of a pipe, in a glass or in his bed. He was never satisfied with what he called her church loving. Kendall always wondered why a good woman like her married the likes of Zeke Preston. Back then, he didn't care about whom he loved either, as long as the drugs were plenty they would find someone to play with. Viola was sweet, but she too had a habit. When they tired of her, there were others.

Kendall didn't sleep well the night before thinking of those they bedded together. There were many nights he got his friend home just before Brenda returned from work. Kendall understood Zeke, but he loved Brenda. He tried to be a friend to both of them but his desires were redirected. He wanted to bed his friend's wife. A line he wouldn't cross as long as Zeke was alive. After her husband's death, she dated Randall to spite him. Kendall believed that. The brothers would fight verbally and threaten each other physically until Estelle, their mother, stepped in and went to Brenda with her concerns. A fine widow was trouble to two inexperienced men. Her sons were off limits. The relationships dissolved.

Trouble found Kendall, he left town to conquer it all. Returning home would be good for Brenda, Dommi and him. He thought of her more and more while he was away. The challenge of having a relationship with Brenda gave him a rush. He would be who she wanted him to be. He would go through it all to have her. He would have to convince her to forgive him. He wasn't' the addict, the home wrecker, or the street bum she cussed at on Friday nights. He had expressed his feelings, declared his love; he was a committed friend. He proved his loyalty. After all he was there with her the night of the murder.

Nineteen

The earliest appointment for Westlene was usually at ten on Tuesdays. After the call from her office expressing Dominique's need to see her, Westlene told them she wouldn't be in until twelve. She would work late. She immediately called Dominique and told her she would love to come and sit with her in her home. She would be there in less than an hour. That would give them three hours, if necessary, to talk in a different environment. When she asked was there anything she could bring her, Dominique asked for the herbal tea.

Dominique hurried, getting herself together and rearranging items that weren't really out of place. She stopped just before the bell rang content with what would be another first impression. She invited the doctor in and immediately excused herself leaving Westlene to find a seat at the island in the kitchen. Again she didn't have the normal yellow pad that accompanied most therapists when evaluating patients.

Westlene scanned the counter for a teapot. Her eyes found a coffee brewer, toaster and other appliances, but there was no pot for the tea. She noticed the water cooler with the hot water spout. She smiled to herself and used the coffee cup in the drain to prepare Dominique a cup of tea.

Dominique walked into the room, pleased to see steam coming from the cup on the counter. "I know I sounded like a drug addict on the phone. That tea is so comforting. You said it didn't contain any medication but the effects are like a drug."

"Nature's way of calming the system, I'm really glad you called. I think we may get better results outside of the walls of the office. How are you, you've slept better?"

She listened to Dominique describe the massage therapy, the first week of sound sleeping she had in months and her new fear. Her facial features changed. She described the feeling of depression that crept upon her when she realized the tea would soon run out. She began to talk rapidly, pausing and excusing herself as she explained how she tried to tire herself out the night before. Tears began to fill her eyes as she explained having to lay her head down knowing the nightmare would return.

"And so it did?" Dominique stared at Westlene, surprised she would ask that question.

"You knew it would. Why didn't you tell me, why didn't you give me enough tea to last?"

"The tea has nothing to do with the dreams. It is you and your state of mind. Your anxiety brings on the dreams. You were tired, restless and needed to relax. The massage gave you comfort and the tea gave you a sense of security. The tea is similar to when you would have company stay with you."

Dominique's anger was building; she thought Westlene understood. Reality stung, her problem wouldn't be solved with a few days at the spa.

"Well your spa treatment didn't work. Did you think it would? Had you decided I was faking? This is real, it keeps me up at night; it haunts me and as I told you before, I can't go on like this. I guess I would need stock in herbal tea, huh?" Dominique's questions brought on silent tears. "I need help Westlene, real help. I believe something happened to me and that's why I'm having these dreams. Now I'm able to put together bits and pieces. I never remembered parts of the dreams before. Will you be able to help me or should I just commit myself?"

"There is no reason for you to be committed. You are not sick, or going insane. Yes, I will be able to help you, but you must understand you have to face those night terrors. We have to talk about those fears, both present and past. You can get over this, but it may reveal an ugly reality. Have you talked with anyone about your dreams last night?"

"No, I wrote down some of the things I remembered."

"Well, let's get started. Are you comfortable here, in your sitting room, or where would you prefer to talk about this?"

"Can we go to my bedroom? I think I would feel better if we go through it step by step." Dominique led the way. She told Westlene about her apartment hunting adventures. She knew it was a blessing when she inherited this home. She wanted her to know why she chose to live on the opposite side of town. She didn't know why her mother wouldn't move with her. "I thought maybe a new area would break the hold that house had on us. The murder of my father took place in that home. My mother and I moved three years later, but she lives only blocks away from our old home. I needed more distance."

The therapist listened as they ascended the winding staircase. She touched the walls and breathed in the scented air, filled with the mixed fragrances of air fresheners. The home was well kept. Pictures of family adorned the walls. Her contemporary furniture was accented with vases filled with shells, and rocks; a picture for home décor magazines. There was a feeling of comfort, and Westlene agreed, Dominique had made this her sanctuary.

Her bedroom was the only room that had not been tended to. The bed wasn't made; the covers were strewn as though she left momentarily and would return to continue sleep. Her slippers were apart as though they had been kicked off. Her pajamas were thrown in the chair that sat near the window. Westlene didn't know how to evaluate the noticeable difference. Dominique had taken time to prepare her home for a visit. However, she invited her to the room, knowing it had not been staged. She stopped at the foot of the bed, unsure where Dominique would want her to stand or sit.

"Here," she said as she moved her pajamas from the chair, "Sit here, I'll be moving around. I want to play out as much as possible."

Her anxiety had begun. This would be the first time she could openly recall her dreams. She could quote what she heard while describing her actions and what she saw. She paced back and forth, not knowing where to start.

"I'll tell you about these dreams, the ones in the past. Then I'll describe the one last night unless you can suggest another way"

"No, you make this comfortable for you. If you become uncomfortable pause, take your time. It is better for your memory."

"Okay, I am so sorry do you want water, juice or anything?"

"No, you may start when you are ready." Westlene wished she had brought her briefcase in with her. She would now have to remember the particulars from this visit without notes.

Dominique began speaking about the dreams in her younger years. She sat on the edge of the bed, her voice and expressions changed with her emotional levels and overtones. She spoke of her disappointment with her mother and the doctors who didn't believe her nightmares weren't just bad dreams.

"Now I believe there is a message. I don't know; I've always believed that God brings you the same problem or situation until you do the right thing to solve it. It will haunt you. It's no longer a dream. I'm being haunted by this; it's unfolding when I sleep."

Westlene didn't want to discourage her, but she knew from experience the resolve Dominique sought would not come quickly. She didn't make any comments as Dominique continued.

"Ms. Adashay, I mean Westlene, I'm so glad to finally tell this to someone. My father was killed in the house we lived in and no one even looked for his murderer. My mother won't talk about it and I think my dreams have something to do with it."

"And how do your dreams connect to your father's death. I know we talked vaguely about that night. Do you now remember more?"

"Not about that night. I have notes."

The two women talked about the dreams Dominique had over the past few months. The darkened shadows that crept into her bedroom were detailed. Dominique cried as she told of the man looming over her, the smell of his breath, and threats of what she knew would be rape.

"Have you, or shall I ask, do you know that you were touched? Do you think you have been?"

"That's what I don't remember."

Twenty

Estelle hung her coat in the hall closet. It was close to six. Rehearsal would start in another hour. She was usually early with time to read the scriptures and talk with members as they entered and left the church. She needed to talk to Brenda. Randall told her that Kendall spoke about apologizing to anyone he had ever harmed. Brenda Preston was on that list.

Estelle spent most of her life keeping Kendall out of jail. He was her youngest and she wouldn't see him behind bars. She demanded Randall protect him; even lie for him to keep him on the straight and narrow. Kendall's choices, from booze to women kept him in front of a judge. Even though they were adults, Estelle felt her duty was to her children.

Zeke Preston and Kendall were friends, *"Thicker than thieves"*, she always said. Estelle knew Brenda had been abused. Her thoughts were Brenda blamed anyone but herself. Her husband played the streets hard. He kept plenty of drugs, had no qualms about who he sexed, and paid good money for a good time. Zeke made several advances; suggested to Estelle she should try his bed once or twice. He teased and taunted her; she imaged his tight body entwined with hers. She needed to boost her ego. Being an older woman when he offered to taste her nectar, she willingly allowed him to fulfill both their pleasures. She wasn't sure if Zeke had blurted her name during his drunken rages, but her relationship with Brenda wasn't the same. If Brenda would find comfort in revenge, her boys would be the targets.

A warning from his mother was more than enough to keep Randall from involving himself in a grieving widow's affairs. When Estelle gave Kendall the same warning it seemed to fuel his desire for her. Kendall was a bad boy who matured to be a bad man. His habits mixed well with the husband Brenda couldn't keep at home. He had his own needs and motives for revenge. Estelle knew his return home was more than the completion of a twelve-step program.

She could hear the voices from the sanctuary. Choir robes were draped across the back pews. The chatter from the members of the Mass Choir was a mixture of opinions. From the solos to be sung, the robes that didn't quite fit, to the upcoming event, the discussions began to grow in volume. The conversations overpowered the music from the organist who seemed to ignore the noise. There was a tapping on the microphone to get the attention of the crowd.

"Is Sister Jones here yet?" One of the choir members asked backing off the microphone to avoid the static feedback.

"Not yet Sistah Jeffries." The answer came from a few members standing in the corner of the church. Once the question was answered the chatter began again. Estelle stood in the back scanning the choir loft for Brenda. She thought about asking if anyone had seen her. Dismissing that thought, she went down the hall where she passed a group of children in leotards and colorful scarves. Estelle took the time to compliment them on their Sunday performance. They giggled responding to her smiles and compliments. Ms. Myers, the dance coordinator, came to the door beckoning for them to enter the room.

"Hey Sister Stevenson, I didn't know why they were out here keeping up so much noise." She put her finger on the nose of the smallest girl in the group and pinched her cheek.

"Yes, they are just dolls in those outfits," responded Estelle, "How are you Ms. Myers? I'm here for rehearsal. Have you seen Sistah Preston?"

"She's here. I think she and Randall are with Pastor. I noticed Kendall is with us now. How good is God, huh? He's returned with a new spirit.

Looking good too, I sure hope he's beneficial to that new ministry. They went toward the nursery about ten minutes ago."

Estelle tried not to make it obvious that she had no concern for Kendall's involvement in the church. She told Randall he would only have problems working near Brenda. She would have to wait for Brenda to return to her office. She would be upset if this meeting would make her late for rehearsal.

She walked through the halls surprised at how busy things were. There were classes going on, group meetings and of course rehearsals. As a member of the Mass Choir and the Sick and Shut In Ministry, she hadn't thought of being involved in any of the other core groups in Pastor Turner's Truly Blessed Ministries. Her time serving the Lord was personal. She felt she didn't need to be a part of every group or the secretary to be saved.

She didn't knock on the secretary's door. Brenda wouldn't mind her waiting. She looked around the room for changes. It had been months since she stepped into any of the church offices. She was impressed. The colors in the room were still a bit bland for her taste. The pictures included news clippings of events Pastor Turner had attended, baptisms and Dominique. The furniture had been rearranged creating the illusion that the room increased in size. Brenda had made the office her space away from home.

Estelle turned and faced Brenda, who stood in the center of the room watching her. The minute of silence said more than words. Estelle took a seat near the desk and waited for Brenda to speak first.

"You're here early, did they change the time?" Brenda stepped around the desk certain the visit had a purpose.

"No actually, I stopped in to see you. I didn't think you would be long, so I waited."

Brenda heard her uninvited guest, but knew there was more to it. She thought about the conversation she had with Kendall. He wouldn't have told his mother. Her precious sons, the dirt from their past, Estelle covered it all. She had always been against their friendship. Brenda wondered how her earlier conversation would provoke her to visit.

"What can I do for you?"

"I wanted to make sure we understood each other. I mean with Kendall working here now…"

"Estelle, we went through this when I was dating Randall. Your boys, and I do mean boys, are of no interest to me. I understood you when you said you would always be involved. It was your involvement that Randall and I didn't need. I never liked Kendall so again, what can I do for you?"

"You and I both know your husband was a friend of Kendall's. I know you blamed him for your husband's indiscretions." She crossed her legs, and sat back thinking she had the upper hand. "It's really time to face the facts. Kendall had nothing to do with your husband's addictions. He was just like my son, lost. No one can blame another for the choices they make."

Brenda got up from the desk and shut the office door. "Don't you ever come to my office with this mess again! You act as though you have some secret to tell, something about my husband or his life. Estelle if you do, tell it, if not leave me alone. I don't want your sons. No woman would, you've ruined them. You're right, I have no reason to blame Kendall, but I don't like him either. I have my reasons and I don't care to share them with you. Is there anything else?"

Estelle took in the silence between them and stood determined to have the last word. "I guess you feel the same way about Kendall as I've always felt about you. I couldn't blame you for being a part of Zeke's life. You know he talked about you often when he visited with Kendall. Just as you said, I never liked you either." She walked out of the office glad she cleared the air.

Brenda was stunned. She didn't want the conversation to turn into an argument. There had been talk of Zeke and Estelle sleeping together. Brenda didn't care who he screwed. It kept him from beating her and wanting to make love ignoring her emotional and physical bruises. Estelle wouldn't have been one she would have put on his list of choices.

Kendall's relationship with Zeke was only a tip of the problems she had in her marriage. Kendall always felt he could get next to her behind Zeke's back. It sparked many arguments and caused many black eyes.

Kendall always found a way to come over to their home afterward and try to comfort her. He was the catalyst to Zeke's anger many times. Brenda ignored his apologies then and had no intention on accepting them now.

The night of the murder, Kendall said he knew Zeke was headed home to start trouble. Brenda was too upset to go over the details. After the police left, hours after the investigation tape was taken down, Kendall helped scrub the floor. The blood of her husband was mixed with cleanser and water on his friend's hands. There was a wretched feeling in her gut that Kendall's blood should have been shed too.

Twenty-one

Westlene finished her comments on the last client's chart, grateful to cancel their appointments after the schedule was pushed back. She opened the bottom drawer and fingered through the file. Dominique's file was thin but she was sure it would be one that would more than double the size of the others. She filled out the form that gave a quick glance of the information the folder contained. She turned her attention to her computer clicking onto a template that was set for client information and began to type.

It was too early to pass judgment on Boat's friend, but she had seen many cases of abuse. Dominique's nightmare's indicated that she had been abused, possibly molested. Westlene was sure, although Dominique didn't say it, she had blocked out the abuse over the years. She begged Westlene to help her understand why she couldn't connect the people or the place in the dream with what she knew was her childhood. She didn't know how to tell her that the nightmares were her connection. The dreams did not lie. Westlene's experience taught her that the nightmares would get worse if Dominique didn't face reality.

The session concluded with Westlene suggesting she speak again with her mother. Maybe visit the home she grew up in and talk about the relationships that were a part of her early childhood. Dominique didn't remember much about the years immediately following her father's murder. She remembered being unable to sleep, the medication and the treatment. She wanted to remember, which was a lot more than Westlene anticipated.

She logged off the computer and put the file away. It was time to go home. She was interrupted by more thoughts. Dominique had described her family as stable. More stable than most African American families the doctor dealt with on a daily basis. There were no uncles, brothers, or other male family members who would have violated her, or was there? She pulled the file again. Dominique had only named three men, her father, the pastor and the deacon of the church. Whoever it was that was still touching her in the middle of the night had a great influence on her. She didn't recall ever telling her mother. She hadn't discussed the details of her recent dreams. Her mother knew she was seeking help and Dominique wanted to leave it that way. Brenda had been no help in the past, other than lifting her daughter in prayer.

Westlene decided her questioning would have to be more direct. Maybe a meeting with Dominique and her mother would shed some light on the matter. Boat's concerns for his friend were no longer the priority. Dominique's problem could become serious. She had seen others lose their sense of self, and in the worse cases become suicidal. Westlene wouldn't be speaking to Boat until she felt it necessary.

During the session, Dominique mentioned her love for both Claudia and Boat. Their friendship was important to her. She admitted there was a fear of becoming too close to either of them. She described it as uncomfortable. Westlene noted it. It was another indication that she had been in an abusive relationship. Claudia and Boat knew about the dreams, they would be the first people Dominique would turn to. Westlene wrote their names as contacts and closed the folder again.

Claudia sat feeling numb, her response to Dominique's recollection of her latest dream. After her appointment, she called Claudia and invited her to have dinner. Dominique cooked their favorites, smothered steak, rice and stir fried vegetables. Claudia, glad to have a night away from her apartment, brought the wine. Dominique wanted another opinion, one that didn't agree with Westlene's conclusion of her being abused or molested as a child.

"I don't know Dommi, she may be right. You've blocked out so much, it could have been the trauma. They say the subconscious blocks out what may be of danger to us. It could have been the only way for you to get through it. You simply blocked it out."

"Claudia, I don't know the people in this dream. I can't recognize the voices. I don't know where I am. Maybe I'm seeing someone else go through these things."

"Well how do you explain the wet pajamas, the heat from the man over you?" Claudia cocked her head waiting for the answer. She contorted her lips putting emphasis on the question. "Come on, think about it. You don't know how to explain the house. Who lives in that house now?"

Dominique answered after a moment of deep thought. "I guess Ms. Brooks still live there. She bought the house from my mother. We went there a few times afterward. She and my mother were close. I guess she knew her from the church. I haven't been to that house in years. Claudia, I remember not wanting to go in that house after we left. I actually cried the last time my mother took me there."

"Your mother took you there to visit after your father had been killed there?"

"I guess my mother didn't think much of it. We never stayed long." She began to talk slower, trying to reminisce. "Maybe it was her cousins who bought the house."

"So you do remember them?"

"Sorta, I don't know if they still live there. I think they moved or maybe they didn't live there long. Yes, Claudia that's it. Ms. Brooks bought the house and then rented it out to her cousins. My mother was upset because she thought…" Dominique paused deliberately. "Ms. Viola wanted it for herself. That's her name, Viola Brooks. She was my babysitter for a while. I remember her now."

Tears began to fall from her eyes. Claudia went to the bathroom and brought her friend a few tissues.

"Dommi, what's wrong?"

"The woman's voice in the dream is Viola's"

"Are you sure?"

"I think so. This is so frustrating. Maybe it's just a dream. Maybe it has nothing to do with my past. People dream all the time about things happening with people they know."

"You're right. Don't let it upset you. Westlene's right, you need to talk to your mother."

"She'll never admit to anything Claudia. Will you come with me?"

"Come with you where?"

"I need to see that house. I need to walk through the area that I saw in the dream."

"No one's gonna just let you walk through their home. I don't know if that will work. Do you know where Viola is now?"

"No, and asking my mother won't work either."

"What about someone else who knows her?"

"That's it. Mr. Stevenson would know. He's a friend of my mother's. I'll ask him about the house and Ms. Viola buying it. Maybe he has some answers."

"Are you going to tell him your reason for asking?"

"No, he'll tell my mother. I'll think of something. I just hope Westlene is wrong."

"Dommi, what if she's not?"

Twenty-two

Kendall sat at the bar nursing the second drink he ordered. The bartender smiled as he waved his hand across the top of the glass, understanding he didn't want another refill. There was a little vodka and cranberry juice that settled in his glass barely above the ice. He took another deliberate sip as he canvassed the dim room.

The bar hadn't changed much. He recognized some of the frequent customers shooting pool, and making noise about the football game. The sports channel was on each of the plasma televisions mounted on the walls. It was during half time when Kendall began to walk the length of the bar getting reacquainted with friends he hadn't seen in years.

"When did you get back man?" A dark complexioned man asked as he passed his stool. The stool sat further back than the others allowing the robust man room to sit comfortably. He put out his puffed hand greeting his buddy from the past.

"Hey Pep, what's up man?" Kendall was glad to see his friend was up and around. He heard about his fight with diabetes and never knew what happened to him.

"It's all good brother, how you? You looking good. I see you back on the stroll."

"Nah, nothing like that man. I'm done with that bull. Got to take it easy, or it will take you out, know what I mean?"

"No doubt, you talking to a witness. I'm still battling this weight thing cause of my diabetes, but I lost quite a bit." He stood to show off his lost. Despite his huge size Kendall was impressed. "I've lost close to fifty pounds or more. It's coming off slowly; they had to change my meds to get this thing under control." He positioned himself slowly sitting back on the stool. Kendall watched realizing the effort Pep put into standing to impress him.

"Hey, Pep man, I'm proud of you. It's coming off. Listen, where's the rest of the crew? I mean do you still see many of the card players?"

The weekly card game brought people from all over town. The years that passed hadn't change the players. Those that loved bid whist, spades, and sometimes a good chess game, loved Friday nights. The regulars were those who drank with Zeke, Kendall, and Pep.

"Well since you've been gone a few of us have been in and out of the hospital, myself included. Dean and the boys changed their spot. Word is they hang out on Bergen near Hawthorne. Small spot their but plenty of women. You know your girl Viola was sick here a month or so ago. They said she had pneumonia. She works downtown, man I can't remember the name of the spot. Upscale joint though, she's a waitress or hostess there. The rest of em' will be here Friday."

Kendall had the information he needed. Viola was still around. She was known for dancing, being a waitress or hostess must have been a cover. He laughed to himself thinking of her dancing at her age.

"Man, you know what the bartender at The Lounge on Central Ave. can tell you where she works. He's dating her now."

"Rich? You ain't talking about Rich are you?"

"Yeah, that's him. Listen, I've got to get outta here man. I've had my limit and talking with you will certainly take me over." Pep put his hands on the bar to support himself as he stood. "Be good man, it was good seeing you."

Pep downed the rest of his beer and left a twenty-dollar bill on the bar. He waved to a few people as he slowly waddled out of the front door. Kendall watched him leave before he took his seat. He ordered a beer, putting the glass he held on the counter. He pulled the stool closer to the bar satisfied. He'd look for Viola a little later. He pulled out his wallet and laid another twenty to begin his rounds. If he was lucky he wouldn't have to spend it all and go home alone.

Through the smoke filled air, he spotted three women in the booth across the room. They looked too young to be in the bar, he could tell by their whispers and giggles they weren't regulars. The stools were filled with men enjoying the game. There were a few women who looked out of place standing and sitting at the end of the bar. Their huddle was interrupted with drinks passed to them from men attempting to get their attention. Kendall wasn't willing to compete.

The laughter of the young women in the booth boomed over the music and the cheering crowd on the television. Kendall repositioned his stool, allowing him to have a visual of the women and the pool game that occupied the space between them. He hadn't had a woman in his arms in weeks. A romp in the bedroom had been even longer. The women in Florida wanted a man who would stay in their bed Sunday through Saturday. The thought was inviting but he who accepted the invitation had to leave his money there too. Kendall didn't want any part of the pay to play plan.

He turned up the beer bottle savoring the last of his third beer. There was five dollars left on the counter. The young women had danced, sang and drank themselves into mellow moods. One flirted with Kendall from a distance and his manhood told him she could satisfy his urge. He sent her a drink and waited for her to make eye contact, an acknowledgement of thanks.

She stood, greeting the barmaid, who pointed to Kendall. Her walk was deliberate. Each step was an invitation for him to meet her as she sashayed closer to him. Kendall was patient, enjoying the slow roll of her hips. Her jeans hugged each of her curves. The figure-fitting sweater was simple, black and low cut, giving him a visual of her forty c's. She stopped in between his legs that parted making way for her to walk right up to the stool's edge.

He could smell her perfume, Red Door, a fragrance his nose was familiar with. She was a pretty girl. Her face showed a faded scar, a marking of a vicious fight from what had to be her high school years. Her complexion was what his mother would call "hi-yalla", she wasn't light enough to pass for white. The yellow tone of her skin and her full lips, gave away her black heritage. Her eyes were dark brown almost black; her lashes were done accentuating her sexy demeanor. Her hair was natural, dreads that glistened, the length of her shoulders. They were thin and designed perfectly to fit her small face.

She touched her lips with her manicured nail placing a kiss on the tip of her finger. She slowly took her finger and placed it on his partially opened mouth. Kendall knew the gesture well and put his tongue out touching the tip of her finger gently. There was a responding pulse in his pants. He knew he was full. He hoped her teasing meant she was willing to fulfill his needs.

Her nipples hardened. The drinks and the view of the lump in his pants took over. Her intent was to tease him longer but her body began to crave him.

"Hello, and thank you for the drink." She held up the glass and put it to her lips.

Kendall didn't want to order another drink and he hoped she wouldn't mind if he asked her not to finish hers. The game she was playing was leading to a satisfying night, but it couldn't be rushed. There were a few things about this sensual lady that he had seen before.

"You're welcome. Do you live around here?"

"Don't you remember me?"

"Should I?" Kendall looked into her face again hoping she wasn't someone from his past. She held no resemblance to anyone he slept with or had shunned off.

"I used to watch you, Pep, and Zeke play cards here when I was younger. I'm all grown up now."

Kendall thought hard; his body reacted. He was losing his erection; scared she would reveal unpleasant memories of his past.

"Don't tense up now Mr. Stephenson. You always flirted with me and my sisters. We'd be here helping to clean up and stuff. I'm Noani, you said you would never forget us."

His heart fluttered as she said her name. The three teenage girls that cleaned the bar on Friday and Saturday nights were cousins of Dean's. They lived with him and his family and came with him to the card games often. The young men in the bar enjoyed their company and they learned at a young age how to handle them all. The back of the bar became a room of training for them and the young male virgins. Dean didn't mind, they weren't his daughters, and he got paid. He shared the money with the girls and that kept them from telling girlfriends, wives and their aunt. Kendall wanted to visit that room with the three of them often but Dean had his rules, young men only, virgins preferred. He was sure that the timid males would be gentle with the girls.

"How you been, how's your sisters?"

"They moved out of Newark, got married. They're doing good. I'm doing good too. I live in West Orange now. Got my own place, I'm working, you know." She put her glass down and sat on the stool next to him.

"You're looking good." His penis responded as he looked at her aroused nipples.

"Kendall, I've always liked you. My cousin told me to stay away from you because of your age. I'm grown now. I remember you telling me things would be different if I was older. Not that I waited just for you but, I always wanted to know what you or any of Dean's friends had that was so different." She smiled and stroked his middle finger.

"So, you remember me flirting with you, huh. You ain't got a man? I mean like you said, you haven't been waiting for me to come through the door."

"Of course not, but some things just give you a feeling that you can't describe. You've always made me tingle, you know throb. Listen you know what went on in that room." She gestured to the closed door behind the bar leaning into him brushing her breast lightly across his hand. "There were many times that I imagined the boy on top of me was you. But I knew you wouldn't be giving me that sloppy loving they gave. You would know what I needed. Dean turned us out. My sisters jumped on the first ones that would marry them. Me, I ain't looking for no husband. I haven't found a man that could satisfy me on a regular, so why would I pretend and get married. I guess I'm still looking. What about you?"

"Can't say I'm looking for a wife, I get around too." He picked up her hand and held it. "There were many times I saw myself in that room with you. We can make this real."

Noani blushed. She could feel her body quiver at the thought. Kendall was always a sexy older man to her. She knew about his drug habits, the women, and his goal to be rehabilitated. She wanted him to touch her all over and appease her curiosity.

"You still deal with Viola, or what was her name, Brenda?"

"No, Viola and Brenda are friends but we're not close like that. I haven't seen Viola in years. I need to talk with her though."

"She works downtown. I go there often and see her. D & L Lounge, she's the hostess there. Do you know where it is?"

Kendall didn't care for the distraction. They could talk about Viola later. His penis jumped again.

"So what about me and you for tonight? I mean can that happen? We both look like we're holding it in."

Noani smiled, "My place or yours."

Kendall didn't have a place to offer and didn't want the questions from Randall. "West Orange baby."

Twenty-three

Boat checked his watch hoping he had time to stop at his apartment. The game was worth attending but his mind kept drifting to Dominique. Westlene didn't answer his questions and she ended the conversation by saying the situation was deeper then he thought.

He phoned Dommi from the game and told her he'd stop by if it was okay with her. They hadn't been alone to talk for the past two weeks. She claimed her schedule was tight. She told him they could hang out in New York all day Sunday; she would enjoy that.

It wasn't as late as he thought. It was eleven; he could get to her place by eleven thirty. Claudia would be gone by then. He was glad she had become a close friend. He hoped with their friendship Dominique would get through her therapy and they'd live happily ever after. Westlene put a damper on his dream when she told him it may take more than a few sessions to get to the root of her problems.

He didn't want to keep guessing at what the problem may be. If he questioned her she would know he spoke with Westlene. He'd have to battle his nerves. He had a fear of the unknown. His cell phone rang as he locked his door leaving his apartment.

"Hey, what's up lady?"

Claudia paused before speaking. "Are you home yet?"

"Home and leaving to get with Dommi. Why?"

"Oh, nothing. Good, you're going to be with her tomorrow?"

"What's up? You sound like there's a problem."

"I'm not sure and I don't know whether I'm stepping over the line here. You talk with her and see what you think. Her dreams are telling a story of some sort and I'm scared for her. I don't know maybe it's just me. Listen, ignore this call. Boat, I know we agreed to keep each other informed about Dominique's behavior but I'm not comfortable with calling you behind her back. It's me being scary that's all. You talk to her and tell me what you think."

The call was disconnected before he could respond. The thought of calling her back crossed his mind. As he sat in the driver's seat of his car, he decided against it. The lights of the oncoming traffic glared as he drove through the streets. Westlene's voice repeating "deep issues" had become the answer to his questions. Claudia's call gave rise to his existing anxiety. The traffic lights seemed to be giving him time to decide about his visit. Although the thought of redirecting his vehicle became an option, he didn't stop until he was parked in Dominique's driveway.

He was surprised the light was on in the living room. He rang the bell and heard the welcoming yell of, "It's open." He shook his head, but decided not to mention his concern about her inviting any stranger in her home.

"What's up Boat? Listen, we can't keep this distance between us", Dominique yelled from the stairs.

He was confused, but if Westlene had given her meds to ease her normal defensive reactions, he wouldn't complain.

"You've been busy remember? I'd love to close our distance."

His smile gave her the signals she loved when her body screamed for arousal. She was prepared, candles, wine and condoms. Her talk with Claudia put her at ease. Her friend agreed to go with her to her old home. She was sure it would put an end to her dreams. Westlene was sent by God to help her and the visit to the house was the missing link.

The women drank tea and talked about men until Claudia got a call from her boyfriend. It was a booty call she wasn't gonna miss and she suggested Dominique call Boat and seduce him. Boat's call made it evident that she needed him to work his magic.

Dominique took his hand and led him to the bedroom without a word. He attempted to shed his coat and gloves as they reached the stairs. He followed her, dropping the coat on the banister, he watched her butt bounce to its own rhythm, as her feet hit each step. Her cut off shorts revealed both cheeks of her smooth bottom. The top of her thong sat above the shorts. He let his imagination fast forward to the bedroom, anticipating what she had prepared for their prelude.

Dominique smiled as she opened her bedroom door. It took her less than an hour to set up the room as a backdrop to a sensual escapade. During a moment of verbal foreplay, Boat told her he had a fantasy of the two of them making love on satin sheets filled with rose petals. He bought the wine, petals and sheets, giving them to her as gifts on one of their anniversaries. She was stuck in a snowstorm in Seattle and never made it home. The gifts were on her bed when she returned. Dominique neglected to call him the next morning to explain the flight was canceled and her phone didn't work from the airport. The note he left said enough. It took them a while to put the event to the side, but she never returned the gifts.

Boat remembered the snowy night as the candles flickered softly. He was taken aback for a moment amazed she would attempt to fulfill his fantasy after the argument they had about the gifts. She kept them; he knew she would. Maybe their relationship was now on another level.

They stood at the foot of the bed facing each other as they had many nights before. It seemed to be their starting point. The romantic stare; they both gazed at the others beauty and smiled. Her buttons were undone, Boat didn't know when she opened them, and she simply let the tank top fall on the floor. Her hardened nipples now exposed in the open air. Boat moved closer to touch her neck with his lips.

The softness of his mouth caused Dommi to quiver. She giggled in spite of herself holding his shirt fumbling for the buttons. He took his time exploring her ear and neck with his tongue. He teased her moving it in and out kissing her ever so softly. She loved the feeling and knowing the man she had made love to many times before, she wanted to be selfish and allow him to please her first.

Boat thought about his normal foreplay. The moves she enjoyed and moaned for. He wanted her to beg him. He wouldn't kiss her nipples, navel or waistline until she asked him to. The thrill would be explosive and worth the intensity. He stood upright and helped her remove his shirt, pants and boxers. His manhood grew in her hands.

She stood in front of him in her thong and worked her magic as she turned slowly and bent over. She removed her thong as he watched. He took his hands and wrapped them around her waist pulling her closer to him. Her butt made the perfect mitt, but he wanted her to beg him. He fondled her breast, appreciating the firmness. His penis began to enlarge as he brushed it against her warm skin.

Dominique waited wanting the first round to begin when she bent over. She anticipated his approach and entry. She had been moist since she held him in her hands. Boat was an average size but he seemed to grow more once the ride began.

The roses were spread over the sheets just as he described but they both hesitated to move to the king sized bed to play. Dominique sat at the foot of the bed and opened her legs hoping the sight would give him an enticing view. The pink walls and her erect clitoris was all he needed to see. He fell to his knees and began the foreplay that made them both moan for more. Dominique raised her legs, wrapping them around his shoulders. He lifted her as he stood, not allowing his mouth to leave her inner thighs. He positioned her cove onto his penis as he realized it was him, that couldn't take the teasing any more.

Dominique let out a scream of pleasure, "I'm…I'm… oh… ooo…"

Boat could feel her heat. He would have to pull out. It would only make the both of them turn on each other. He remembered seeing the condoms on the nightstand.

"Baby wait, I—"

"Shhhhit…ummm…"

Dominique repositioned herself in the bed, waiting for him to return. The nightstand held the wine and the condoms. Boat took the bottle and drank from it. Hoping it would be a quick fix for his thirst. He massaged his penis as he put on the condom, silently saying "thank you" to no one in particular. It had been months since they made love like this.

Boat returned to the bed, slowly approaching Dominique who had turned her back to him. He kissed the back of her neck and whispered softly, "I can't wait to give you what I got for you, baby. I've been waiting for this a long time."

Dominique rolled over happy to accept his package and the load he carried. As she turned the face that met her wasn't the man she loved. She could smell the liquor on his breath, the stench of his breath made her want to puke. It was too late he had entered her. She watched as his face became contorted. There were minutes where she thought she saw Boat and her body reacted and then she was petrified by the appearance of the stranger. She screamed. Boat continued he was reaching his peak. The lips of her vagina held him close, and he could feel her pulsating. She screamed again, he ejaculated pleased that he finally had given her more than she could stand.

"Get the fuck off me!!"

The condom fell on her leg; sperm spilled onto the sheets.

"Oh God, no!! Get the fuck off me! What the fuck is wrong with you! You come in here every night haunting me for sex, what the fuck, you raped me!"

Boat shook his head in confusion. His penis was still erect. He was embarrassed that he was still feeling the passion of the moment.

"Dommi, baby what's wrong? Did I hurt you?"

It was as though she came out of a daze. She broke down crying. Boat got up and went to the bathroom. He brought back a warm cloth and began to wipe her legs. Carefully he patted hoping he hadn't hurt her in any way.

"Are you okay, I didn't mean to…."

"Oh my God. Boat, I need help."

"Was it me, did I hurt you. Baby, I would never…"

"I think it happened before."

"What?"

"He tried to rape me."

Twenty-four

Kendall tapped his feet to the music Noani had blaring from her Boise system. She offered him a drink from her well stocked bar. Her place was simple, nothing fancy, basic furniture and not many accent pieces. It was clean with the exception of the dining room table that held books and papers scattered in no particular order. She kicked off her heels, wiggled her toes and gave him a smirk when she noticed his stare.

"Guess you saying, I'm too slow about it huh?"

Kendall was enjoying the music, the idea of having a drink when and if he needed to, and a woman in the bed. The thought of making her home a temporary rest stop was dancing through his mind. If he could clear himself of the guilt he felt about Zeke's death, he could move on.

"Take your time, I'm good."

"I haven't had company in a while. You can tell huh? I'm a loner. Those chicks you saw me with, I run into every now and then. How about you? Are you back here for good?"

"If I can find a reason to stay. I'm staying with my brother now, but I ain't got no strings."

"I'd love to be tied up." She brought the mixed drinks over, placing them on the coffee table. Her body spoke louder than the music, which was taking them back a few years. The Isley Brothers harmonized through the next song and Noani tapped the remote lowering the volume. She took a seat at the other end of the couch, and stretched her legs touching Kendall's pocket teasingly with her toes.

He reached for his drink and mentally began to plot his approach. It was too easy for him to just unzip and release. She wanted it to be special; he'd make sure she couldn't forget it.

"How long have you lived here?"

"About four years. I work at the hospital. I have weird hours, hard to keep much of a relationship. But the people here are cool, it's a garden apartment for now but I've got plans. So did you and my cousin turn out any other young girls?"

"That was your cousin's doing. I didn't know too many young girls as you call them."

"If you say so. You know Dean is registered right?"

"Registered?"

"Yeah he was charged for pictures of some high school girl and trying to sell them, some shit. Anyway, they caught him with the pictures and charged him. So he's registered as a sex offender."

"Damn, he was like that?"

"Kendall come on you know what y'all did in the bar with us was illegal."

Kendall tried to suppress his anger. "So you brought me here to tell me you think I should be registered too?"

"No, I just hope that you didn't do no shit that will haunt you now. That shit can come back on you." She shifted on the couch and didn't give any regard to her blouse falling open. Kendall took her feet in his hand and began massaging her toes.

"Listen, anyone I ever laid was of age. So I'm good."

"Y'all did a lot of shit, I hope you didn't come back to get it all together for it all to fall apart."

"You know something sweetheart? Let's not go there, I ain't Dean and we both know Zeke is dead."

"Yeah did they ever find out who killed him?"

Kendall was beginning to get bored. She talked too much. He wasn't used to a woman's chatter.

He leaned over her feet, which now had a place in his lap, reaching for his glass. He'd have to be blunt to get her to focus on his reason for being in her home. He sat back and released his belt and the button on his jeans. She wiggled her toes over his zipper pleased with his actions.

Twenty-five

onday morning found Dominique dragging out of bed. She hadn't slept long the entire weekend. She spent most of it apologizing to Boat. He said he accepted her apology but she wasn't sure if he was avoiding the truth. She yelled rape, a word that would unnerve any man who thought he was pleasing the woman he loved.

It was close to six, she had an hour of Boat's time before he left for work. She convinced him to spend another night. He was persistent about sleeping in the guest room. She agreed with the arrangement afraid he wouldn't visit or return her calls if they didn't get another chance to talk. He had been distant on Sunday and if he hadn't paid for tickets to a matinee on Broadway she was certain, he would have left early that morning.

It would take more than a conversation to convince him that she didn't mean what she said. She repeated her dreams to him explaining the man's touch, smell and what was said. Dominique didn't believe she had been raped. The thought became a part of what could be real; the man was there to rape her. When Boat asked had she been raped in the past she firmly answered, "No".

"Babe, I'm trying not to dwell on this. I know it's bothering you but I'm getting madder and madder the more we talk about it. Could you have been raped and don't remember it? I just don't understand that."

"I wasn't raped, I know I wasn't. But Boat, that doesn't mean, I don't know, maybe that's what all this is about. This man has been haunting me for months. He keeps getting closer and closer in my dreams. I don't know what stops him. Maybe someone walked in. I know he sneaks into my room. I know I'm a child. Maybe it's not me; maybe it's another girl that got raped. I don't know. You've got to understand, I was drifting off relaxing and I guess I picked up my dream where it left off. Maybe it was an attempt. I'll call Westlene and ask her."

"And tell her this revelation came in the middle of making love to me?" Boat sighed and began to butter the toast Dominique prepared for him. His breakfast was more than what she usually made after his overnight visits. She was definitely trying to please him. He put the toast down on his plate. His appetite was gone. "Dommi, maybe if you ask you mother, you know, before talking to anybody else. I don't know though, she would have told you before now. I mean, you know if it really happened."

Dominique didn't know what to say. It was apparent that Boat didn't believe her excuse. There was no need to debate with him. She knew she hadn't been violated, but what if someone had made the attempt when she was younger. She understood his point.

"I'll see her this afternoon. Claudia and I are going to the house we lived in."

"The house? Why?"

"Westlene says it may trigger my memory; just what you're saying, if it happened."

"I'm not saying it happened, I mean, I hope it didn't. Dommi, this is not what I thought would come from your dreams. I still say you should talk with your mother. It may be more than the memory of the house. What about your memory of the murder?"

"I don't remember the murder."

"My point, suppose this nightmare is what went on the night of the murder?" He swallowed the rest of his coffee. He took the last bite into the toast as he removed his plate from the table. Putting the dishes in the sink, he ran the water rinsing his hands. "Go see your mother first. Prepare her before you walk into what could be your biggest fears. You always said you've had these nightmares all of your life. What was your age when you first had the nightmare?"

She held her head and shut her eyes. She couldn't remember how old she was. The nightmares weren't the same she was sure of that. Boat was right. She would call the church first. She wanted to know the answers before her mother had a chance to lie to her. Randall would be in the office by eight thirty. He would be able to help her. The sound of the chair moving as Boat pushed it in caught her attention.

"Boat I'm sorry. Can you forgive me?"

"Call me before you go to the house. Baby, if you need me to go…."

They walked to the front door engrossed in their own thoughts. She kissed him on his cheek, giving him a coy smile as she opened the door. The chill of the air made her push it closer, leaving only enough room for him to lean in and kiss her on her lips.

"Call me." Boat pulled the door closed and turned his collar up to block the wind. His thoughts were confused with an emptiness he didn't quite understand. The "what if's" were beginning to creep upon him and he couldn't give an answer to any of the questions.

The leather upholstery in his car was cold. He sat motionless waiting for the car to warm up. He stared at the bay window of Dominique's home. He couldn't believe his mixed emotions. He was numb, not knowing how he would feel if the woman he adored had been violated in some way. He put his car in gear, convincing himself that whatever she had experienced it wasn't her fault.

Dominque turned the lock, and allowed her head to fall gently against the door. She took a deep breath and mouthed a prayer, hoping it wouldn't be the last time she saw Boat. There was so much she should have said before the weekend. She realized now, she loved him. Returning to the kitchen she picked up the phone and put it back in the cradle. Her tears flowed freely.

Twenty-six

It was close to ten thirty before Randall answered his phone in the office. Dominique closed her eyes, rolling them in disappointment after hearing the answer machine begin the recorded voice message. She was stunned hearing his baritone voice interrupting the prompted script.

"Good morning, Deacon Stevenson, how may I help you?"

Dominique's voice cracked as she began to speak. She cleared her throat as the Deacon repeated himself.

"Good morning Mr. Stevenson, it's me, Dommi."

"Well, good morning, how can I help you?" He questioned minus the professional demeanor.

"Mr. Stevenson, I have a question about the house on Rose Terrace where my mom and I lived."

"Your mom would be the best person to ask about that." His response told her he had the information she needed. She ignored his answer and continued.

"Do you know if Ms. Viola still owns it?"

"I don't think she ever bought it. Hold on." She was put on hold. The voices of the choir chimed through the phone. Dominique found herself humming softly feeling a little guilty that she hadn't been to a church service in months. The singing stopped and a commercial with the times of Sunday worship caused her to smile and shake her head. The message gave her an unexpected jolt, but she understood the work of the subconscious. She wondered if the Deacon had forgotten about her as the choir began another selection.

"Dommi, I'm sorry, I wanted to be sure of the information I was giving you. The church bought the property from your mother and your mother moved the two of you into an apartment on the other side of town. Well, Viola wanted to buy the house, when the church put it up for sale. I don't know what stopped her from going through with it but a family member of hers rented it for quite some time. Now the rest you would have to ask your mother."

"Did the church sell the property?"

"Oh no, it's still the church's property. We thought about selling, than there was talk about a day care center. Nothing was done with it until about five years ago. A member uses it as a library and resource center for the school children in the area. I don't know if they are still there. Again, your mother would know."

"So the house is occupied?"

"Daily from eight in the morning until seven at night, I don't know that anyone's there over night."

"Thank you, one more question?"

Randall closed the file and pushed it to the side of his desk.

"Do you think my mother would have a problem with me wanting to walk through the house?"

The silence on the line gave Dominique a queasy feeling in the pit of her stomach. She waited hoping she wouldn't have to repeat her question.

"What are you looking for child? You don't want to go there. It may not be good for you. I mean you still have those nightmares right?"

"That's why I want to walk through that house. It may answer a few questions."

Randall ended the conversation simply replying he understood. There was nothing else he could say. Brenda had made a decision years ago that she would tell her daughter about her father's murder, if she should ever ask.

Dominique's decision to drive past the house on the other side of town didn't include walking onto the porch and ringing the bell. The address, she had recited so many times in grammar school, was easy enough to find, although she had limited travels in Newark's Southward. She called Claudia repeating the deacon's warnings. Dominique's argument included the fact that the house was occupied and vibrant. There wouldn't be a cause for alarm.

The peeling paint and creaking porch told there was a lack of care given to the edifice over the years. What seemed to be a large home during her childhood took on a different appearance. Dominique rang the bell again listening closely for noise from within. A teenager opened the door, smiled and turned away without uttering a word.

"Who turned the lock on the door? People can't get in if you lock the door. Where is Robert? Your job is here at this desk, that's why the door was locked. If you think you're being paid to roam around…"

Dominique stepped in and looked around trying to get her bearings. The woman, obviously annoyed closed the door allowing Dominique to take another step away from the entrance. The house looked more like a library or learning center. The two front rooms were filled with books from the floor to the ceiling. There was an executive desk at the door where Robert was assigned to greet visitors. His nameplate sat proudly in the middle of the desk. The robust woman wiped her hands on her apron and turned the book toward their afternoon guest.

"I'm so sorry Ma'am, these here kids will make you go crazy. Welcome, have you been here before?"

"Well, no not really. I guess you could say I was here years ago."

"We ain't been here that long, are you sure?"

"Oh no, not while you were here."

"Well then I'll need you to sign in first. Robert, you get over here and do your job. Do your job, or I'll get your pay!"

Dominique signed the book and waited for directions. Robert a frail boy, who looked to be no more than twelve or thirteen, came running, pulling up his pants.

"I told you about those pants too. You ain't gonna be satisfied until your job goes to someone else. You musta forgot you asked for a chance, don't mess it up. Now introduce yourself and do your job."

The woman turned, leaving Dominique in front of the boy who was still adjusting himself.

"Hello, my name is Robert Willis, welcome to The Neighbor's House. What brought you here today?"

The boy's efforts made it worth answering his questions but Dominique knew she needed to speak with an adult. She wondered why the woman walked away without introducing herself.

"I wanted to see how my home changed. I lived here years ago."

"Really?"

"Yes, really. Can I look around?"

The boy didn't hesitate to tell one of the other boys to cover his desk while he took her for a tour of the house. Dominique couldn't tell if he was excited about her visit or the fact that he could move away from his post. They started in the front rooms where he proudly told her about the donations of books from neighbors, and other outreach programs. Robert was knowledgeable when questioned about a few of the afternoon programs The Neighbor's House provided. Dominique could tell right away why he held the desk position.

There were no familiar settings in the front of the home. They walked through the hall to the dining room, which held a large conference table. Young children around the table were doing homework with teens who were texting on cell phones until they saw Dominique enter the room. Immediately they became attentive, asking questions and correcting mistakes. Robert continued his rehearsed description of the room's use.

"Did you have dinner in this room or the kitchen?"

"Mostly the kitchen, we ate in here for holidays. Our Christmas tree stood over there."

Her memory kicked in. She could see the tree and the presents; her father and mother sitting at the dining room table as she tore open the wrapping paper. Christmas mornings were so pleasant, it wasn't long before the night brought the fights and arguments. Her mother would beg her father to stay home with his family. When the begging began to annoy Zeke he would tell her he needed some air, only to return after the lights were out. He'd stumble up the stairs and the argument would resume.

"Miss, are you okay?" Robert tapped her gently on her hand. She had stopped walking at the bottom of the staircase as they approached the kitchen.

"Yes I'm sorry."

The kitchen was busy. There were two other women making trays of food while the woman who greeted her at the door stacked them on rolling carts. Two boys not much older than Robert wheeled the carts into the dining area. Dominique understood the urgency; it was near twelve. The woman who greeted her at the door paused to speak.

"Ms. Preston, I am so sorry. You've come in the middle of our noon rush. Kids are out of school this week and we try to serve them lunch as well as the homeless that drop in. My name is Ms. Brown."

Twenty-seven

"So you went upstairs right?" Claudia couldn't wait for Dominique to get through her thorough descriptions of the rooms and what the home was being used for. She memorized most of the information her young escort conveyed to her.

"No, wait. We got to the kitchen door. Now the dining room, kitchen and the staircase meet at a certain point. Do you know what I mean?"

Claudia was trying to keep up, imagining the house, as it was when Dominique was young and the new description she gave her. Without being there she had no idea if her interpretation was correct.

"I think so. Is there like a small hall at the base of the stairs?"

"Yeah, I guess. Not big enough for a lot but there's a small closet there. My mother kept the mop, vacuum and other odd supplies there. I hid there often playing with my father. Wow, I forgot about that today. I thought that hall was huge when I was small. There was a table and chair there too. My dad sat in it before climbing the stairs many nights. Drunk as usual and without the help from his friends; they were gone by the time he would attempt to join my mother in bed."

Claudia didn't want her to lose her again. "So you didn't go upstairs?"

"Uh, oh yeah, no. We talked there in the hall. Ms. Brown asked if I could come back after hours any day this week. She would sit with me if I wanted to talk. I told her I would go back tonight."

"Tonight, isn't that rushing things?"

"What, what am I rushing? I'm yelling rape in my sleep Claudia. I need to find out what happened."

"Did you call Boat or your mother?"

"No, I'll talk to my mother after I go there. Are you available around seven thirty?"

"Yeah, but why not call Westlene?"

"Are you scared? Ms. Brown will be there."

"Isn't that your mother's friend?"

"No, that's her cousin. She works there. She told me the same story Mr. Stevenson told me. Viola didn't buy the property and she couldn't afford it. The church met with a few people in the neighborhood and they worked it out. They rent and have a place for the children."

"Dominique, did she mention the murder?"

"I don't think she realized who I was. I didn't want to tell her, just in case she would tell the raw version of the murder."

"Raw version."

"Yeah, the version my mother and others won't tell me; the version that's in my dreams."

Twenty-eight

Dominique didn't feel nervous until her mother called. She had a way of telling when her daughter wasn't quite herself. After rambling on about undone projects, her weekend with Claudia, and what her schedule would be the next few days, she knew her mother was patiently waiting for a pause to question her.

Brenda took a seat on her couch and patted her foot keeping her thoughts to herself until she had a chance to speak. The silence spoke for her.

"Mom, what's wrong? Have you been listening to me or are you watching the television?" Dominique hoped it was the latter.

"Have you been listening to yourself? Why did you need to know about the house on Rose Terrace? Why didn't you call me?"

"I was going to speak to you about that. It was suggested that I talk with you and maybe revisit the house."

"For what Dommi? What would that solve? Why would you want to stir up the past like that?"

"Stir the past up for who? There's no one there that knows about the past? Ms. Viola is not there and I don't think her cousin recognized me or knew why I was there?"

"You went there?"

Dominique felt like a child again. She had wronged her mother in some way. In an hour she would wrong her again. She would be visiting the house again, hoping to tour the home in its entirety.

"Well did you? Dominique, what are you looking for? What did you tell that doctor?"

"I told her about my dreams Mama. You won't discuss them. When I was younger, did I ever tell you about a man coming in my room, or the woman whose voice I heard?" Dominique paused, waiting for her mother to interject. "You won't tell me, and it's about time someone or something did."

Brenda heard her daughter's fears. At night she would rock her child to sleep, cradling her as though she were an infant. She would pray, sing, and console her each night the dreams returned. Brenda asked; what did the man do to her; who did she see; who did she hear? The man, the shadow, the voices, the terror, left Brenda to question what went on in their home while she worked nights. Viola would only say that Zeke had his friends with him and they kept Dominique from sleeping. Brenda would rock her until her face was soaked with her own tears and her baby girl was asleep.

"Mama, I've got to go there. Don't you see? I can't live like this. I'm in love Mama and I can't love him when…."

"Him, who Lawrence? Is that what this is about? Is he pushing you to relive your past? What is he implying happened to you?" Brenda hadn't thought of others influencing her daughter to face the past she and the pastor hid so well.

"He has no idea what may have happened, but Mama, it may ruin my future with him or anybody else. I think there's more to this than you or the pastor want to admit."

Brenda felt the air leave her. She fell back on the couch unable to speak. Pastor would have to help her. Dominique couldn't survive the truth and neither could she.

"Baby, come by the house tomorrow. We'll talk about this and I'll tell you all I know. There was times when the doctors talked with you and didn't tell me what was said. If it will help, I'll tell you all I know."

"Okay, that will help. Westlene suggested we talk. I just thought you wouldn't be willing to revisit the past because of Daddy, you know. Mama, I really don't want you to have to go through this, but I can't deal with it anymore."

"It's okay. I've dealt with it before."

"What do you mean before?"

"We'll talk tomorrow baby. Promise me you won't do anything until then. After we talk, you can tell your doctor what I know. Maybe she can help you without you visiting that house. I really don't think that's wise."

Dominique listened to her mother. It sounded as though she was hiding what the visit would reveal. It wouldn't stop her. She had an appointment at 7:30.

"I will talk with you tomorrow. I'll come by your house before it's time for you to leave for your meeting."

"It won't matter. I can miss one meeting."

Twenty-nine

Viola played the voice message again, it was Brenda Preston. She couldn't believe her ears and although the message brought tears to her eyes, she understood the urgency. She called her cousin immediately and told her she was not to meet with the young woman who wanted to tour 134 Rose Terrace. She would explain her reasons later.

She got up early the next morning and dressed quickly to meet her friend who obviously had not forgotten her. She couldn't remember the last time they had lunch or chatted on the phone. It had literally been years. The last time she talked with her was a few weeks after Zeke's funeral. Brenda would barely speak to anyone above a whisper; scared someone in connection to the investigation would be listening. She told Viola the police were looking for anything that would link her to the murder. Viola knew different. Brenda hadn't killed Zeke; she loved him in spite of his ways. Viola knew her friend sought forgiveness, she asked for it daily. Long after the police stopped snooping around, Brenda still asked to be forgiven.

Zeke's death gave Brenda a reason to keep to herself. She told Viola she was quitting her job. She wouldn't need her to be home with Dominique. Viola offered to sit with her, but her somber mood was more than she could bear. She had her own guilt to face.

Their early morning meeting would be refreshing, or so she hoped.

Brenda told her where they would meet. The restaurant off Springfield Avenue in Irvington would be less suspicious. Viola never asked her why it would be suspicious or to who. She sighed as she turned the key locking her apartment and proceeded to her car.

Dominique dialed the number to The Neighbor's House again. She had been told that Ms. Brown was not available and wouldn't be taking calls until later in the day. She couldn't believe she had been stood up and wanted an explanation. The extension rang and just as before the voice mail spoke.

"Ms. Brown, this is Ms. Preston. I would like to speak with you as soon as possible." Dominique reluctantly recited for the recording.

"Hello, hello, this is Ms. Brown." Ms. Brown answered annoyed by the persistent ringing of the phone.

"Ms. Brown, this is Dominique Preston. We were supposed to meet last night." Dominique was questioning herself at this point.

"Yes, I had an emergency and I'm still in the middle of a small crisis. I am so sorry but I didn't have any number to contact you. I'll be leaving here in ten minutes and I don't know when I'll be returning. Can we set your visit, or tour for another date?"

Dominique shook her head. She wanted to scream; instead she took a moment to think. "Would it be alright if one of the staff just walked with me around the house?"

"No, that won't be okay. I am so sorry Ms. Preston. Contact me next week we'll set something up."

Before Dominique could comment the dial tone sang in her ear. It seemed strange, but she refused to become frustrated. She would get the answers she needed from her mother and visit Westlene before visiting the home again.

Viola sat listening to Brenda's updates. The tension between the two women was obvious. Viola watched Brenda's expression change when she spoke of her mixed emotions about the Stephenson brothers and their mother. She had her arguments with Kendall and her feelings were mutual, she wouldn't believe that his time away had changed him. She didn't want to interrupt, but she couldn't continue to listen to Brenda repeating the lies he told during the time of Zeke's death.

"Brenda, you know Zeke, Dean and Kendall were into that mess together don't you?"

"What mess?"

"Dean is in prison. I'm surprised they didn't take Kendall in too. I've always believed that's why he high tailed it out of here."

"Wait, Dean is in jail? I wondered what happened to the bar. Is it still running?"

"Oh yeah, same crew on Friday's. They still drink, play cards and gamble. New people running it though. I don't know who bought it. I don't go over there much. I work with Rich now. I couldn't stay there anyway."

"Viola you can't be still dancing, tell me you ain't dancing girl." They laughed as the tension eased.

"Girl, any wiggling to be done won't be done around those cheap bastards. It don't pay like it used to."

"Shame the devil and tell the truth. You can't move like you used to." The women snickered louder than expected. Brenda stopped laughing and tapped her friend's hand. "Seriously, what did Dean do? I've been to myself for years."

"Brenda, you know what they were doing to those girls. His nieces finally told it. One of the customers, some young man from up the hill was there quite often. His woman followed him and wanted to fight whoever he was seeing. Well when she saw the girl was no more than fifteen she went and got the cops. Operation shut down, owner of the bar locked up. I heard he also had some problems with the school. Probably messing with those high school girls. They all was in and out of jail, I guess you never paid it much attention."

"You're right. I figured they closed it down for the once a month fighting, the drugs, or something. I never thought about those nieces of his being used like that though. Viola, did Dean ever come to the house while I was working?"

Viola took a drink of her Pepsi. She allowed the seltzer to trickle down her throat. She was beginning to understand the meaning of the urgent call. She promised she wouldn't relive the nights she argued with Kendall, Dean and Zeke. The fear she had for Dominique and Brenda at times was unbearable. She hoped to rekindle their relationship without the past resurfacing.

The waitress noticed they both needed refills and stepped in asking if they wanted to order anything else. Viola was grateful for the pause in their conversation. Brenda shook her head at the waitress and continued her questioning.

"Did he? I mean, I know Zeke and Kendall would come in plastered but did Dean ever come with them?"

"Dean and others too, I would leave them in the kitchen and tend to Dommi. I'd read her a story or watched a little television with her until she fell asleep."

"Yeah, that's the problem." Brenda continued explaining why Dominique wanted to visit their old home. Viola wanted to cry. Instead she fought the back the anxiety that crept upon her emotions. She didn't want to believe that she wasn't there or had gone home too soon, leaving a seven-year-old child to defend herself against her father's perverted friends.

Thirty

Brenda promised Viola she would call her after talking with Dominique that afternoon. She was certain there would come a time when she would need her to explain their friendship. Dominique would remember Viola and wonder why her mother spent so much time alone. Dominique would ask why the woman who babysat for more than three years left her mother alone to mourn the death of her husband. As an afterthought, Brenda wanted to know as well.

The wind was picking up as the weatherman predicted. A storm was brewing. Brenda hoped the rain would hold off until she got home from the church. She didn't want to be chilled in the brisk air mixed with rain. She entered the front door, closing out the cold air and welcoming the comforting heat.

It was too early for the clients in either of the programs. She walked past Randall's office hoping she wouldn't have to deal with Kendall. She heard voices coming from the office. The conversation was barely above a whisper and her instincts told her Kendall had a woman visitor. Brenda tipped past the partially opened door making sure she missed the floorboards that would squeak. She cringed remembering what Viola told her went on at the bar. She pondered about Zeke and Kendall's participation in the sexual antics with Dean's nieces. She would talk to Randall about the visitor and Kendall's personal visits being kept out of the church. She wished she could have convinced Pastor Turner that

Kendall was not a good choice for the position he now held. She closed her office door; grateful she wasn't tempted to eavesdrop on the hushed voices.

"So will I see you this evening?" Noani smiled hoping Kendall was satisfied with her performance the night before.

"Is that what you want?" He stopped pulling the folders to see her expression as she answered. She wasn't as naïve as he thought and if she was extending an invitation, he would accept.

"It's really up to you. I mean you said you were tired of your brother's company."

"Well yeah, but I don't want to wear out a welcome. I don't want to be too pushy." Kendall laid the bait hoping she would bite.

"How 'bout you call when you're getting off?"

"Look sweetie, I think you got me confused with a man that wants to chase you. I'll be here. I'm available most nights or any night you want, but only if you want."

"Okay, so what time do I pick you up?"

"Four, I'm out of here at four. Thanks for the ride this morning."

Noani turned slowly giving him a view of what would be a treat later. Rubbing her cleavage with her finger she leaned over the desk and kissed him gently on the lips. Her deliberate slow motion allowed him to view her breasts as she stood up.

"No, thank you for the ride last night. I'll be outside at four."

Kendall smiled; pleased she was willing to admit he had pleased her. Randall passed her as she waved from the office door.

"Potential Client, good morning, I haven't seen her before."

"That's one of Dean's nieces. She worked at the bar before he got locked up."

Randall didn't make any indications that he paid much attention to the answer as he prepared his folders for the morning rush.

"I've got a few meetings at City Hall this morning. Then I'll be going to those properties with Pastor. Did you say Dean's niece?"

"Yeah, Noani. She's a fine one right? I know what you're gonna say and it ain't like that. She's a grown woman now and besides I wasn't into that mess like them."

"Keep her out of here. Don't bring that mess in the church doors."

Randall left without waiting for any comments. Kendall lifted his head from the file cabinet to respond as his brother was closing the office door. He never told him the truth regarding his arrest three days after Zeke's death. Randall and his mother assumed he was guilty. Dean was the only one who really knew the truth. Randall came to bail him out gave him an order. Not much changed, Randall never asked for an explanation.

The police gave him a receipt for the bail he paid. They asked him if he knew Kendall's whereabouts on the night of the murders for both Rita and Zeke. Randall had no idea. It was said after Zeke was shot Kendall spent the next two nights with Rita, a young woman in the neighborhood. The girl was found dead and Kendall was arrested. Randall made calls through the church connections and had his incoherent brother released. Without any concrete proof, the church's lawyer got him off. Kendall promised to go to a drug and alcohol program after Randall told him he believed he killed the woman.

Kendall didn't remember much. He consoled a friend. Rita was Zeke's mistress of five years and his death delivered her an emotional blow. She begged Kendall not to leave her. He didn't for two days. Dean called to say Brenda was looking for them to be at Zeke's funeral. The rest was a blur. Kendall couldn't remember where he went, who he saw, or what drugs took him away from the reality of losing a friend.

He remembered leaving Brenda sleeping on the couch, once they cleaned the last blood splattered stains. The police stayed longer than either of them thought was necessary. The scene repeated, reminding him that parts of Zeke's body were matted on the floor. He scrubbed until his knuckles were raw as Brenda sat in a daze. With no one watching he wanted to cry, to yell, to cuss, but Brenda was there. It was as though she knew the killer or the reason, but she didn't say a word.

He left her, knowing he had to tell Rita and Dean. Rita was feeling better and promised to call him later that evening. He had just come out of the liquor store and crossed over Irvine Turner Boulevard. A police car pulled over and the officer's jumped out and put him face down on the ground. He was read what he thought were his rights and brought to the station. He didn't speak, knowing in his condition he would be facing any charge they wanted to give him; the charges included Rita's murder. He missed Zeke's funeral. Kendall felt Brenda never forgave him for not being there. Shortly after his burial, Rita's murder was in the paper and again he was blamed. He agreed to the program, out of state hoping it would clear the bad air.

Dean visited him a week before he left. He confessed he missed Zeke's funeral too. He stopped at Rita's hoping to catch Kendall there after he called him. Rita was irate, hysterical about Zeke being shot. She blamed Dean for being jealous. Dean confessed he and Rita had been lovers once and he desperately had been trying to get her back. He had begged her to leave Zeke; after all he was married. Rita didn't understand the difference Dean was married too. He cried as he told Kendall they fought, she hit her head and he left her there. He was sorry the police didn't care that Kendall hadn't done the crime. Dean gave them an alibi, but it wasn't until Kendall's lawyer began investigating that he was released. A few of the card playing crew agreed with the story Dean told. Kendall was playing cards that Friday as he had on many Friday nights.

Kendall went on a drug binge until it was time for him to leave. Randall refused to talk to him and after Dean's arrest it was clear to the older brother, Kendall had more problems than drugs.

Thirty-one

Brenda couldn't wait for Westlene Adashay's return call. She left a message on her answering machine when she arrived in the office. It was now ten and she was beginning to regret making the initial call. Pastor Turner left their conversation periodically to answer his expected calls and now she stood in the middle of her office stressing.

"I'm sorry Brenda, today seems like one of those days."

"Don't claim it Jacob, 'cause I sure don't need it to be, one of those days."

"She didn't call, huh? Look why don't you relax, you'll work yourself up for nothing. I'm sure this, psychiatrist…"

"She's not a doctor." Brenda cut in disturbed she even thought about talking to her. "She's a dream chaser or catcher or you know the one's that look into a crystal ball, I would guess."

"What does Dominique think she can help her with?"

"Jacob, I don't want this woman snooping around my past, our past. Who knows what will come up? I want to know what she's looking for and where she's looking."

"Did Dominique go to the house?"

"No, I spoke with Viola and she called her cousin to stop that so called tour."

"How far did she get? I'm surprised nothing jarred her memory."

"That's just it, I don't know what she's remembering. Just dreaming about this man being in the room night after night, she thinks she was raped."

"Raped, by who?"

"That's what I want to know. I don't want it to be true at all. I mean maybe the dreams are in pieces that she's putting together wrong."

Brenda went to her desk and sat down. Jacob could see the worry on her face. It had been a month since she told him that the dreams had returned. He wondered how much sleep she got since Dominique told her.

"Pastor." Kendall called from the hall through the closed office door. He dared not intrude.

Jacob opened the door expecting Kendall to enter. Instead

Westlene reached for his hand and introduced herself. Her smile was soft and her appearance eased the tension he felt as she stated she was a dream catcher by nature but a psychologist by title.

"Good morning to you both. I received several calls on my way to a board meeting this morning. I am sorry Ms. Preston. I could not return your call. I was worried there was something not right with Dominique so I stopped here first."

Brenda didn't know how to answer. This woman was not who she expected to fit the name Westlene Adashay. There was nothing that looked like the insane witch doctor she imagined. Even her speech, though broken was understandable. It was obvious she was too quick to judge this woman who apparently had a solid background. Jacob continued speaking to her at the door. He was intrigued by the title she held, and how often it was confused with those who read palms, and claimed they knew about the future of their desperate clients.

"There are those in my native country, Pastor Turner, that have that innate ability to do such things, however, I've not seen many of them here in America. That is a great burden and I only wish to help stabilize the mind that is temporarily lost. Similar to what you do with one's soul. I give mental guidance and peace. There are those who seek peace in their dreams only to find chaos that they have to face. But I do not seek them, they seek me."

"How did you meet my daughter?" Her making light of evaluating her client's dreams didn't charm Brenda.

"I met her at a celebration for a mutual friend, a co-worker of mine. I gave her and others my card as an introduction. She called me later. We have talked in session and out."

"Westlene may I call you that or do you prefer doctor?"

Brenda asked although she had no intention on referring to her as a doctor. She was unsure what credentials the self-proclaimed dream catcher processed.

"No it is whatever you prefer. I am comfortable with both."

"Come in and sit down." Jacob took her coat and they sat across from Brenda's desk. Brenda went to the door and secured it not wanting to be disturbed. She was glad Jacob didn't leave them alone.

"Westlene, I called you this morning because I was concerned about these dreams Dominique has been having. She told me she decided to seek your help. I want you to know that I suggested she talk with Pastor Turner and pray. Prayer brings peace. I don't know what your treatment will do for her."

Westlene hesitated. She had questions of her own, another reason for her visit. Dominique was cautious when speaking about her mother and the home they once lived in. She understood her mother's statement, but she wasn't certain that Brenda didn't have another reason for her doubts.

"Ms. Preston, I assure you that as you say prayer brings peace but good sleep brings comfort as well. Dominique is not sleeping. She has had some sort of trauma that is hidden deep within her subconscious. I think she wants to find out what happened to her as a young girl. You may be the one who can help her. The house may be the place where this trauma occurred."

"She told you that or is that what you read in her dreams?"

Brenda was becoming fearful that Westlene was leading Dominique to the night of her father's murder. A topic she didn't want to discuss.

Since her conversation with Viola she had questions that she wanted answered. She hoped they weren't revealed in Dominique's dreams.

"No I don't read dreams. I don't hypnotize anyone unless they ask. We talk about the dreams, what she sees, what bothers her, and where she is in the dream. Nothing commercial about what I do. I am a professional and I have credentials you can check if you like. Your fears Ms. Preston; are they of guilt, doubt or worry that something will be discovered?"

"You ask as though you have suspicions…."

Westlene rose to her feet. "It is not I, nor is it my place to be suspicious of anyone or anything. You need to talk with your daughter. Tell her the truth as you know it. Let her visit this home that haunts her. Go with her Ms. Preston, you know the house better than anyone. Tell her what went on there that night. Show her where it went on. Walk her dream with her and you will find out about the nights that haunt you the most. I must go. I have as you say patients that want to know their fortune."

Annoyed, Westlene proceeded to the coat rack. Pastor Turner and Brenda watched her as she prepared to leave in silence. They stood in awe, understanding she knew more than she told them or Dominique.

Thirty-two

Boat waited, as directed, in Westlene's office. His day ended with his last client at two o'clock. Westlene had one last client scheduled. She called him right after lunch asking to stop by her office around three. He sensed the tone of urgency in her voice.

He tried to get her to reveal what was so important, but he knew from past experiences she wouldn't answer his questions until they were face to face. He also knew it was regarding Dominique. Their earlier conversation was short but her concerns now included Brenda. After meeting with Dominique's mother, she was certain the source of Dominique's nightly terror was known, yet kept secret.

While waiting, Boat tinkered with his blackberry, checking sports updates, the news and his emails. Dominique, Claudia and Eric had left text messages. Claudia's message caught his attention.

"Boat, Dominique wants to go to her old house. Her mother persuaded her to wait until they talked. Maybe we should talk her out of it. I've got a bad feeling about how she may react, you know, maybe the dreams have to do with her father's murder. She's not saying much, but you know how crazy she gets. Anyway talk to her and tell me what you think. She's really upset with her mother. She won't say it, but I can tell she's scared Boat."

Eric's message was the simplest to answer. He typed quickly his response, telling him something came up and he wouldn't be able to meet him at "The Spot" later. A few of their friends were getting together. Boat was sure Eric would use it to tell the four of them he wanted them to be in his wedding. Dominque's message was sweet. A text to say she was thinking of him. If she only knew, the balance of his day would now be dedicated to her. He would call Claudia after talking with Westlene.

A petite woman, her features lead Boat to wonder if Westlene dealt with teenagers or college students, passed him in the hall as he walked toward Westlene's office. The woman kept her head down, a deliberate action, avoiding eye contact. Boat didn't let it bother him. There were always those who felt uncomfortable being "clients" of Dr. Westlene Adashay.

Her perfume left a distinct aroma. Boat smiled, the scent of a woman always perked his manhood. Again, his thoughts began to race. *"Why would Ms. Preston fear Dominique's visit to their old home? Is that where her daughter was raped? Was she raped?"*

"Hello Mr. Boatright" called out one of the secretaries from another office as Boat approached Westlene's office door. He leaned back to see her smiling and waving.

"Hey lady, how are you today?"

"Busy", she answered. "And if we're busy, I can imagine what your part of the building is like. Is it me or do people just have more problems around the holidays?"

"I never thought of it that way, but you're right it is busier around that time. Take care."

Mrs. Masters worked with Boat briefly when he first started as an intern. She showed him how to deal with a lot of clients that refused to believe any state agency could or would help them. He didn't see her much and gave a sigh of relief knowing she had returned to work after her battle with an illness. They had become as close as a mother and son on the job, but neither strayed from being professional at all times. She was Mrs. Masters, and he was Mr. Boatright. He made a mental note to call her later in the week and update her about Eric's engagement, another one of her favorite interns.

"Ah, Lawrence Boatright, I heard your mother announcing you."

"Is that what Mrs. Masters does now, announce your unscheduled appointments."

"Boat, you forget, I called you." Westlene teased. She was clearing her desk preparing her briefcase with files to review for the evening.

"Do you take work home every night?"

Westlene gave her friend a stern look.

"Okay, my bad. I just don't think you should work as hard as you do. You know what they say about all work and no play…"

"You play enough for me and you."

"Westlene, you know me better than that. I've been serious about Dominique for what, let's just say too long."

"And that is bothering you now?"

Boat hesitated. He knew she had a reason for her question.

"I never said it bothered me."

"You didn't have to. You wanted me to talk to her. Her problems affect you as well. I see that now. You, Mr. Boatright, are a part of those *"issues"* as you call them."

"And you say her mother is too. I don't see the connection with me, maybe her mother, but not me. I don't know what happened to her when she was younger."

"Her mother may not either. But as I said to you on the telephone earlier, she knows something."

"Why not just say what she knows, it may help her daughter?"

"It may destroy their relationship."

Boat was confused. Westlene got up and closed the door to ensure their privacy.

Thirty-three

Brenda had not been herself the entire day. Breakfast with Viola and the meeting with Westlene confirmed her fears. Dominique would remember something while in the house where they once lived. Would she remember it all and had she been violated, were the questions that brought on a multitude of questions for Brenda throughout the afternoon. She didn't get much work done and now an hour before leaving, she prayed the answers weren't going to worry her the rest of the night.

Zeke swore to his wife months before his death, that no one had harmed his little girl. Brenda paid close attention to their only child's behavior. It had changed. She could tell something had her baby shook. She had begun to wet the bed. Viola held on to her story, even then. She didn't understand why Dominique was wetting the bed. She stopped all fluids at seven thirty as per Brenda's directions. She was in bed by eight, at the latest eight thirty. She never sat up with Zeke or any of his friends. Viola couldn't stop Zeke from bringing his friends home drunk or sober, but she never let Dominique out of her sight. She promised.

When the nightmares began, Brenda couldn't pinpoint the reason. Zeke's murder, the loss of her father, the stress of the police, family, and friends secretly asking questions constantly taunted her. Brenda consoled her child each night with prayer.

Westlene knew, but how much did she really know? Brenda sat behind her desk with her bible, praying she and Dominique would connect without digging up the past. She would convince Dominique to move on and by all means get rid of the Witchdoctor. Jacob agreed, Westlene might have become Dominique's external support since Brenda no longer seemed interested in her dilemma. Jacob should have understood, she hadn't lost interest; her fears had increased.

Dominique hadn't called, which indicated she was still annoyed with Brenda's request to see her. Her meeting with the Shut-In Ministry was canceled so they had the entire evening to themselves. She could hear the sound of the lock on Randall and Kendall's office door. It was just another thing she needed to talk to Jacob about. Why did Kendall find a need to lock the door when he left? They never locked interior doors. She shook her head and rolled her eyes thinking about his despicable ways.

"Rough day?" Brenda's eyes diverted to the door where Kendall stood. They hadn't spoken in more than a week and she didn't want his conversation at the close of any day.

"Not really, just a little tired. How 'bout you? You were here bright and early, I would have thought you'd be gone by now."

"Hmmm, I knew it would snow so I thought I'd better get a few things done. We may have to cancel the program for tomorrow."

"It never snows much this time of year."

"Well you'd better take a look outside."

Brenda sprung from her seat rushing to the window to see how much snow had fallen. She couldn't believe she hadn't noticed the large flakes that danced in mid-air before touching the ground. It was obvious it had been snowing all afternoon. Her preoccupation with Dominique, Westlene and Zeke's death kept her from noticing the snow as it fell outside her office windows.

Kendall didn't move from the door. He was well aware of Brenda's surprise and it brought a grin to his face. Randall and Jacob were gone leaving the two of them to lock up. Noani called asking could he get a ride to her apartment after the threat of the snow became a reality. He would get a chance to be alone with Brenda. She wouldn't see him walk in a blizzard.

"Well, I guess your brother and Pastor will be here bright and early pushing the shovels. Did Randall mention that the men that work here help with the shoveling?"

"Yes, and the leaves in the fall, the grass in the summer and the trash year round. I'll be here in the morning. Just wondering, I mean if you wouldn't mind, would you give me a lift home?"

Brenda's hesitation was noticeable.

"I promise I won't bite or talk you to death. Maybe we can come to agree to be a little friendlier to each other."

"I ain't promising all that Kendall, but I'll drive you home if you clean the car off for me."

"Sure thing."

Brenda grabbed her coat and took her time putting on her hat and gloves. Kendall walked ahead of her leaving her to lock the door to the foyer and the porch. The snow was sticking to the ground and coming down at a faster pace. The storm was quickly approaching. It would take her thirty minutes to get home. Randall's apartment wouldn't take her out of the way. Besides she had some questions about the evenings Kendall shared at her home with Zeke, Dean, and the others.

Thirty-four

There was a time when Dominique loved the falling snow. As a child she longed to play in it until she was chilled to the bone. Her teeth would chatter, as her mother would question her reason for staying out so long. Her hands would be stiff, unable to take off her wet garments.

"Child, you are soaked. Snow angels, huh? Didn't you feel wet? You'll catch your death of cold. Mother Nature won't tap on the window when you're hacking in the morning. Give me those wet socks."

Dominique would touch the snow filled socks with two fingers, too cold to respond. The other children promised to meet after lunch as they went to their homes to listen to the same speeches. They played all day, throwing snowballs, making snowmen, lying in the streets pretending they were snow angels. Each year they prayed for blizzards. Living without large yards or fields, the unplowed streets became their playground.

The winter scene brought tears to her eyes. It snowed the day her father was buried. The family stood at the gravesite as the snow flurried around them. Now each flake whispered her name, Dommi. Her father had a special way of calling her. Even if she was in trouble, his voice never startled her.

She remembered the arguments he would have with her mother. The names he would call her after being out with his friends. The sound of dishes crashing against the walls, her mother's screams for him to stop, the sound of her being smacked and knocked around.

Dominique missed her father, the man without the bottle. The man who was different Monday through Thursday was her father. Zeke without the wild card parties on Friday nights was quiet, and reserved, the man her mother must have fallen in love with.

It was snowing the night they carried his body out of the house in that stiff black bag. She watched from the top of the stairs, from the window when they wheeled him out on the gurney. She strained to see through snow filled windowpanes before the black car, marked County Coroner drove off. She missed her father.

Brenda had to understand her need for closure. The visit to their old home was important to ending her pain. Something happened in that home. Not only did she lose her father, she lost part of who she was. She drank the rest of her coffee. It was her fourth cup of the day. She needed to call Westlene for more tea. She hadn't thought about it before draining the coffee pot. Maybe Claudia was right; she had become addicted to the caffeine.

She put it to the back of her mind as she opened the closet to find her boots. Her choices took her deep into the closet. She heard the faint sound of the doorbell. She grabbed her blue "Uggs" and closed the closet door.

"Westlene! What a surprise, come in."

"I did not want to simply call you. I believe we need to sit once again before you meet with your mother. I hope I have come in time."

Westlene took her time closing her umbrella after shaking off the snow. Dominique reached for her visitor's coat and umbrella. She was unsure why Westlene made an unexpected visit. What more their talk would reveal?

Thirty-five

The storm caused the traffic to move slowly. Brenda, who hated bad weather and driving in it, allowed the conditions to be her excuse not to engage in a deep conversation with Kendall. He hummed a few of the songs that played on the radio. The melodic moment was no disguise for his anxiety. He needed to ask her why she treated him the way she did.

"Hey." They both chimed in and laughed simultaneously.

"I'm sorry, go ahead." Brenda turned the volume down to hear him speak.

"No, I was just going to ask how Dommi was doing. Is she still working in New York?"

"Yes, she's still there and doing fine." Kendall could tell she was nervous. He decided to let her lead the conversation between them.

"That's good, real good."

"What about you? Are you planning on staying with your brother long or are you passing through?"

"I'm from here Brenda, I'm not passing through. I left to get it together. I know it seems like there's a lot of people who need to leave and never come back."

He made the comment in jest but got no smile from her. She continued to look into the traffic although they sat at the light waiting for it to turn green.

"I don't know Kendall if your return is good for any of us."

"What is it that I've done Brenda? One of the reasons I've returned is to resolve this feeling between us. What did I do that was so wrong? I mean to you, what did I do to you?"

"You took my husband, you, Dean and the others." Her response brought on a stern demeanor, one he didn't know she possessed.

"He never came home the same. He was a beast in the home after being with you and the others. I believe you all became beast, drinking that clear poison, pushing yourselves on women, and then fighting anyone and everyone. Well in our home Kendall, I was the punching bag. I received the blows and when the bastard laid there in his blood I said thank you. Who thanks God for their spouse being murdered?"

The horns blared and Brenda floored the gas pedal. The tires spun causing the car to fishtail up the narrow street. Other car horns blew as she crossed the intersection and slammed on the brakes. She put the car in park and cried the tears she never cried looking at her husband on the floor. The pedestrians mouthed obscenities as they crossed the street uncertain of her intentions.

Kendall jumped out of the car and helped her to the passenger side. He buckled her in as she shouted about the abuse she endured. Her ranting and raving turned into sobs and more tears as Kendall pulled off before the traffic light changed for the third time. He drove slowly, hoping she would stop crying before they reached his apartment. Brenda's crying was silent; the tears continued to fall, and her pain spoke volumes. He hurt for her and for the first time Kendall understood her pain.

Zeke would never worry about getting home. Kendall and the others thought their marriage was headed for a dead end. He treated the girls at the bar as though he was single, not caring who saw him touch their bodies. He paid for lap dances and never stepped into a private room. There were a few he dated, a few he sexed, and a lot who gave him spurts of pleasure. Since Brenda worked nights, he spent his nights out until he was too drunk to drive home.

Kendall was usually his escort home. Brenda had it wrong. He didn't approve of his friends behavior. He had no idea she was being abused.

Dean and a few of the others didn't care. Zeke would brag about Brenda, his daughter, and his living when he was sober, but the liquor painted another picture for him.

Kendall parked the car hoping Brenda would understand his concern. "Brenda, I can drive you home. I don't think you should drive like this."

"Is that what you said to him, night after night? Get out Kendall, oh before you go…which one of you raped my daughter?"

The question hit Kendall in the chest. His own questions entered his mind. *"Did someone rape Dommi? Who?"*

"Brenda, I had no idea—"

"Get out of my car Kendall!!" Brenda began to climb over the center console, as though she was chasing him. Quickly he got out as directed and tried to talk through the opened driver's door.

"Brenda, we need to talk. We need to talk to Viola, the three of us need to sit down."

"We will you bastard and if the cops don't lock your ass up, you'll be just as dead as your friend."

"Brenda, I didn't touch Dommi."

Brenda slammed the door as the tires spun while she sped off. Kendall watched her slipping and sliding away from him. He'd have to speak to Viola and maybe even Dean. Kendall stood on the curb watching the car until the snow made the view impossible.

Thirty-six

The storm continued through the night. Dominique left a message on her mother's phone knowing she would be mentally worn from her ride home. She didn't want to clean off her car to drive across town to hear her mother's complaints about the traffic, the drivers, and the predicted weather for the next few days. She assumed The Neighbor's House would be closing early. She decided she would call Boat and hope he would want to talk until she fell asleep.

She closed the blinds and secured her front door. The accumulated inches of snow brought out her neighbors who began to shovel their sidewalks and driveways. Boat would ask if she paid the neighborhood teens to shovel before he left for work in the morning. Annoyed that her mother hadn't called after eight the thought brought on worry. It wasn't like her not to return a call during a storm. She fought off the thoughts refusing to make the second call to her home.

Boat hadn't returned her call and it was after ten. She was beginning to feel sleep creeping upon her, but she wanted to be sure she would be tired enough to sleep through the night. She remembered Westlene leaving her more tea and boiled the water with a smile. The phone rang and she rushed to answer, glad her mother didn't let the night pass them by.

"Dommi, I'm so sorry we couldn't get together, with the weather…."

"Mama, did you listen to your messages?" Dominique interrupted as she poured the water into her cup. "I didn't know how bad the storm would get so I'll just go to the house tomorrow."

"I don't know, you may have to wait for this weather to blow over. It's pretty bad out there and we haven't had a chance to talk. We really need to talk sweetie."

Dominique looked at the phone inquisitively. "Uh, well yes, that's what we need to do. I don't know if I'm going in tomorrow, but if the snow has slacked up will you be home?"

"Yes, I don't plan on going in. There's nothing that can't wait on my desk. Randall and….." Brenda's voice faded away. She thought about Kendall and what he may have known about her daughter's dreams. She should have never accused him.

"Mama, are you okay. You don't sound right."

"Tired, just tired, snow and rain will do that; not to mention no sleep."

"You're not sleeping either?"

"Just lately, there's a lot going on at the church. I'm just mentally tired, that's all." Brenda didn't want to let on to the argument she had with Kendall.

Dominique recalled her conversation with Westlene. She was certain her mother had answers about her dreams. She suggested Dominique question her mother before going to the home. She even asked her to visit the home with her mother.

"Mama, would you go with me to the house? I mean, I'd like for you to walk through it with me. I'm sure they have people there to show me the rooms but you could help me remember the rooms and what went on before dad's murder."

The question Brenda feared had been asked. She paused and sighed realizing there was no way around it. She would have to reveal her nightmares to her daughter before they went to the house on Rose Terrace.

Dominique felt better after the talking with her mother. Brenda agreed to talk with her as soon as the weather permitted and visit their old home. The tea had begun its magic and the warm shower set the tone for a peaceful night of sleep.

She cut off the lights on the first level of her home and proceeded to her bedroom. She reached for the light switch and as it clicked there was a flash in both lamps. Dominique couldn't believe that both light bulbs blew simultaneously. She would have to get new bulbs from the hall closet. She turned to go out the door and it slammed close. She began to panic and realized she was not alone in the room. The air was cold and a pungent odor of cigarettes passed her nose. She frowned reacting to what had become a familiar smell; she knew he was in the room with her. The stench forced her back on the bed and she pressed her body close to the headboard protecting her face from his anticipated approach. She closed her eyes afraid to look into the darkness. The smell decreased and vanished at the same time the door opened.

Dominique jumped up from the couch in a sweat. She looked around the room only to find it as it was before she dozed off. The television was on, though the volume was barely audible. The lights were on in both the living room and the kitchen. It was clear she hadn't made it upstairs. She looked toward the staircase knowing her bed wouldn't see her again until morning.

The clock read two. Brenda had been fully awake for an hour. She prayed again for peace of mind. Kendall had stirred reality and it just wouldn't settle. Zeke knew about Dominique being touched, he had to. Whenever he was drunk he talked about Dean and his nieces, and the money they made at the bar. Brenda thought Dean had the girls playing the sexy waitress roles. Viola gave her the truth. Zeke didn't want that for his baby or did he? She couldn't be sure what he would do when he was under the influence. She shook her head again thinking she should have let Kendall explain. Maybe he knew more. He was right they all needed to meet.

She walked to the window and put her hands on the cold glass. The chill seemed refreshing as the tears began to flow. She needed to talk to someone about her intentions. She needed to repent for the sin she would commit if she found the man who violated her only child.

Westlene came to mind. The woman knew there was more to the dreams, something that connected Brenda and Dominique although neither of them knew the others pain. Brenda couldn't remember the details of her last dream. She knew it was Zeke, he caused her to toss and turn, scream and call out Jacob's name. She shuddered at the thought. The ghostly image was Zeke's but the man in the bed with her was Jacob.

In her dream state Zeke continued his threats. He spit at her laughing from his grave. It stopped the night Jacob became a part of her midnight dream. Zeke interrupted her soft moans of pleasure snatching Jacob from her bed as though the scene was real. Jacob stood bleeding from his nose, his eyes swollen from Zeke's powerful blows. She screamed for Jacob, told him she loved him and how sorry she was. The ghostly image of Zeke's vanished and she hadn't dreamed of him since.

He had returned. The memories would begin haunting her again. Zeke was determined not to let them live in peace. Jacob and Westlene were right. She would only gain peace if the truth were revealed.

Thirty-seven

Jacob answered the call as he had the others during the day. "Pastor Turner, good afternoon."

"Good afternoon," Brenda said rushing through the pleasantries. "Jacob, did anyone come in today?"

"Hey Brenda, no I told them it's too bad. The men did show up to shovel, including Kendall. I was surprised about that. Anyway, I think they left about an hour ago. How's your area? This is the strangest thing for early November. A real blizzard just ain't usual for this time of the year."

Brenda listened still on an emotional edge. She didn't return to her bed and now fatigue was setting in. She hadn't changed from her nightgown certain she wouldn't have company in the bad weather.

"The boys came around and did the sidewalks. I'm sure the plow has me blocked in."

"Don't worry no one has come for any of the scheduled programs. I cancelled them and called the members phone line. Kendall and Randall called the board members and told them to call and check for tomorrow's schedule. I don't think we'll be here then either." He answered knowing she'd be concerned about unfinished paperwork and getting to work the next day.

"Good, good, Jacob can you please come over. I need to talk. I need to talk to you, Viola and Kendall. I need to talk to all of you before

Dominique wants to visit that house. There's some things that need to be aired and I need your support."

Brenda's request surprised him. He didn't expect her to want to meet with Kendall or Viola about Dominique. "Are you sure?"

"Jacob, Zeke is taunting me from the grave. I know it sounds crazy but I need to know what Zeke was talking about after he was shot."

"Brenda, you never mentioned Zeke saying anything, do you really think they know anything? I thought they didn't know about the murder."

"They don't, they need to know. I've carried this burden only to find Zeke betrayed me Jacob. Please say you'll come."

"Betrayed you? How, never mind, what time do you want me there?"

"I've got a lot of talking to do, but I called you first. I'll have to call Viola and apologize to Kendall. I lost my temper driving him home yesterday. I'm sure he'll come though."

Jacob hung up the receiver unsure what was going on. He looked at the phone reminiscing the call from the police the day Zeke was shot. *"She's calling your name Pastor Turner, can you get here right away?"* The officer told him the circumstances. It wasn't unusual for a minister to be called, but Jacob had to control his emotions before responding to the officer's request.

Jacob drove hurriedly across town. Zeke was shot, that's all the police told him over the phone. Brenda was unable to talk and the child, yes, Dominique was with a female officer. They took her out of the house to spare her the vision of her father lying in a pool of blood.

The house was corded off and television cameras and reporters were preparing for the statement from the Captain of the police force. Jacob walked through the crowd escorted by a female officer who was posted awaiting his arrival.

"Reverend can you tell us what has happened?" The reporter shouted into the microphone before she shoved into his face.

"No, no I can't please."

Dominique ran to his side as he entered the front door. She didn't say a word, but he could tell she was shaken. The strangers in her home had scared her beyond telling a friendly face the gruesome details. Brenda was answering the questions asked by the officers who Jacob assumed called. She was pleading with them to call Pastor Taylor and ask him to come quickly.

"I'm Pastor Turner may I speak with Ms. Preston before you go to the station?" Jacob asked the question to no one in particular hoping someone would provide him with their intent.

"She won't be questioned there until maybe tomorrow. We're taking a description from her. The intruder left out the front door so we'll be dusting for prints momentarily."

"Where is Mr. Preston?"

"I'm sorry to say Mr. Preston is dead." The officer continued into the kitchen where Jacob could see the black body bag. Jacob stood in the hall stagnant, what he later described as shock. Brenda joined him as they strapped the bagged body to the gurney. Jacob put his arm around Brenda and looked for her daughter. Turning at the front door he saw Dominique was standing on the staircase looking out the window. In the crowd that gathered on the sidewalk he saw Viola. He waved his hand for her to come and join them. Officers tried to prevent her from stepping out of the crowd but Brenda yelled her name seeing her friend and the officers stepped to the side. Dominique joined her mother who surrendered herself into Viola's familiar arms.

The confusion of that evening hadn't left his memory. The intruder was never caught. Brenda never asked why the police hadn't found her husband's killer. Kendall was there when Jacob arrived. He was there before the police, but then he seemed to fade into the crowd. He was gone before anyone noticed. Jacob often wondered why he was there at all. The questions, from the officers, family, and church members went on for months. The hushed voices spoke of the suspicions, and the rumors. There were no answers and no one asked why. Jacob closed the door to the offices and prayed hoping the visit to Rose Terrace would put an end to all the sleepless nights, including his.

Thirty-eight

Dominique called her job only to find that the offices would have a delayed opening. She wanted the weather to be her excuse but with the approved delay she decided to make the attempt to go in. She put on her snow gear prepared to shovel her car out of her parking space. She made a call to Claudia and they agreed to talk before meeting each other at Penn Station.

The sound of shovels from the neighboring homes told her she was one of the few who got a late start. The plow had pushed mounds of snow around the cars who neglected to move. The snow was still soft but more than the predicted forecast. Three inches and it was still falling off and on with another two inches promised before noon. Thanksgiving was the following week and Dominique knew she wouldn't be standing in the crowd at the Macy Parade if the snow was still present.

With her shovel in her hand, she put on her gloves and went out the door. Clearing the sidewalk was easy. She had paid two boys earlier to clean the sidewalk and the steps. They asked her about putting down salt but she told them she would put it down. Dominique shoveled as did her neighbors for most of the morning. The snow got heavier by the minutes. After digging out her car, she remembered the salt. A neighbor shouted her name and waved to say hello. Dominique responded and missed her footing. She stumbled and slid on the stairs. The fall was sudden and she wasn't sure she could get up. The neighbor, a woman the age of her mother, screamed alerting the men who were talking across the street.

Dominique refused to go to the hospital, but it was certain that she wouldn't be going to work either. Her neighbors helped her into the house assuring her they would throw the salt on the walk. She called Claudia and Boat, and told them about her slip and fall.

"So is Boat coming over, if not I can be there in an hour." Claudia dialed their job from her house phone and told them about Dominique's accident.

"I told the job I'd be with you until you were settled. I thought about it. Girl that may be at the end of the week; thanks for the vacation."

"I really don't think I'm that bad off. I hurt like hell but that's normal considering how I fell."

"What's swollen, other than your butt?"

"My back hurts more and my ankle is big but it didn't turn colors. You know they say a break will turn the skin blue."

"You need to get an x-ray just in case."

"Boat is on his way. I'll go if I have to when he gets here."

"Call me." Claudia hung up the phone certain she would get another call from Dominique.

The x-rays were negative and with the medication, the pain in Dominique's back and foot eased. Boat carried her into the house just before the snow began to fall again. Her frustration showed as she hobbled through her home.

"You should really use the crutches. The doctor said you shouldn't put your weight on it for a couple of days. I don't think using them on the snow and ice would be a good idea but indoors you need the support."

"Boat, this weather has ruined everything. Not to mention my clumsy ass slipping outside. My mother won't drive in this mess, and going to the house is out until the ice and snow is cleared."

"What's the rush? Listen rest, stay off your leg. Call your mom and talk things over. Call Claudia about your work; take a few days off for both reasons. You need a few days."

"Not really, these nightmares have given me enough time off. Now this, Claudia is not going to believe this. How long did they say it would take for this to heal?"

Boat brought her a much-needed glass of juice and the remote for the television. She refused to go to bed it was too early and even with the medication she feared the nightmare would return.

"The swelling will take a day or two. You almost broke it. They say a bad sprain is worse than a break. You'll need at least three or four days. Hey it gives me a chance to pamper you."

He smiled as she rolled her eyes. She puckered her lips and sent him a kiss. "Thank you, I guess I could use some pampering."

Dominique did as Boat suggested. She called Claudia, her mother, and Westlene. They all understood and wished her a quick recovery. Each of them promised to stop by over the next few days to check on her. The couple spent the rest of the evening watching movies.

"I guess there's only so many reruns to watch huh?" She was bored with the new regiment. Dominique adjusted her leg on the couch as she surfed through the guide on the television.

"What did you have a taste for? Are you hungry?" Boat called from the kitchen.

"Boat, can you go with me to the house?"

"What house? No, you can't mean on Rose Terrace."

"I can't rest without knowing what it is that went on."

"Dominique ask you mother, isn't that what Westlene said?" He stepped around the kitchen counter and saw her face. Her annoyance was obvious. "Alright, I'll take you there. Give your leg a few days of rest, we'll get with your mother and go to that house. You'll sleep fine until then. What's in the kitchen, any of your favorites? I'll cook some dinner, you'll take your meds, and we'll call it a night."

Boat left her in thought. The leftovers he heated up were more than enough for the two of them. They watched another movie and it wasn't long before the medication did what it was supposed to do. Dominique didn't argue or complain when Boat helped her to her bed. He stayed the night willing to be her comfort if she needed it.

Thirty-nine

Noani hadn't heard from Kendall. After being snowed in for two days she didn't understand why he hadn't called to see if she was okay. As usual she had set herself up to believe there may have been a connection between them.

Her uncle warned her about Kendall Stevenson, he was a friend who was off limits. The others, like Zeke were frustrated married men and after sex didn't want more. Noani was always curious about her Uncle Dean, Zeke and Kendall. She only needed a chance with Kendall. She dreamed about him many nights after he left the bar. He became a distant fantasy.

The thoughts of a teenage girl, her uncle would say. She had that chance and now the man wouldn't answer her calls. She'd make her visit with her uncle and go on with her day. Kendall would have to continue to be a fantasy. She was sure she would see him again. He would tell her the weather was the cause for his disappearance. He would admit he missed her touch and tender care. She thought of stopping by the church office but turned the corner toward her destination, the county jail.

Kendall fumbled through his pocket for his cell phone. His intention to call Noani earlier in the week to set up a date fell behind keeping the snow shoveled and the programs needing to be rescheduled. His attempt to see Viola at her job failed as well. He needed to see Viola and Dean before talking with Brenda again. The thought of Dominique being raped or used seemed impossible.

Questions of when, where, and who, kept coming to his mind. Zeke was so protective of his little girl. Dean often talked of Dominique as he had his nieces, comparing their size as they got older. Dominique was younger by seven years or more. Dean would wait until Zeke asked for a lap dance from the young girls.

Once he had his fill of Vodka, Dean would make reference to his precious daughter. Kendall never heard Zeke argue when Dean mentioned tricking Dominique or the money that could be made. Zeke would get his thrill and find someone to finish the pleasure since Dean wouldn't allow his nieces to fulfill his needs.

Kendall dialed Noani's number prepared to explain his absence. "Hey sweetie, are you home?"

"Hmm, who is this?" teased Noani.

"You know who this is. This weather is trying to mess up my chance to get with you. I've been at this church for the past two days. You'd think I was a Deacon or something."

"I bet. So what's up Deacon?"

"You, ain't nothing changed. I do need a favor and I mean I need it today if possible."

"I don't get down like that. You had your taste, ain't no need for us to waste time. I've got plenty of brotha's that can fulfill my need for a night."

"So what you saying, I ain't worth another round?"

"I told you, I put you in a different category. I'd rather continue to have a fantasy about us being in a relationship then ruin it with another romp in the bed. My uncle played enough of those games with us. I don't fuck for free and I really don't need an attachment without batteries. You know what I'm saying. It's either a relationship or a dildo, don't matter to me."

"Well it's a good thing I didn't want to fuck, as you put it. I need to get with Viola and your uncle. I tried that spot you said she was working, but she won't be there until tonight. Do you think we could stop there for a few drinks? Maybe we could have dinner and then stop there. Oh yeah, I need you to tell Dean to put me down for a visit."

"I was on my way there. His visits are on Wednesdays and the weekend. I don't know if you have to be on his list 'cause it ain't a contact visit, plus it's the County Jail. He'd be glad to see you. Stay there I'll pick you up in a few."

Kendall sighed as he closed his phone. He wasn't sure how glad Dean would be to see him. It wasn't long before Noani pulled into the space where the sign stood for church staff. Kendall shook his head wondering if it made a difference to her that she wasn't a part of the staff. The programs ended early as they had for the past two days. It had been a long day even with the time changes due to the weather. Randall spent his time with Pastor Turner visiting the elderly and making sure they were taken care of during the unexpected storm. There was no need to report his departure time. He locked the front door and got in the car glad to feel the heat.

"Whew, it's cold. I guess I've missed this climate. Florida doesn't get this cold."

"So close the door. If you can't get in to visit you'll have to sit and wait."

"I'm good with that. I really hope I can get in though. I've got to talk with your uncle."

"So what's the rush? You didn't mention visiting him the other day. What's come up now?"

"C'mon girl, don't act like that. I'm running a program, new at it too. This weather threw me off. I had no idea that I would be working this hard."

"Hmm, your phone don't work?" Noani put the car in gear and swerved out of the parking spot. "Y'all need to put down more salt too."

"Listen, I'll make it up to you I promise. You know you're cute when you're angry. Got some spunk with you; I like that, but seriously me, and Dean got some things to talk about. I don't know that you should be with me when we talk."

"No you listen, I visit him once a month that's it. This is my visit, share it or come on your own." She gave him a questioning look wondering whether she should stop the car.

"Alright, I'm good. I'm with you but don't be shocked with our conversation."

"Don't you be shocked; it can't be worse than the conversations at the bar."

"Noani, did Dean have other girls? I mean other than you, your sister, and cousins?"

"Probably, we were teens, I'm sure he had a few women."

"Any other kids or teens?"

"Nah, I think we just got turned out like that 'cause he had to watch us from time to time. I don't know, we don't talk much about it. Why you asking about that?"

"Viola would know if he did right?"

"Yeah, she knew all the girls that worked for him. There was a group that worked cross town, I didn't know them though."

"What about Zeke, did he have girls too?"

"That was a rumor, but I don't know it to be true."

"We need to find Viola tonight."

"You act like there's some type of rush. Are you running to something or from something?"

"Baby, listen I stepped on something and now its blowing up in my face."

Noani listened as Kendall told her about his friendship with Zeke and Dean. He told her about the women, the drinking, drugging, and Brenda. The card parties, the gambling, Zeke's habits of being drunk and violent were described as though he was reliving each moment. They arrived at the Essex County Jail and parked while he finished his story.

"Zeke was shot, killed in his own house. Brenda blamed me, your uncle, and the others for bringing him home too drunk to know an enemy from a friend. An intruder shot him when he opened the door. But that ain't all of it, there's something that nags at me saying it's more to it. Now Brenda is saying somebody violated her daughter too. Noani she accused me. I ain't never touched that child. I talked to her sometimes when she couldn't sleep, but I never touched her. Viola watched over her while Brenda was at work. But somebody got to her and Dean might know who."

"Damn." Noani didn't know what to say. "You're right maybe my uncle won't talk if I'm with you. You go in. I'll wait for you. You'll see the officer registering people. Just follow the procedures."

Kendall and Noani entered the facility and kissed as they separated. Kendall registered for his visit and followed the officer and other visitors to the designated visit hall. The distant sound of voices became louder as they approached the area where the visitors were being processed.

It took longer than Kendall expected for Dean to come and sit across from him in the booth with the Plexiglas window. He smiled surprised to have and unexpected visitor. Pointing to the receiver that hung on the wall, the men picked up and simultaneously said, "What's up?"

The booths on both sides of them were empty allowing Kendall time to ask his questions. He rushed Dean through the small talk and catching up.

"I've been back about two months now. I'm working at the church. Randall hooked me up with Pastor Turner."

"Good, your brother's always looked out for you. How's your mom?"

"Good, but listen, I've talked to Brenda. She works there too."

Dean didn't respond which gave Kendall a strange feeling. He got closer to the window and whispered into the phone. "She seems to think her daughter was touched, maybe raped. What's she talking about Dean?"

Dean responded looking around as he answered as though someone else was interested in their conversation. "Why would you come here with this shit? Did Noani tell you why they got me in here? I don't know nothing about that child or any child. Look at me damn it!"

Kendall dropped his head realizing he shouldn't have asked the question while on the prison's phone. He raised his eyes to meet Dean's. Dean shook his head. "I got money coming man; I'll be out in a week. Then I can talk to you."

"What? Do you know who, where? This woman thinks it's me."

"You or her husband, that would be 'bout right. Zeke wouldn't let me near her but the two of you spent time in her room telling her goodnight stories and shit." Dean laughed at the fear he saw in Kendall's face.

"I didn't touch that child." Kendall whispered harshly through clenched teeth.

"Then why you here? If you thought I did it, or your dead buddy why come here? Tell Brenda you didn't do it and the hell with the rest. Nah, my man, you're here to get confirmation of how sick your ass was before you left. Kendall you were so high most of the time you didn't know who or what you was fucking. That's why I didn't let you and Zeke touch my girls. One of y'all did it and Brenda just woke up."

"What is that supposed to mean?"

"She was so out of it when he got shot I guess she just forgot a lot of shit. You were thrown out of their house many nights. You'd claim you were bringing Zeke home but you like kids Kendall. That's one of your problems. Ain't shit in Florida killed that urge. You and Noani done hooked up huh? You always wanted them young."

"What they got you on Dean?"

"That don't matter, ain't none of your business. I'll be out in a week."

"What's your bail?"

"Why, you got me covered? Brother, tell her it ain't you. You don't remember anyway. She don't remember. Zeke is dead. Who's gonna point a finger at you? I got to get out of here, so don't come telling me to admit to that shit!" Dean's outburst brought an officer to their booth.

"What's the problem?" The officer asked looking at Kendall waiting for Dean to respond.

"Nothing man." The officer continued past them to the next occupied booth. "Listen Kendall, I can't help you from here and you can't help either one of us if you playing investigator. We all guilty man, even if you didn't do it, you was there."

"So what you saying Dean? Who did it? You, me, Zeke, us? You're right, I don't remember ever touching that girl or seeing anyone touching her, besides Viola was always around."

"And what about when old boy was there, her man, getting his from her. What was her old man's name? Rich, that's it. You don't remember them getting busy right there in the living room? Zeke would be high as hell by then. All of us was, but Viola wouldn't know shit either. Listen, keep your mouth closed and we'll be alright."

The officer nodded at Dean, a signal that he had another ten minutes. "Let Brenda figure the shit out on her own. You don't owe her nothing, especially heads on a platter. How is Dominique? I saw here a couple of times before I made this hell hole my home."

"Man, you got me spinning now I know I didn't hurt that girl."

"Ask her then. Ask Brenda no better yet ask Viola and Dominique. But when they come talking to me about it, you know what I'm gonna say."

"What, what could you say?"

"You and Zeke liked them young."

Forty

Noani sensed the visit hadn't gone well. The two left the building without saying a word. Kendall turned looking at the structure as they walked to the parking lot. The size seemed to dominate the block giving the surroundings an eerie shadow.

"I ain't never going to jail, never." Kendall walked looking at the outer walls and barb wire. He visualized the gray walls of the visit hall, the heavy metal doors, and the officers with the handcuffs. He still had the stale smell in his nostrils and the echoing of the intercom in his ears. He compared the Miami Dade Rehabilitation Center to a prison when he was there. Now he knew there was a distinct difference. He looked past Noani and shook his head slowly.

"Why would you? Was Dean alright? Did you get the answer you needed?" Her questions brought his thoughts to the matter at hand.

"No baby, we've got to find Viola." Kendall lied. He didn't believe Dean's story. Noani's black Maxima was parked farther than he thought. As he began to feel the chill of the afternoon air, he turned up his collar and put his arm around her shoulder as they continued to walk.

"Cold huh? The temperature dropped. Do you have time for us to stop by that place you said she works?"

"What happened to the dinner you promised? Can we still do that?" Noani questioned wondering if he had used her again.

"Sure can."

Noani drove to the diner of her choice. Tops had always been her favorite. It was close enough to the downtown area of Newark for them to catch Viola before the evening crowd came into The Spot. Kendall watched Noani as the waitress led them to their seat. He took her coat off for her and waited as she slid across the seat in the booth. Dean was right he liked Noani, but as he thought of the women he dealt with in the past, age had never been an attraction. He didn't care about their age, but they all were legal. He wasn't into prostitutes or one night stands either. Coke and alcohol was his only addiction and then he'd have problems with the women he was dating. Too high to remember his commitment to them, he'd forget to show up, pay bills, or work. He'd make promises and never keep them. His time always included Zeke, playing cards, and of course getting high. His mother and Randall knew it would lead to problems after he began to fight a few of the guys at the bar and hit his last girlfriend. Dean's arrest woke up the community and pointed fingers at the group that was always together. Randall and his mother talked him into leaving.

Noani smiled while sucking through the straw in her soda. They carried on a mental and visual conversation, which allowed Kendall's thoughts to flow freely. Florida was good for him. The treatment was strenuous but it didn't take him long to shake the drugs and realize he had to come home to reconcile with his family and a few of his friends. During the sessions he spoke of Zeke, the murder, and his love for Brenda. After being with Noani, he realized he wasn't good enough for Brenda or a woman who had that close of a connection to God. He hadn't been to church in years and didn't think God would wait on him. After visiting Dean he prayed for the first time since leaving Florida. He was a believer, just not one for church worship.

"Who do you think raped her?" Noani touched Kendall's hand to get his attention. "Do you have an idea who might have raped her? She was a little girl when her father died right?"

Kendall wiped his mouth, after eating the last bite of his roast beef. "She was about seven or maybe eight. I can't tell you who would do that. Your uncle claimed…." He stopped in the middle of his sentence. He couldn't repeat what Dean said. He didn't want to think about what Dean said. "We need to talk to Viola. So where'd you say we could definitely find her?"

"So you ain't telling it all?" Naoni was younger than Kendall by twenty years or more but she wasn't dumb. "Kendall, I told you games is for kids and some of them wannabees in the street. What you and my uncle got gonna on that Ms. Viola is a part of?"

"Nothing, I just need to find out the truth. I've been chasing my past since I got back. I'm trying to come clean with myself and that includes family and friends."

"That sound like some ole' twelve step program shit."

Kendall chuckled thinking how many times he heard that over the last year. "Seems like the only people that look to clean up the past and look toward the future is recovering addicts. That's a sad thought. Why don't people that go to church looking for salvation fit into a twelve step program?"

"I don't know I guess salvation is salvation, anyway you can get it. So you trying to save your soul and Viola is the key?"

"No, I'm the key. Nobody can fix me but me, well me and God." He didn't believe he said that, but he realized if Dean was telling the truth, then only God could help him.

Forty-one

Viola looked closer into the mirror. The signs of aging could only be covered with good makeup. She made a mental note to purchase more foundation on her next trip to the mall. She took a deep breath and began the ritual of putting a "face" on. It didn't cover the years well, although Rich spoke of her beauty often. She was still vibrant after years of entertaining in the bars around the city and she was one of the best at it.

Viola didn't graduate from high school and as a barmaid she took care of her family and her children for years. Both her daughter and son finished college on the money she made. She would proudly tell anyone she never had to prostitute herself for any of it.

Viola Brown was a highlight on Friday and Saturday evenings. Monday through Thursday she was a mother and a babysitter for friends who worked odd hours. Brenda worked those hours at the hospital, hoping to become a full time nurse. Viola saw her passion and agreed to help. After Zeke was killed the dream died too. Viola couldn't convince her friend to continue school. The thought of becoming a nurse was second to protecting her child and the memories of Zeke's death.

Viola heard the men talking about Zeke's Friday night card parties and it brought on a new fear. A young child shouldn't be in the house with men drinking, cursing, and talking about what they wanted do to women. She quit working Friday nights and told Brenda she would watch

Dominique on Friday's too. Grateful for the help and relieved that she didn't have to depend on Zeke, Brenda agreed. As the schedule at the hospital rotated Viola changed her days as well. Dean fired her after he found out her real reason for limiting her hours at the bar. She worked for Rich at The Spot the very next night. The crowd followed her once the word got out she was at Rich's place.

Viola danced freely, entertaining the customers and the tips grew. The downtown crowd was more sophisticated; a welcomed the change. She saw the regulars on Friday's at Brenda's house playing cards with Zeke. They stumbled in after twelve and left before six, the time Brenda would be returning home. Zeke fussed throughout the week about a babysitter being in his home. After his objections regarding his wife attending school and becoming a nurse, Brenda knew he would argue about her internship hours at the hospital. Her duties wouldn't include pay; they were merely hours to finish her course of study. Zeke wasn't pleased regardless of the benefit it would bring the family.

Viola knew Zeke and Brenda had problems in their marriage. He told it all at the bar every time he drank over his limit. After talking loud and luring some young girl to his lap, he'd go in a back room for pleasure. Dean set up the back rooms to make extra money. Zeke set up his home for the same thing. Viola would go to Dominique's room and read to her until the child fell asleep. She would then stand guard keeping the company from disturbing her peace. Zeke allowed them to use the den, the guest room, and the living room. They'd meet at the bar and continue their escapades in his home.

Viola never told Brenda. Zeke's threat held her tongue and now years later she would have to tell it all. Brenda called for the second time. She wanted to meet with her and Kendall. She needed to let Rich know ahead of time. He'd have to have a person to fill her spot. It was Wednesday. Thursdays and Fridays brought the end of the week crowd. She told Brenda to get with Kendall and she'd call her back.

She applied her lipstick and stepped back to get a full-length view. Her body was well preserved for a woman in her fifties, late fifties at that. Viola made sure her outfit would be a compliment to the event Rich was having at the club. The businessmen and women loved the treatment she provided and she loved her work. Although she no longer had no desire to dance, she loved to socialize. She smiled in the mirror, admiring herself. Rich would be pleased. She grabbed her purse and keys. She'd have to hurry to beat the rush hour traffic.

"Viola should be here any minute can I offer you a drink until she comes?" Rich didn't understand why Noani or Kendall asked for him. The after five networking event would be starting in another hour and he had to prepare for the expected crowd. The Spot wasn't like the bars in the south or central wards of Newark. It was downtown, an area that now held promise for the city and its visitors. Rich didn't see much of the old crowd and didn't miss any of their after hour's antics.

Kendall and Noani ordered their drinks, and positioned themselves where they could see the entrance. Kendall didn't give any explanation for their visit. He did mention that they had talk to her at some point during the night. There were a few customers that arrived early in their suits and business attire, which made him feel uncomfortable. Both he and Noani would stand out in their excessively casual attire. The bar was lined with lights and the counter was marble instead of the wooden top counters he was accustomed to. Individual tables for couples were centered on the large floor and booths lined three of the walls. There was a dance floor and stage area with overhead lighting, speakers and a microphone that sat center stage. After scanning the room, he soon realized there was difference in the clientele as well. Rich was no longer a bartender; he was an owner, a host. Kendall nodded his head impressed by his success.

"What are you nodding your head for? You like this atmosphere or the music?" Noani asked. It was apparent she disagreed. The music in the background could have been heard after midnight on any R & B station. The classics — oldies but goodies — nothing for the dance floor. It gave the elite group a chance to talk and mingle.

"I'm liking all this. Rich is doing his thing. I know now why you don't see him much up the hill. So what does Viola do here?"

"She's in charge of the barmaids and the bartenders. You know, greets the customers, gets them talking, and keeps them satisfied. Rich does the same in the cigar room in the back."

Kendall gave her a blank stare.

"No, nothing like the back room at Deans, these are businessmen. They make their business deals and such back there. I tried to get a job here when he first started but he said Dean ruined it for me and the others. Our reputation spoke before our mouths did. Guess he didn't want that mess to follow him. You know Rich used to come by every now and then."

"Rich? Rich got with you and your sister?"

"No, my cousin, she was about seventeen then. But yeah, he frowned on all three of us when we wanted a job. He didn't mind the job she did for him though. I can't stand his ass."

Rich approached the couple again offering his apologies. "I'm sure she won't be much longer. Would you prefer to wait for her in the lounge?"

"I think you'd prefer for us to wait in the lounge." Noani abruptly replied rolling her eyes.

"No thank you. I'm enjoying the music and the drinks thanks." Kendall replied ignoring Noani's rude response.

"The music can be heard there as well." Rich sounded desperate.

"Man we ain't here to embarrass you. I see some of your people are casually dressed. What's the problem?"

Noani bucked her eyes waiting for Rich to answer Kendall. He smiled and began to wave at the door. Viola saved him.

Forty-two

The weather slowed traffic but there was no rescheduling of appointments. Boat called Dominique to check on her before packing his satchel to leave after what had been a tiring day. He made a comment to Eric earlier that there must have been a full moon because all of his clients and Pam were acting strange.

For the past few days she seemed determined to get him to go out with her on Friday night. He didn't want to repeat that he didn't date women he worked with. Eric teased him saying he'd better be careful before he lost a receptionist. Pam gave him the "treatment" when he said he'd be busy and she hadn't changed her attitude toward him even after he bought her lunch.

"Pam, do you know where the notes for Ms. Chavis are? I have to turn in the monthly report tomorrow."

"No and the report was due today."

Boat looked at the calendar. Pam usually alerted him days prior to the deadline. He shook his head realizing she was paying him back in her own devious way.

"Thanks. You have a good evening."

"Yeah, you too." He heard the office door close. He would have to explain the delay for the report, without the file he couldn't complete it. He went to Pam's desk and checked for the folder in the bin labeled signature needed. The file was there, awaiting his attention. He would have to talk to Pam. She couldn't ignore work simply because he wouldn't date her. His cell phone rang and he ignored it allowing it to go to his messages. The office phone rang and the light blinked next to his name. He picked up the phone hoping it wasn't Dominique.

"Did you find the folder?"

"Why are we playing games?"

"You're playing the game sweetie. You know what you want but you've made the choice to play nursemaid to that psycho you're dating. Wait. Can you call it dating? Does she even attempt to satisfy your needs? I don't think so. If she did I wouldn't be able to tell your full size when I get close."

"Pam, listen, I don't want you to take this the wrong way. It's not that you're not attractive or you're not...."

"Save it baby. I'm like you. I need someone to talk to, understand what I'm going through, and whatever that leads to, fine. Even if it doesn't, I was only offering a few drinks and good conversation."

"I'm not saying…"

"You said it already. Westlene called, she said call her. I asked what it was in reference to and guess what. She told me Dominique. So I guess the African got her piece, Dominique got hers and me…well I'll wait. Have a good night."

She hung up the phone. Boat sat thinking about her last comment. If he could only have them all; Westlene the exotic woman, Dominique the professional, and Pam the around the way girl; he'd definitely tell Eric about that fantasy.

He looked at his cell. Pam had tried his cell number first. It was close to five. Dominique would wonder why he was taking so long. She told him she would cook dinner for the two of them if he brought the wine. Her foot wasn't much better and after three days the swelling gave an indication there may be another problem. The visit to her mother's house would be pushed back until she saw the doctor on Friday.

Boat called Westlene while walking to his vehicle. Soft Caribbean music played until it was interrupted by the beep of an incoming call. He looked at his phone and clicked over.

"Yeah Claudia what's up?"

"Spoke to your girl today?"

"Earlier, I'm on my way to her house. What's up?"

"Is she still talking about going to that house?"

"Claudia, did you talk to her?" He hated playing *"guess what I know"* with females.

"She called them today Boat. She's planning on going there on Friday."

"She's got a doctor's appointment. He foot is still messed up. I'll be with her."

"She talked to the woman while I was on the phone. They agreed to meeting Friday or Monday. I guess she'll call if or when she finds out about her foot. I just thought I should let you know."

"Thanks Claudia, I'll talk to her."

"Don't tell her we talked, you know she'll get mad at me."

"Yeah, thanks." Boat put the keys in the ignition and dialed Westlene's number again.

"Lawrence, my friend, how are you?"

"Fine lady, how 'bout yourself?"

"Blessed my friend, blessed. Did you contact Dominique today?"

Boat felt as though he missed something, first Claudia then Westlene. Dominique didn't call him back to discuss any problems she had. Maybe the dinner was to persuade him to accept her decision to go to the house.

"I did, this morning."

"I see. Well your friend is having thoughts about going to her old home. I don't recommend she go alone. I get the feeling there was something going on in that home and the spirit has not left there. It may answer her questions, but she may need support to get her through it."

"I told you her father was murdered there."

"It is not her father's death. It is other things that went on there. Her mother knows, there is more, I can't see it and she has blocked it. I tried telling her mother to go with her. Obviously they didn't go together."

"They didn't get together because of the weather. I think Dominique's foot is another problem."

"The dreams will continue. She will have no peace."

"Westlene, she may have been raped."

The silence on the phone came across as cold as the winter air. Westlene simply said goodbye and hung up. He wanted to call her back, but didn't know how to ask the questions he felt she could answer. He put the car in gear and headed toward Dominique's house.

Forty-three

"So Viola agreed to come over tomorrow. Are you waiting for Kendall to be there with the two of you?" The Pastor wanted to understand what Brenda was anticipating.

"Yes, and you, I want you there too. Jacob if Dominique was raped Viola knows. If it was one of the men they played cards with, Kendall knows who they are."

The two sat at the kitchen table talking about Zeke, the card games, his drinking and the company he kept. It was the first time they spoke about him since his death. Brenda cried as she told Jacob that she should have married him, even though she was pregnant. Pastor Jacob Turner agreed, but he couldn't look into her tear filled eyes and tell her he was committed to being a man of the cloth. He didn't doubt his love for her or God, but he chose God. Now he prayed he could live with his choice.

"Well, I understand we've all had our burdens and I am blessed to have you in my life. But Jacob, I've made mistakes and not marrying you was one of them." Brenda wiped the tears as they fell. "And now my daughter has suffered because of it. I don't want her to remember any of those years Jacob. If she was harmed I would have known it, how could I have missed my daughter being raped? Then her father's murder, she can't relive that night."

Jacob stood over her and lifted her slowly out of the kitchen chair. "Let's sit on the couch. Come on, calm down, it's gonna be alright. You'll see. God has made a way for you both through all of this."

"God has a way of showing you the truth. Pastor she's not ready for the truth. You know that. She can't handle what happened that night."

She sat on the couch and Jacob went back to the kitchen and got her a glass of water. "Here, drink and relax. You're working yourself up. You don't know Brenda, maybe it's all coming back to her now."

"Oh no, don't say that Jacob, no!"

"Brenda, you never said why Kendall was here that night. Why did he come back to help you clean up? Why was he here before any of us? Did you call him?"

"He was here, he came in with Zeke. I didn't go to work that night and told Viola she didn't have to come. Zeke didn't know I would be home. Kendall came over, I guess looking for the usual fun they had night after night. Viola had begun sitting for us even when Zeke told me he would be watching Dommi. She insisted that Dominique had become accustomed to her schedule and she tried to keep her on it while I was working. Zeke would let her stay up, eat whatever and whenever. She'd be tired in the morning, dragging and running late for school. I didn't suspect anything and agreed with Viola." Brenda paused and her tears began to fall again.

"It's alright Brenda."

"No, no it's not. I don't know if Dominique was touched, violated, raped, or who knows. But you know what, I believe Kendall and Viola know and that's why I told them to come here. We'll go to the house on Friday like Westlene said and we'll all stir up some memories. Jacob, pray for me."

Pastor Turner took her hand into his and bowed his head. Brenda closed her eyes. She couldn't tell him the truth. She couldn't tell him that Westlene had seen through her and she stirred the suspicions she had as Zeke tried to talk with his last breath. Brenda remembered the night in flashes during her dreams, and like her daughter, the picture of that horrific night was almost complete.

Jacob whispered his prayer asking God for the strength Brenda needed to see her through this turmoil. He let her hand go but continued to pray silently. His suspicions were haunting him and he hoped Kendall had not been an intricate part of the murder. He always thought Kendall avoided charges when he fled to Florida. Maybe it wasn't the murder he was running from, maybe he was the one fondling the child that Zeke failed to protect. Jacob needed strength himself, the strength to refrain from killing Kendall if the truth matched his suspicions.

Brenda sat with her eyes closed. The tears were still falling. She and the Pastor held hands in silence for a moment allowing the moment of prayer to refresh their thoughts.

"Jacob, how does one forgive when the pain is still there? As a Christian, how do I forget? Kendall Stevenson had parts in the devil's work. I know he did. I just don't know what part he played. He and Zeke were as thick as thieves and if Zeke…Jacob did you know that my child was scared of her father?"

"What do you mean scared?" Jacob handed her the glass she reached for. Although her voice didn't quiver her hands were unsteady. "Brenda, are you okay?"

"No, I feel sick. Excuse me." Brenda rose to her feet and headed for the bathroom. She went in and closed the door. Feeling lightheaded she put the top down on the toilet and sat. She could feel the anger and pain again. It was the same the night Zeke was killed. "Lord, give me strength. This can't be the reason. Lord, help me. Lord, help Dominique."

"Brenda, Brenda are you okay?" Pastor Turner stood outside the door calling her name. He tapped on the door lightly hoping she would respond.

"I'm sorry Jacob, I'll be alright. Can you see yourself out? Please come back tomorrow. Viola and Kendall should be here around seven. Say you'll come, I need your support."

"I'll be here. If you need me before then call me."

He stood at the door waiting for her response. He could only hear the hollow sound of her sobbing. Jacob understood her pain was deeper than he thought. Westlene touched the surface of her raw emotions and now she was facing the process of healing again. He went to the closet and retrieved his coat. The thought of staying crossed his mind. He put the coat back in the closet and sat on the couch. He wouldn't be able to sleep if he left the woman he loved again.

Forty-four

Viola and Kendall shared memories and talked for hours before Noani began to become weary of the conversation. She saw a few people she knew but felt out of place when she compared herself to the others who had filled the room. She sat watching the networking and buzz of the customers; it wasn't her type of crowd. Kendall didn't seem to mind, engrossed in the walk down memory lane, he ordered another drink.

"Kendall, are we gonna be here long?"

"Oh, I'm sorry, we must be boring you. Viola, girl there's so much to catch up on, but there's a real problem that brought me here. I went to see Dean today after Brenda accused me of possibly raping Dominique. I went to see him because I know I didn't touch that girl. He tried to make it seem like I was too high to remember. I know I would have remembered some shit like that. I was wondering if you and I could go talk to Brenda. Part of my recovery is to atone, you know. I do feel that I did her wrong, you know. Zeke did some foul shit and I knew about most of it. I was in love with her and fantasized about being with my friend's husband. I know that was wrong as well."

Noani turned to focus on their conversation with a frown. She took a slow deliberate breath catching Kendall's attention.

"C'mon babe, it ain't like that now." He reached for Noani's hand and continued. "I just want to clear the air. Viola you know I didn't have nothing to do with no rape."

"Kendall, you and Zeke tried some things. That's why I volunteered to babysit. Zeke was trying to do the same thing that Dean was doing. Noani can tell you the money that was made prostituting those young girls. Well Zeke wanted the same thing. Dean didn't like it 'cause some of his customers would come over to the house to see what girls Zeke had lined up for the night. It was dipping into Dean's business."

"Wait, you telling me that he was letting men touch his daughter?"

"Not while I was there. But I don't know what went on when Brenda left that child with him."

"You never said nothing to Brenda?"

Rich came over to the table. It was close to six-thirty and Viola hadn't greeted any customers or did her usual welcome to open the after hour mingling event. She excused herself from the table promising to be back. The crowd applauded her arrival on the small stage. The volume of conversations and the DJ's music decreased as Viola invited the guests to the buffet and free drinks for the cocktail hour, which would begin at seven. Kendall turned his attention to Noani who turned up her glass and pushed it to his side of the table.

"Noani, did you know about this?"

"I didn't know you was in love with Brenda. Is that what this is about? I'm helping you reunite with the widow?"

"No, listen. I ain't gonna lie. I thought about it when I got here. She was one of the reasons I came back. But I realize things have changed."

"What changed was you got your first lay in years from me. Listen, I told you I don't play those games."

"This ain't no game. I'm with you on that. I need to be sure she understands I didn't touch Dommi. I'm sorry I didn't tell her about Zeke and some of the shit he did to her."

"You don't owe her no apology for how her husband treated her. That man did what he wanted to. You, my uncle, Viola, Brenda and Dean; we all were touched by that demon."

"You? He did something to you."

"Yeah, he tried. My uncle wanted to kill him. You know how he used to want the girls to do him right there at the bar. Well he pulled me one night and my sister another. Dean pulled his gun on him."

"Do you think your uncle killed him?"

"Wouldn't be surprised, but if it was him, Brenda knows what my uncle looks like."

"True."

Viola returned to the table after they had another round.

"Listen, Brenda is willing to meet with us on Friday. Let's get this straight then. I'll tell her what I know and you'll get your chance to tell her your side."

"Sounds fair, where are we meeting her?"

"At the house on Rose Terrace; she wants to meet where it happened around eight."

"That's some weird shit there. Why would she want to be in that house again?"

"Noani, if that's where she wants us to meet her, its fine. Viola, I'll be there at eight."

Viola smiled and left the table tapping on the next saying hello to the couple who sat next to them. Kendall and Noani finished their drink keeping beat to the music and trying to enjoy the atmosphere. Noani felt a buzz from the three Martini's she downed, but it didn't give the surroundings a better appearance.

"Let's go. I don't really like this place."

Kendall gave her a questioning look. "What do you have in mind?"

Noani stood allowing him to assist her with her coat. "You can't tell?"

"I don't want to be wrong."

"You're not wrong."

The two left, smiling. The cold air hit them in the face and they quickened their pace to the car. Kendall thought about Viola, the nights she babysat for Brenda. He thought about Zeke, the nights he fought with Brenda. He began to feel guilt creeping upon him. He couldn't deny what he knew. Every weekend there had been another girl, woman, fulfilling a man's pleasure in the Preston's home. Kendall couldn't stay the night with Noani. He had a sick feeling in his stomach. For the first time in years, Kendall longed for his mother.

Forty-five

The sound of the neighbor's car tires on the hardened snow woke Dominique from a sound sleep. She was pleased Boat stayed the night. As usual with the warmth of his body next to her she didn't fear the shadowy image haunting her in the middle of the night. She stretched without removing the comforter and rolled over to see the clock on her nightstand.

She and Boat talked late into the night. Now at nine o'clock, she only had two hours to shower and get to West Orange for her doctor's appointment. The nurse heard her complaint and decided to squeeze her in early. Normally Friday appointments were booked but she had one opening.

"Dommi, are you eating before we go?" Boat called from the bottom of the stairs. "The coffee is ready. I can make you toast or something if you want."

"The coffee is fine," she replied as she carefully moved her injured foot from the bed to the floor. Her foot was still swollen and she now believed Boat. There was something seriously wrong. She slipped on her robe and hobbled slowly to the staircase. It looked as though it would take her most of the morning to reach the bottom. Boat met her midway assisting her balance holding her arm as she grimaced in pain.

"I don't know babe, there may be a tear or something…" Boat caught her look before completing the sentence. "I'm just saying you keep walking on this thing. You didn't go to the doctor and you know the hospital doesn't do more than x-rays."

"We're going this morning, between you, my mother and Claudia, you all would have me on the table under the knife."

"Not me, I love your stubby toes." Boat sat her in the chair where the steam of her food met her nose.

"Thank you Mr. Boatwright. Breakfast in bed would have been the bomb," she teased.

"You would have missed the appointment. Claudia called too; you can call her after eleven, something about a meeting." Boat sat across from her and blessed his food.

"Did she tell you about the visit to the house?" Unsure how to answer he let her continue. "She's been trying to talk me out of going, but Westlene said it may be the answer I need. Well tonight is the night."

"Did Ms. Brown say she'd be there?"

"No, but she said there was someone else coming by and they made arrangements with Ms. Viola to see the place. She didn't say who. Just that Ms. Viola would be there. She may have answers I need as well. So after this appointment I'll be resting this foot so I can get around on it tonight."

"Yeah well let's just wait and see what the doctor says. You'll need someone around the next few days, so if you don't mind?" Boat stopped buttering his toast awaiting his answer.

"Thank you, but that's not going to stop me from going to that house. My mother knows something. You would think she'd arrange to come here and talk. She's using my injury to avoid my questions. She hasn't even called. Did you notice that?"

"Listen, you and your mother can talk right after the doctor's appointment. If you still want to go to the house then you both can go."

"No, I don't want her covering things up making excuses. If she calls we'll talk but if not, I'll go to the house get my answers and call her later."

"Let me help you with that." Boat moved her seat as she attempted to steady herself as she stood from her chair. "I'll clean this up, you get ready and then we'll go."

Dominique didn't move, she smiled knowing he read her mind. He walked with her to the stairs. Noticing her pain, they paused. She began her climb again as he watched each methodical step.

Forty-six

Kendall called the church, as he had done each morning after the first winter storm of the season. There was no answer, which he found unusual for the nine o'clock call. He had overslept, tired from his mind racing the night before. Viola's answers to his questions as well as Brenda's accusations worried him. He dialed Randall's cell number assuming he was at the church, but not at his desk.

"Good morning, rough night huh?" Randall's sarcastic greeting touched Kendall's nerves, but he held his tongue.

"No, I was home before you, just couldn't sleep. Is it possible for me to take off today? I want to talk to mom about a few things."

Randall sensed the sincerity in his tone and became concerned.

"What's wrong? You don't sound right."

Randall listened as his brother explained his reasons for wanting to talk with their mother about the conversations he had with Dean, Brenda, and Viola. It was a part of the past he hoped his brother would never have to revisit. Kendall had been so high, whether it was alcohol or drugs, that he never got a straight answer about where he had been or who he had been with. The same accusations came up with Zeke's death and Dean's arrest. Kendall didn't remember much about either incident. He stayed high and always had a woman to satisfy his needs. Randall often prayed his brother wouldn't die from an overdose of his pleasures.

"So what do you really expect her to tell you? Ma wasn't with you and she sure as hell didn't come to get you."

"Randall, I'm not looking for excuses, I'm looking for the truth. I've changed. No matter what you or anyone else thinks, I'm not the same person. Have you noticed anything different about me?"

It was true; he had changed. This was the first day he wasn't at the church on time. He was home before twelve and if he stayed out he told Randall where he would be. Lately it was with Noani. Randall couldn't complain about how Kendall kept himself or the apartment. He spent his pay on household items and food. He even offered to contribute to the bills. He went to his mother's on Sunday's after church even though he didn't attend the services.

"Yeah, I noticed, but why are you involving her in this mess. You know what she went through when you left here."

"Where are you? I called the office, no one answered."

"I'm at mom's house."

"Stay there, I'm on my way."

Randall wasn't sure what he would tell his mother. He had told her so much over the years about his brother's mistakes and misfortunes. He told lies that painted a fading picture; a façade for Estelle, who thought nothing but the best of her boys. He couldn't hide the addiction to drugs, but Kendall's lust for young women was a well-kept secret. Randall often questioned their ages but was brushed off by insults and comments about his inability to keep a relationship. Reality caught up with Dean and now his brother was once again on the run. There was no evidence to prove Kendall had been with any of those girls that took the paychecks of most of his friends including Zeke. Randall told him time would tell; the clock seemed to be chiming.

"Was that Kendall?" Estelle entered the room drying her hands on the dishtowel she used for the morning dishes.

"He's coming here to visit," replied Randall dryly. He stood debating whether to stay, leave, or warn his mother of what was to come.

"Oh good, you know it's not often that the two of you are here together. How's he making out at the church? He's not trying to talk with Brenda is he? You know…"

"Mama, leave it alone. He's coming over to talk to us. He said something is on his mind."

"So you think something is wrong?"

"When has he ever wanted to just talk to us?"

Estelle didn't know what to think. Randall seemed despondent. He always was when Kendall reached out for support. He had issues and was on his way to her home seeking what she was sure would be their help.

Forty-seven

Westlene flipped through her notes. There was no other way to deal with the Preston's than to talk with them together. Brenda obviously knew what went on in the house and didn't want her daughter to relive the trauma she had been through. Dominique had been reliving it for years.

The doctor thought about the torment brought on by the dreams. She referred to them as haunting shadows. Westlene wondered what her feelings would be if she found out her mother knew about the attacks all along.

She looked at her scribble, words that expressed Dominique's emotional rage when she described what she felt. What happened to this man who violated her as a child? Was he apprehended? Did he surrender, or was he still involved with her and her family? Boat didn't confirm she had been raped. Brenda didn't seem anxious to talk with her daughter. Her response to Westlene's suggestion seemed nonchalant; not what she had expected.

She dialed Ms. Preston's number deciding to dig deeper. The mental and emotional state of Dominique would depend on her mother's support.

"Good morning, Ms. Preston?"

Brenda recognized the accent. She could feel her anxiety building. "Yes, doctor, good morning."

"I guess my voice gave way to who I am. I say good morning to you. How are you feeling this day?"

"I'm well, as well as can be. You know Dominique has injured her ankle. I'm a little worried about her. She'll have to see a doctor today, I believe."

Westlene could sense she was talking in an attempt to keep the conversation from the obvious matter at hand.

"Oh, I see. Have you had a chance to speak with her as we discussed?"

"No I am still waiting to talk with her, maybe after the weekend. The snow and ice should be gone by then."

"I see, Ms. Preston, I wouldn't prolong this conversation. Your daughter has been hurt enough. She will need your comfort and words to get her through the truth."

"What truth? What is it you think you know about the truth doctor?"

Westlene paused before answering. Telling patients the truth before they faced the reality themselves had never proved to be beneficial.

"I'd rather you tell the truth Ms. Preston. I am not involved to solve this issue for you and your daughter. She is searching for peace of mind and she won't get it being haunted by the past. I believe you are instrumental in helping her with this. Again, I am merely suggesting you speak with her before she enters that house again."

"Doctor, I am a Christian and I don't believe in black magic, palm readings and such. If my daughter wants to seek help through this type of therapy it will not include me."

"Ms. Preston, I can assure you my practice does not include what you call black magic. I too am a Christian woman. Unsettled spirits exist and for whatever reason there is a spirit that is haunting your daughter. Something happened in that house that included that spirit. Let the truth be told, all of what happened in that house includes this spirit. Let Dominique have peace of mind. Tell her about what went on in your home. Are you suggesting that my involvement would interfere in you helping her or telling her what you know?"

"I don't believe that me telling Dominique about what has been put to rest years ago will cure or prevent anything. You have been chosen to help her. I am not a part of the prescription. Sprinkle dust; call the spirits if you like, but don't call me again with this."

"I don't mean to disrespect you or your feelings but I am a Doctor of Psychology. My work is in mental health. Your daughter is mentally and emotionally affected by these dreams. As you well know she has had them since childhood. You know when they started and you know the root of the problem. If you care not to be a part of the prescription, I understand. Maybe your emotions and mental state has been affected as well. Know that this problem is not at rest. It lives with you and your daughter. You are bothered and live with this taunting from your past. Ms. Preston your daughter is tormented by it. I will not bother you again. Just know that this will not go away without your input."

"Goodbye doctor."

Brenda held her tears until she put down the phone. She clutched her chest feeling the pressure and stress. She never thought about her husband's spirit being the cause of Dominique's nightmares, her pain. She moved from the home hoping it would bring the child peace. Westlene was right. Her emotions and mental state had been frayed, although she made it through each day, she barely slept each night. She too was tired.

It was still early. Pastor Turner left after breakfast and Brenda convincing him she would be fine. She took the day off to clean her home preparing for Kendall and Viola. She was certain they would need to talk after visiting the house on Rose Terrace. She would ask them to meet her at her home, a more comfortable setting. Her conversation with Dominique would be filled with questions. Questions Brenda was sure Viola and Kendall could answer.

Westlene had touched a nerve. She put a checkmark on her pad next to Brenda Preston's name. She had reached a dead end. Boat would be asking her what was next. She wasn't sure, but she was determined to exhaust all her options before telling him there was nothing she could do. She dialed the number Dominique had given her. It was the number she said she would answer anytime. The phone rang twice before she heard her voice.

"Hey Westlene, how are you?"

"How are you? Are you up and about?"

"Yes, I'm on my way to the doctor to see about this foot. It seems there may be something else wrong. Boat thinks so and to be honest it feels like something just isn't right. Did I miss an appointment or something?"

"No, I am just checking with you. Have you been sleeping better lately?"

"Not really. I am going to the house this evening. I'll get to the upstairs this time, I'm sure. My mother hasn't called so I'm assuming she doesn't want to be a part of my discovery."

"Discovery? What is it you think you may discover? I thought your visit to the house was to reflect on the past. Are you trying to solve something, what are you looking for?"

"Westlene, I think I was raped, in my room, in my bed, in that house. I think that's what the dreams are about. I don't know what happened but I think once I find out I will have peace of mind."

"Peace can bring trouble my dear. Are you ready for that?"

"Trouble? What trouble?"

"If someone raped you in your home, could it not be said they knew you, your family, they were not a stranger?"

The response to Westlene's question was silence.

"You must remember, I said speak with your mother. Talk with her before you go into this house again. She should be with you."

"So is it true? I was raped is that what you see doctor?"

"No, no my dear. I see nothing of the sort. I see you are in turmoil about your past. The time you spent in that house was painful for you. Your mother should talk with you about this house, this turmoil, and help you through this pain."

"Doctor, can you hypnotize people? Would you hypnotize me? My mother won't tell me anything about the past. She never talks about it or my father."

"And what do you expect from this visit to the house?"

"I don't know. Can you hypnotize me?"

"I don't know. Call me when you've finished with your appointment. Call me before you enter that house."

"Will you hypnotize me today before I go to the house?"

"You may not want to go in the house afterward. Just call me."

Forty-eight

"Why would Brenda or Dean say those things? I don't know. Mama you know I would never have touched that girl. Brenda didn't say I did anything. She assumed I knew what went on when she wasn't there. I don't remember Zeke having nobody go into his daughter's room. I would have said something."

Randall watched his brother reach for his glass. His nerves were rattled. If he had been a part of an interrogation, one would have said he was guilty. Estelle looked at her sons wondering who had been lying. Randall never mentioned the antics that he knew went on in the Preston home. The drugs were enough. She sat across the table trying to put the pieces of the story together. The picture Kendall painted wasn't clear.

"Kendall, did you know that girl was touched in any way. You know that woman ain't been right since that night. Wasn't you there?"

"I was Mama. I never denied that. Zeke invited me there but I got there after the murder. Brenda said it was an intruder. I stayed to help her clean up the blood."

"Didn't the cops want to look for evidence?" Randall never understood why they cleaned up the scene the same night. "What was the rush to clean up?"

"Dominique, Brenda didn't want her to see the mess. The cops did what they had to do and told her we could clean it up seeing that it was an intruder. They believed her story and waited until after the coroner moved Zeke and they left. I think they told Brenda they'd be back to question her the next day. Wasn't much evidence that the blood had been stepped in by Brenda; I guess she stepped into it trying to be at his side. That's where I found her."

"You were there before the police?" His mother was stunned never hearing this part of the story.

"Brenda called the police I guess when the intruder left. I walked in and found her on the kitchen floor holding Zeke in her lap whispering to him."

"Where was the child?" Estelle didn't remember the story being told the same way when Kendall was asked about it before.

"She was sitting on the top step. She was crying but she didn't move."

Randall shook his head and sighed. "Kendall, you didn't tell us this before. Mama, do you remember what he said when we asked him?"

"What did I say before?"

"You said you were upstairs in the bathroom and came downstairs when you heard the shot. You kept screaming about Zeke was dead and it was your fault."

"Baby we shut you up before you put yourself in trouble." Estelle patted his hands. Kendall snatched his hand from her touch and looked at them as he stood.

"No, no that didn't happen I would have seen the intruder. I would have seen who it was."

"I don't know man, you were high. You came to my house after cleaning up that mess with Brenda. You said you and Brenda drank your way through cleaning up that mess. I knew you had more, coke or something. You were gone. I changed your clothes and told Mama you had to be admitted into the hospital. A few days after Zeke's funeral you were on your way to Florida.

"Randall, then why is Brenda blaming me? We both saw the intruder? Is that what you're telling me? Why didn't Brenda tell the cops she knew what he looked like?"

Neither his mother nor brother answered.

"No, no are you saying I shot Zeke? I would have remembered that and why would I do that?"

"You loved Brenda son. You knew Zeke was mistreating her and that child. She didn't tell on you, she let you get away with it."

"Mama, Randall, y'all don't believe I did that. No, then why is she accusing me now? No, that's not it." Kendall paced the floor. "Why can't I remember?"

"It will come to you. It will take time but it will come to you."

"Mama, I don't have time. I can't go on like this. I need to know. Dean seems to think I touched or raped Dominique and all this time the two of you thought I may have murdered Zeke?"

Kendall slumped into the kitchen chair and held his head between his hands. His brother began to mumble. The name of Jesus was between every other inaudible phrase. Estelle got up and poured them all a drink. She looked at the clock. It had been years since she drank before noon.

Forty-nine

Boat helped Dominique into the car. He was glad she agreed to go to the doctor. The bone was fractured in two places. The swelling hid the tiny cracks that would keep her off her foot if it was to heal properly. Dominique waited to get in the car to speak about her prescribed bed rest.

"I know what you're going to say, but I have to do this or I won't get any rest. And that's what the doctor wants right?"

"Dommi, you're gonna do what you want to do anyway. If I say no, you'll wait until I'm not around to hobble your way over to that house. So, let's get this over with."

"Westlene's office is our first stop. Then we'll go from there."

"Westlene's office?"

"Yes, I've agreed to see her before I go to that house."

Her emphasis on the words "that house" added to Boat's confusion. He kept his thoughts to himself. Westlene knew more and the requested visit proved it. He wished he had spoken to her in depth. She hung up the phone before his mind caught up to what she was saying. Westlene knew about the rape and the murder. He wanted to ask her would she tell Dominique.

The radio played the mid-day mix, which seemed to ease Dominique's nerves. Boat was edgy enough for both of them. She told him Westlene was willing to hypnotize her. Now he understood the fears Brenda Preston held to herself over the years.

The air was changing with the winds blowing atop the shoveled snow mounds. Dominique wrapped her face with her scarf before stepping out cautiously onto the sidewalk. There was no room in the parking lot since the trucks plowed the snow on one side. Boat recognized many of the cars as co-workers who would wonder why he wasn't in his office.

"Are you stopping at your office?"

"Not unless you don't want me to come with you. I'm off until next Friday, maybe longer." He raised his brow an indication her condition would be the deciding factor for him to return to work.

"I don't know if Westlene will allow you to stay while she hypnotizes me."

Dominique stopped, to take smaller steps as she approached the salt covered stairs. Her toes began to get cold as the air came through her stocking covered cast. The crutch, provided by the doctor, seemed to be more of a hindrance than assistance.

"Whew, my toes are getting numb. It's cold out here."

"Lean on my shoulder you can get up the stairs quicker."

The heat hit their chilled faces as they paused after coming through the heavy door. People passed giving them nods, acknowledging the couple adjusting to the warmth of the lobby. Boat helped Dominique reposition herself before they walked to the elevator. Eric spotted the couple and hurried to catch them.

"Mornin' people. What's up? Whew, Dommi that can't be a good thing."

"Hey man." Boat pushed the numbers for both Westlene and Eric's floor.

"No, it's not a good thing, but the doctor said I'll only need the crutch a week or so."

"She's supposed to stay off the foot. The crutch is for the sistah who stays on the go." Eric understood nodding his head at Boat as he inspected the cast.

"So what did they say you did to it?"

"Eric, I don't know. I fell on a patch of ice and he thinks there's a fracture, maybe two."

"Ouch." The elevator door opened to Eric's floor. "Hey, Boat man, call me." He looked at the number still lit on the panel and raised his eyebrows at his friend. "Call me when you get a chance. Good seeing you Dommi. Take care of that foot."

They spoke at the same time; Dominique saying thanks and Boat agreeing to call him. Two floors later they got off the elevator and head toward Dr. Adashay's office.

Dominique loved the smell of Westlene's office. It was always refreshing, not like the mixture of colognes, breath mints, or the individual odors that permeated the air of most doctor offices. Boat took her coat and his, and hung them on the coat rack. The receptionist recognized him immediately.

"Good morning Mr. Boatwright, does she know you're coming?"

"No, I'm here with a friend. She has an appointment."

The woman looked up. Her smile disappeared as she recognized Dominique from her first visit.

"Ah, I see, the one who is no patient of Dr. Adashay's." She responded loud enough for Dominique to hear. "That's what all of dem say, you know." She added in a lower voice while winking at Boat.

Not completely understanding her response he simply smiled and returned to his seat. Dominique waited until he sat down to make a comment.

"I like Westlene, but she really needs to get rid of that one. She's upset with me still because I wouldn't fill out the questionnaire. Like I'm a patient or something, I told her that the first time I was here."

"They don't know the reason for you being here." Boat didn't want her to get upset.

"I know, that's what I said, some people. She's got a job, that's all she needs to do, her job."

Boat smiled and Dominique caught on. "I know. That is her job. Okay, okay, just forget it." But she didn't. When called into the office she smiled at the others and gave the woman a stern stare.

Fifty

"So you see it does not matter how it is interpreted. You are de one who must understand your dreams." Westlene began to adjust the lighting in the room. Dominique agreed to continue with the hypnotism after a thorough explanation of the procedure and what the effects may be. Boat left the two of them and was told to return in an hour. She still had her doubts and other questions. Westlene knew it was her nerves, her fear of what the session would reveal.

"How long will I be under, what is it, your spell?"

"You sound like your mother." Dominque sat up on the couch, obviously upset that Westlene may have spoken with her mother about the visit. "Lie down my child. She knows nothing of you being here. But she does believe I sprinkle dust and rub bones." The doctor laughed in spite of herself. "Oh, back in the day, my Grand Mama would throw ashes over de bones and say sum ding about rising up. I would laugh as a child, you know, not understanding what that ole woman pray about. We had wolves that would attack de village at night. She pray for de spirits to protect us. I never see any wolves. They say my Mama was sick, crazy, you know. But yet, if dey hear a howl in de night, de next day dey send for her to pray in front of their home. Your mother de same, she won't admit her belief in this that I do. But she wants my help to save her home."

Dominique listened as she did as she was told. She tried to get comfortable. Her toes were no longer cold and for the moment she had nothing to complain about physically. Westlene gave her a cup of her favorite tea. She said it was to help her get warm, but Dominique recognized the flavor and knew it would calm her anxiety. She missed the calming effect of the tea each night. Westlene wouldn't give her much of a supply. She said the herbs were hard to come by in the United States and promised to order extra for her when she put her monthly order in for the office.

"What happens now? Do I count backwards from one hundred or do you use the watch?"

"De watch?"

"Yeah, you know. You swing it slowly back and forth in front of my face."

Westlene took her seat beside the couch. The chair was positioned next to the end where Dominique would lay her head.

"No, no." The doctor tried not to laugh. Both women allowed humor to take over. "I've never seen such antics. I won't ask what that does. Even my Grand Mama would say that dis is, what do you say, too much drama."

"Yes, I guess it is dramatic. I just don't understand how one falls under."

"Relaxation you just relax. The conscious mind will not block as much when you are calm. We need to deal with your emotions and your memories."

"I don't remember much." Dominique adjusted herself on the pillow provided for her foot. She laid back and turned to listen as Westelene continued to talk.

"The watch is used for movies, funny most people don't respond well to it. It will be okay, you will see." Westlene lowered her voice barely above a whisper. "You'll be aware of what's going on, but your conscious mind will take a backseat to your subconscious mind. I'm hoping we can work our way back to when your dreams first started. You'll hear my voice and talk to me focused totally on our conversation. It will be good, no?"

"Yes," replied Dominique. She was comfortable and her foot's pain had subsided.

"This is a good thing you will see. How do you feel? Weightless, easy, relaxed. That's what I want. There are many times that one cannot relax and this method does not work."

"I can't imagine anyone not feeling relaxed coming into your office."

"Lay there for a moment, think about the colors that surround you now, and listen to my voice."

Westlene began to hum softly. She picked up her pad and pen when she noticed Dominique closing her eyes. Dominique began to hum the repeated melody that began to linger in the air. Her patient's comfort was apparent as she spoke again.

"Dominique what color was the room where you slept as a child?"

"Pink and white, I had matching furniture. No the walls weren't pink and white, just the furniture and the curtains. The walls were white." She opened her eyes slowly and remained still.

"What did you like most about your room?"

"My toys, my dolls; I had a doll house, a tea set and a small table by the window, with Teddie in it." She giggled. "Teddie, we spelled it with "i" and "e" at the end because she was a girl. She was a large bear with a pink and white sweater, hat and booties. My father gave her to me. She was too big to sit in the small chairs at my table. She sat on the floor near the closet."

Westlene noticed her tears as they rolled down her face. "What is upsetting you so?"

"Teddie sat at the closet door to keep the boogie man in the closet. I was scared of the closet at night. My father sat her there to protect me. The boogieman never came from the closet. He came from downstairs. I should have known she couldn't protect me."

Westlene began to hum. The soft tone brought the sense of calm back to Dominique's being. She seemed to drift to the softness of her voice. The security she missed each night when she was tucked in, embraced her as the doctor continued the melody. She had never heard the lullaby; she was sure it was from the island.

She could feel the breeze from her bedroom window. The warmth from the summer night circulated through the air. Her ceiling fan turned slowly above her. She could hear the laughter, the voices of her father's friends having a good time. It was routine, cards, and drinks and then the women would arrive. Soon the laughter would fade and there would be the low sound of music. She strained to hear Ms. Viola's voice. She would be safe. He wouldn't stay in her room whenever Ms. Viola was there.

She remembered the story, her favorite. It was read each night by Viola. Viola made sure she entertained the seven year old, certain that after her animated reading she would sleep through the night. Dominique heard her saying, "You've heard your favorite. Tomorrow we'll read another. I think you just like me acting a fool." Dominique would giggle after receiving soft pokes under her arms and a goodnight kiss. Her father wouldn't bother with tucking her in on Friday or Saturday nights. Her mother took Viola's place on Saturdays and Sundays, but it was never the same.

She loved her mother. The weekdays, after school, and most nights her father shared story time with Viola. He stood watching from the door until he was invited in to be different characters. He was a loving father, until he drank what he called his juice. He'd change, fighting and calling Brenda and Dommi names, obscenities she was too young to understand. Viola was her protection when her mother wasn't home. Viola was always there when he and his friends drank too much juice.

Westlene's voice seeped into her dreamy state. "Is there anyone else in your room?" She asked, waiting for Dominique's answer.

"Ms. Viola, she reads to me each night. She's sitting watching me as I sleep."

"Is there anyone else home?"

"My daddy and his friends are downstairs. They're not allowed in my room. Ms. Viola doesn't like them. I don't like them either." Her voice fades as though she's been a disobedient child. "I can't go downstairs now."

"Did your father kiss you good night?"

"Not when his friends are around." She replied in a whisper.

"Is Ms. Viola always there?"

"Not when he comes to kiss me. He waits until she leaves."

"Who waits, your father?"

"No, his friend."

Fifty-one

Westlene rocked Dominique as a mother would a child. She continued to cry, a muffled sob, which made her fears quite evident. She didn't know the man. She described him to the doctor while in her dream state. The pungent odor of his clothing and breath, the tone of his voice and his threats. He got closer and closer, whenever he could.

He noticed she ran across the hall as he was coming up the stairs to use the bathroom one night. Viola had left her room assuming she was asleep. Dominique felt the urge to go to the bathroom. After flushing the toilet she peered down the hall making sure none of her father's guest would see her in her Cinderella nightgown. Quickly she ran to her room and covered her head. She heard voices calling to him to hurry back to the card table. It was Friday night and the women hadn't arrived yet.

Dominique forgot to close her door as Viola did whenever she wasn't in the room. The shadow that appeared on her wall was not the figure of a woman. She closed her eyes tight. She wanted to scream but knew Viola wouldn't hear her over the loud conversation and music that loomed throughout the first floor.

"I'm just checking in on you, saw your pictures downstairs. Maybe me and Viola can read to you one night."

She told Westlene he came back, no longer talking from the door. He got close enough to whisper in her ear. Where was Viola? Why didn't she know he was coming in her room each week? She waited until he left her bedside and returned to the card table. It was a night when she pretended she was too tired to want Viola to read more. Viola seemed preoccupied with the conversation downstairs and it interrupted her recital of the story. She kissed Dominique and quickly joined the group in the dining room.

The small child got out of bed and sat at the top of the stairs. Dominique recalled being scared she would be caught peeking at the adults through the banister. She heard his voice. He was standing over the table watching her father marking the score sheet. He turned and smiled in her direction. She was caught.

Dominique began to cry, she was getting hysterical. Westlene attempted to soothe her. Through her tears she mumbled Viola's name. "Ms. Viola didn't come upstairs with him. He told me I would be his kitten. I tried to scream but my voice…"

Westlene needed to know who he was. She was sure Dominique would want to know as well. She listened to her cry for Viola. No man's name was mentioned. Her tears dried on her face and she stared at nothing particular on the doctor's wall.

"Who was he, did you know his name?"

"My father's friend, my father's friend tried to touch me. My father came in and stopped him. He told him, 'Not tonight'. Westlene my father sent him to my room, didn't he?"

Dominique pushed away from the doctor's embrace no longer under a trance. She understood fully her childhood fears.

"Westlene, the man came back sometimes later than the card games. He would fondle me. My father watched as I cried. He would sit in the chair after throwing Teddie on the floor and stroke himself as he watched that nasty man touch me. He tried once. My father fought him that night. He told him no penetration with his penis was allowed. I was too young to even know what a penis was. My mother called them private parts. His nasty hands touched me until he and my father ejaculated and then they would leave the room and go in the guest room, together. I don't know his name. I guess I blocked that out."

"Why didn't you tell your mother or Viola? Do you remember if you told someone?"

"My father was drunk each time he watched, pissy drunk. The man seemed to be in charge. I don't know his name, damn, I can't remember. My father threatened to hurt my mother and Ms. Viola if they ever asked him about what happened. He'd say, "Your mother need not know, it would kill her or I would." He began cussing at Viola too. Shortly after my mother started staying home on Saturdays and Sundays, my father would only have company on Fridays. Viola's boyfriend would come around more often. Now that I think of it my father made sure she was in another room before he'd come upstairs."

Westlene was at a dead end. She wanted to suggest another session, but feared the results would bring about emotional trauma. She was sure Zeke Preston watched his daughter be molested or he molested her himself.

"Dominique, did your father ever touch you?"

"No just the man."

"But your father was there whenever this man touched you?"

"Yes."

Westlene wrote on her pad, '*Possibly molested by father*'.

"Is Boat picking you up my dear?" Westlene asked as she poured Dominique another cup of tea.

"He said for me to call him."

"Yes, he did. I remember now. Drink this tea; I will call him. Are you sure about this visit you want to make to the house?"

"Don't you think it would help?"

"You have remembered most of what you wanted to know, right? Why not talk with your mother first, eh? I think she should know what you remember. It's time to tell her. You think about this carefully. Your mother needs to know this matter before you discover another."

"What is the other matter?"

"I am not here to lead you on my dear. This other man, you say, he may be close to your mother, he may be a friend. Dominique, you must understand, this man may not exist. This may be a way of you protecting your father and his vile ways."

Dominique remained silent. She tried hard to remember the man, his face, his name. She didn't know him. Her father's face stood out vividly, but the man remained a shadow.

"May I use your restroom?"

"Yes, let me help you." Westlene allowed Dominique to lean on her as she stood. Her foot seemed to be numb but as she put pressure on it, she could feel a twinge of pain. She grimaced as she positioned herself on the crutch. She managed to proceed to the restroom in Dr. Adashay's office on her own.

The doctor picked up her phone and dialed Boat's number.

"Yes, she's ready. I don't believe she will want to go to the home tonight. We did make a breakthrough." Westlene wanted to end the conversation there.

"So was she raped?"

"Well Boat let's just say—" Westlene was avoiding what had become obvious.

"Was it rape or was she molested." Boat didn't wait for the answer. "By who?"

"She doesn't know. That is still blocked; it is mental protection. I believe she does know, but there's something else that is hidden as well."

"Westlene, what could be as devastating as being molested as a child?"

"The murder of her father."

Fifty-two

Viola opened the front door of 134 Rose Terrace and invited Kendall inside. After talking to Brenda, it seemed they had a miscommunication. She was waiting for them at her home thinking they would talk there first then ride over to the house.

Viola told her she didn't know how to reach Kendall. She wouldn't be able to tell him to meet her at Brenda's. She had told him to meet them at the house around seven. Brenda seemed agitated about the mix up but with two hours remaining before meeting them, she agreed it was better to get it over with.

Kendall stepped in out of the cold, a night that was predicted to be the warmest of the week. The temperature didn't stop the brisk air from having the winter bite. He removed his coat, hat and gloves and handed them to Viola. She placed them over the chair where her winter outerwear rested.

"Still a bit nippy, I don't know what the rest of the winter will be like if we're starting like this."

Viola didn't notice Kendall's reservations about moving from the spot where he stood. He was taking in all the changes made to the home that was filled with his weekend memories. There was a smell of children, paint projects, and candy. The smoke filled air he remembered had been gone years prior, years he spent trying to regain his soul.

"They've really changed this place. Who owns it now?" He asked.

"Let me show you what they've done. It's a community home. They use it for after school programs for the children. They also have programs for the homeless and the elderly. It's a great project."

They walked from room to room as Viola explained the church's generosity and the use of the home. They both stopped in the dining room in awe of the library.

"My cousin says all the books are donated. They serve meals to the homeless here, lunch on the weekdays, breakfast and lunch on the weekend. Seems strange huh, I mean after all of the gambling and sex parties Zeke held here."

"Does Brenda know about the parties? I know she knew about the card parties, but did she ever find out about the girls coming in here? Is that why she's mad at me?"

"I don't know. I never told her." Viola kept moving to the kitchen. "They changed this too. It's more efficient for the cooking they do. They have a lot of children that come through here. They even turned the rooms upstairs into classrooms and media rooms. My cousin loves it. The church provides most of funding and donations come through from various sources."

Returning to the dining room they both slowed their steps in the hall. At the base of the stairs Kendall bent and touched the darkened floor.

"A night I'll never forget. This floor was covered with his blood, there too." He said as he gestured toward the kitchen's doorway. "Brenda was here when I came down the stairs." He caught his words, remembering the story he told his brother and mother.

"Why were you upstairs? I thought you came in the door after the murder?"

"Viola, I remember coming down the stairs."

"Then you saw the murder? You saw who shot Zeke?"

"No, but I don't know why I was upstairs." Kendall sat on the bottom of the staircase. Tears fell from his eyes.

"I just know I didn't touch that girl, Viola. You know that don't you?"

"I never saw any of that going on. I don't know why Brenda thought Dominique was touched that way. But if you say you were upstairs, then how did you not hear the shot?"

"Randall was right. I was too high to remember, over the years I've forgotten so much of what I did."

"So you don't remember where you were, upstairs or downstairs?"

"Viola, I couldn't have been upstairs. I would have heard the shot. I hope Brenda can bring this torment to an end."

"Kendall, seems like she has her own torment. C'mon let me show you the upstairs, maybe it will jar your memory. Brenda should be here shortly. She thought we were coming there first."

"She didn't want to meet us here? I thought…"

"I got it all mixed up. She'll be here, I'm sure."

The two mounted the stairs slowly. Viola pointed out some of the children's artwork that hung on the walls. They entered the room that held scattered memories of orgies and sexual escapades. It had been changed into a resource room complete with computers and a large plasma television.

"Sure looks different, the things that went on in this room."

"Good times and bad. Remember Dean's face when he found out Zeke was using his home the way he was using that room in the bar."

"Viola, do you think Dean would have shot Zeke?"

"He threatened him enough, but you know they argued all the time. I don't think anyone thought much about his threats. Zeke didn't seem upset about them. Dean was welcomed here, just like everyone else."

"True. The cops never did an investigation, they never questioned me. Did they come back to question Brenda?"

"Not that I know of; I didn't keep in touch with Brenda after the shooting. She kept to herself and then shortly after she moved. She didn't return my calls and I knew she wouldn't welcome my visits. So I prayed for Dommi and my good friend from my home. I was glad she called, even if it is to rehash the past."

Kendall stopped as they exited the room. "Is that what this meeting is for, to rehash the past? Viola, I think there's pieces missing. Dommi thinking she was raped or molested; who really shot Zeke and why I can't remember the things Dean insinuated? I hope we're here to put this puzzle together."

Viola opened the door of Dominique's room. The sight of the room startled them. The light from the hall gave them a dim view. She flipped the switch on the wall adding more light to the room. It was obvious the room was for the girls who played with the dolls that were shelved above the Fisher Price kitchenette. The floor was tiled with numbered blocks. There were two small tables and multicolored chairs, a blackboard with chalk, and Dr. Seuss books lined the wall. The room was a perfect playroom for any little girl.

"No playroom for boys?" Kendall teased.

"I'll bet the other bedroom has been converted for boys. My cousin has dreamed about a site like this since her teen years."

"Viola, why would someone?..."

"Don't ask Kendall. Like you said maybe Brenda will be able to fill in the blanks."

Fifty-three

Pastor Turner found himself running late. He promised Brenda he would be with her when Viola and Kendall met her at her home. After preparing scriptures for Sundays service, and his ritual of evening prayer he sat thinking.

The night Zeke was killed a parishioner called him letting him know there was trouble in the Preston home. The police and an ambulance were in front of the house. Sister Mitchell hadn't been outside of course, but from her window, she could see that the incident seemed serious. More police were arriving and the ambulance attendants had returned an empty gurney to the vehicle.

Not many neighbors were in front of the home when he arrived. The door to the house was opened and he could see the flash of the cameras from the porch. Just beyond the front door, a policeman asked who he was. He allowed Jacob Turner to pass without any questions after he identified himself as Pastor of Faith Temple Baptist Church.

There was blood everywhere. The police cleared the hall between the kitchen, dining room and staircase. The body was still on the floor covered with a white sheet. It was then that Jacob spotted Kendall. Their eyes met, neither acknowledging the other. Kendall walked behind the officers and out the front door.

Brenda was seated in the kitchen. Her clothing was blood stained as well as her hands, although she attempted to wash them.

She began to cry when he entered the room.

"Pastor, can you get Dommi out of here please. An officer took her upstairs to her room."

Jacob came closer. "Are you okay? Let them move the body. Did she see this happen?"

"Pastor, we'd prefer to ask the questions." The officer tapped him on his shoulder to make him aware of his presence.

"Yes, I'm sorry. Let them move the body Brenda."

"Jacob, please pray with me. Zeke is dead now, pray for me."

Pastor Turner looked back to the blood stained sheet over the body of the man who tortured Brenda. The whispers outside the home said there was an intruder. He assumed that would be who the officers found on the floor. Numbness came over him. Zeke was dead, where was the intruder? He motioned to the officer as he stood to leave Brenda's side.

"Did you get the intruder?"

"No, she said when he heard her and her daughter's screams he ran out the door. We're looking into how he got in now. Looks like a robbery gone bad. Guess they were lucky."

"What kind of gun?"

"We won't be able to tell until we check the body. There's been a few of these break-ins in the neighborhood. Maybe you can get the little one out the back door. You know, avoid this crowd. We'll be here with the mother for a while."

"Sure." Jacob looked around at the mess he was sure Dominique would have questions about. He took the advice of the officer. He brought her down the stairs and exited through the side door. He was sure to keep her head buried into his shoulder. She was asleep when he entered her room, or so she made it seem.

He hadn't thought about that evening in years. The questions, the memories, and the pain would be revisited he was sure, over the next few days. He looked at his watch as he sat in his car waiting for the chill to leave its interior.

Brenda hoped Jacob would be her support when Dominique arrived. The plans for the evening were changing rapidly. God had truly intervened. Kendall and Viola had gone directly to Rose Terrace. Her daughter called to say she needed to speak to her and was on her way. Had things gone as planned Dommi would have arrived and stumbled upon the four of them discussing what may have been her past. Brenda wanted to know the details before her child could remember who had molested her. She needed to know what Kendall and Viola hadn't told her. She was certain Dominique would think they were covering the truth. The truth that Brenda hid kept to herself over the years had been her secret. She never told anyone, including Jacob.

Dominique seemed upset, or unraveled as she told her mother about the session with Dr. Adashay. She had been hypnotized and as Brenda feared, her memory was jarred. She didn't mention the night of the murder. Brenda wanted to ask about that memory but trepidation held her tongue. Her motherly instincts wanted to protect her child; self-preservation toppled it all.

She would use Pastor Turner as an excuse and quickly leave Dominique and Boat to meet with Viola and Kendall. She would advise Boat that rest would be the best remedy for Dominique's emotional state. After she convinced him to take her home, she and the Pastor would leave. She had already called Viola, apologizing for their lateness and begging her to give her extra time to get there. Viola assured her they would grab a bite to eat and meet her and the Pastor afterward. They both agreed talking with Dominique was a necessary delay.

She put on a pot of water for tea, hoping it would be enough to take the chill off her visitors. She couldn't see herself drinking anything stronger, although she needed it, with Jacob being one of the guests. The bell rang and she quickly took off her apron draping it over the kitchen chair.

Her Pastor hadn't let her down. He entered her home closing the door behind him, trying not to let the night air in. She took his coat turning her back to avoid his questioning eyes.

"What's wrong Brenda, you seem to be a bit nervous?"

"You know me too well. Dominique and Boat are on their way."

"You invited them too."

They proceeded to the living room where she explained the phone calls made over the hours since she spoke with him. Before he could ask any questions they heard keys rattling outside the front door.

"That would be them. Please Jacob, let's hear what she has to say, maybe we can avoid talking about the night of the murder. I really want to talk with Kendall and Viola before discussing it with Dommi."

"I'm just here, there's not much I can say."

The door opened wide and Brenda got up immediately to help Dominique come through the door with her cast and crutch. Boat turned to secure the door.

"Lord, its cold out there." Dominique noticed the Pastor and giggled in spite of herself. "Sorry Pastor, I didn't know you would be here but it is cold. My foot is frozen."

"You need a thicker sock, that's for sure." Brenda inspected her daughter's foot as she helped her take off her outerwear. Boat kissed Ms. Preston and took the coat and scarf from her. Dominique moved carefully across her mother's waxed floor and sat on the couch.

"How are you feeling? That thing looks like it hurts."

"It's not that bad Ma. Pastor Turner, how are you? I haven't seen you in a while."

"We have a stop to make for the church tonight. I forgot all about it when you called. But Pastor said we can go after we talk."

"Yes, we don't have to be there until at least eight or was it eight thirty?" Jacob smiled at Brenda recognizing his cue to speak.

"They said they'd meet us there about that time."

Dominique detected the nervousness but she always suspected them of being a bit too close. She smiled and moved over for Boat to sit next to her. The tea pot whistled from the kitchen

"Would you like a cup of tea? I was making myself a cup."

"I'll make the tea for you Sister Preston, you sit there. Dommi, Boat, tea?"

"Yes please." Boat got up and walked to the kitchen without answering the question. Brenda's palms began to sweat, a sign of nervous tension. Jacob brought tea for both ladies. The serving tray was complete with sugar, milk and slices of lemon. They thanked him as they took what was needed for their individual cups. The men remained in the kitchen. Brenda sighed and passed the sugar to Dominique.

"You've had a full day, complete with having your foot casted. Are you supposed to be on it?

"No, not really," Dominique answered; lowering her voice so Boat couldn't hear her answer. "But, Mama I really needed to talk to you. I think, well I know, I was touched by someone Daddy knew."

Brenda offered no excuse, nor did she comment. She waited for Dominique to continue, certain there was more she needed to say.

"I let Dr. Adashay hypnotize me. Why didn't you let me be hypnotized sooner?"

"Why didn't you tell me your intentions? You were too young. You wouldn't have understood what you were remembering?"

"Even a man touching me? Mama, did you know what was going on?"

"No, no baby I didn't. I heard you say that the other day and I couldn't believe that was a part of your memory." Brenda closed her eyes and whispered, "Jesus keep me". Her fears led her to believe that a child wouldn't remember the horrid night of her father's death. She didn't want to admit that Dominique's horror began before Zeke was shot. Her mind drifted to Zeke lying on the floor, trying to talk after being shot. He'd said enough; the bullet finished his sickening statement. Brenda wouldn't allow her memories to give her details. She wondered if Westlene's session had revealed what she dared to face.

"Jesus has kept you Mama, but I haven't been able to sleep for years. Jesus has kept me up night after night sending these dreams. What happened at that house?"

"I don't know baby. Your father was shot and my dreams ended. I didn't know what your dreams were about. You would complain about seeing shadows, never faces. I asked you time and time again."

"Did I tell you they touched me? Did I cry to you about the nights they crept into my room?"

"I can't believe Viola would let them come in your room. She would never let someone harm you."

"But Mama, he waited until she wasn't there."

"Baby, I don't want to upset you, but whenever Violas wasn't there, I was. We kept it that way so…" Brenda looked into her daughters eyes. Dominique responded with conviction.

"So he wouldn't do it again."

Fifty-four

Brenda cried silently with tissue in hand the entire length of the drive to Rose Terrace. Dominique became angry blaming her mother for hiding the truth. Jacob and Boat entered the room to calm the hysteria that caused them both to yell and scream. Brenda held her tears. She held the story that she wanted to tell. The desire to confess to her failure as a mother came second to her wanting to talk to Viola and Kendall. She too, wanted to know who touched Dominique. She didn't want to add more to her daughter's pain.

She didn't mention her father as she detailed the dreams. The vile treatment Dominique remembered while under hypnosis painted a grotesque picture. It replayed in Brenda's mind as she tried to pull herself together. Jacob found a parking spot across the street of her old home. The lights were on, an indication that Viola and Kendall had returned. Boat apologized for Dominique's abrupt departure. She put on her coat and grabbed her crutch and stood at the front door until he opened it. Boat said goodbye for both of them. Brenda was glad Viola and Kendall were patient. The couple proceeded to the front door.

The door was unlocked. Brenda pushed it slowly; hoping not to go any further than what had been her living room. She heard Viola's laughter and knew she could quickly move on to the dining room. She avoided looking down as she felt carpet under her feet. Zeke never wanted carpeted floors. Each step reminded her of the pool of blood she walked through as she opened the door for the police. There was no trace of the bloodstained floors where Zeke's body was placed into a black bag. The walls were no longer covered with the bloody handprints, her handprints, left where she steadied herself. Brenda couldn't help but relive the moment she screamed, "He's gone Lord, he's gone."

Jacob was amazed with the changes, but he still had an uneasy feeling about being there. He always felt Zeke's presence in the house, before and after his death. Even in spirit Zeke was keeping an eye on Jacob. Maybe he knew how the Pastor felt about his wife. Jacob breathed in deeply. His last visit in the home was before the community center was considered. The church was determined to sell, but Viola's cousin had other plans. She had limited money, but her dream and efforts had been recognized. Pastor Turner signed the papers agreeing to rent the building. He prayed the murder wouldn't overshadow her program. It had been boarded up for years and cost the church to restore the structure. Looking at it now, he was pleased.

Kendall stood from his seat acknowledging their arrival. Brenda promised herself she would be cordial and not give in to her suspicions. Kendall gave her his seat and moved around the conference table to sit directly across from her. Viola hugged her friend before Brenda sat down.

"I'm glad to see you and you too Pastor. How have you been?"

"I can't complain Viola." Jacob responded. "If this weather gets any colder though, I may have to fuss a little. How about you?

Kendall, you feeling better man?"

Jacob noticed Kendall was distant. He was watching Brenda as she positioned herself, giving Jacob her coat.

"Not as good as I could be Pastor, that's for sure. But as you church folks say, God will see me through."

"Well if you need Him, He's always there." Jacob answered. He didn't understand Kendall's sudden reference to church folks, or what they would say.

"I made a pot of coffee, would anyone like some before we get started?" Viola waited standing in the doorway for an answer. Everyone wanted a cup as she assumed they would. She went to the kitchen where she had the tray complete with cups, sugar, and milk.

She brought it into the room and hurried back to get the coffee.

"Anything else? They have some cookies and things in there as well."

"I think this is fine. Brenda why don't you start." Jacob said a silent prayer. He could feel his nerves in the pit of his stomach as Brenda thanked him with a soft touch. He hoped they wouldn't be there long.

Brenda cleared her throat and paused, cautiously choosing how to ask her questions.

"I want to apologize for my delay. Lord, this is so hard. I didn't know returning to this house would have this effect on me. Viola, y'all been sitting here long?"

"Girl, we went and got something to eat. We came back about ten minutes ago. How's Dominique?"

"Well, that's why I called you guys to talk. I didn't know she was coming over and now that she did, it makes it more important that we do talk. I don't want no lies though." She looked at Kendall, who frowned questioning her stare. "I mean it. Lay it all on the table. It's been years since some of these things happened. Dominique has been having these dreams, this torture for years. I don't know if you've been sleeping after some of the things y'all done in this house, but me, and my child have been suffering."

Kendall went to speak, but Viola grabbed his arm softly. "Let her finish."

"Thank you. I just don't know how to say it. You both know how Zeke was. I mean there's no denying, especially now that he's dead, he was abusive." She hung her head and sighed. Jacob rubbed her back to soothe her. "He drank and fought. He fought you guys on the weekends and us during the week. Oh, he didn't hit Dominique; he'd save that for me. But he would cuss at her, call her names and blame me for it. He'd say I made him take it out on her cause I worked, I was never home. I wasn't raising her to be worth anything for any man. I took that from him day after day. It got worse around the time that Viola said she'd sit for me during the week and not just the weekends. Zeke thought Viola told me something.

I never asked him or you what." She looked at Viola who nodded her head in agreement. "I often thought about what he was hiding, what would make him say the things he said."

She sipped her coffee and continued. "That's how we lived. I'd go to work, Dommi would go to school and Zeke would jump from job to job. He couldn't keep a job with his drinking and missing days. So he would be home drinking whenever he wasn't working. He was like a time bomb. Whenever he exploded, I was the target. He never missed. Dommi would yell for him to stop but one look from him and she'd run. But his personality flipped when he was sober. I guess we both wanted him to stay sober. We would play up family time big then. That's one of the reasons I worked the graveyard shift. I could be home with him during the day and early evenings."

Viola poured more coffee in the cups. Seeing an opportunity to speak she asked, "Didn't that help, you being home when he was home?"

Brenda frowned, "No, I was interfering. I was always interfering. I would try to talk to him about his drinking. I'd tell him we seemed more like a family when he didn't drink. He said he understood but when night fell he had to have one after another. He stopped when it put him to sleep or we began fighting. I couldn't take it no more and prayed that I would find a way out. Dominique deserved so much more. She spent half her childhood crammed in that bedroom. If she came out she'd witness him in full rage cussing and hitting me. The day he was shot was an answer to those prayers."

The silence in the room spoke volumes. Each of them drifted off. They held on to their personal thoughts about the shooting. Kendall needed to speak regardless of the consequences.

"Brenda, I knew about Zeke being abusive. I saw it a couple of times with the guys. I didn't think much about him cussin' at his child. He only did it to tell her to stay upstairs. That happened a few times when he was babysitting. Never happened again after I told Viola about it, I thought she told you about it. It was right before she started sitting all the time. I thought that was your way of taking care of it. I can't say I remember everything, you know I was always high and shit. Oh, excuse me Pastor. If I can help you put this puzzle together for Dominique or you…"

"I believe you can." Brenda interrupted. "You and Viola."

"What do you believe we know Brenda?" Viola asked a bit confused. "We don't know why Zeke did the things he did, and I can say he didn't do anything that I saw to Dominique when I was here."

"Why would you say that he did?" Pastor Turner looked at her waiting for the answer.

"Pastor, I think you took my statement the wrong way. I didn't see him or anyone act out of the way with the child. I kept her upstairs most of the time. She'd have her dinner, a little television time and then upstairs she would go. No problems, no one was allowed upstairs, except to use the bathroom. I watched Dommi as though she was mine. Nothing went on, so what could I tell you?"

Brenda attempted to speak but Jacob spoke first. "Wait Brenda, excuse me. I'm trying to understand, you didn't see anything but you volunteered to babysit for a man who was taking care of his daughter fine for the week. On Fridays, you knew he played cards, got drunk and brought in men, so you volunteered to keep the girl safe. Am I right?"

Viola was beginning to feel uncomfortable with the Pastor's questions, but she felt compelled to answer. "Yes, you can say that, I guess."

"So," he continued, "You began watching the child during the week knowing what, the same things were happening? The card games, the drinking the company or was it Zeke. His behavior scared you didn't it? You saw something in his behavior on Friday nights that you didn't want Dommi to be a part of during the week, am I still right?"

Viola didn't answer, she couldn't. Jacob was right. Brenda worked a few weekends for extra money and Viola kept the child on those nights too. She felt the little girl wasn't safe. The men, the alcohol, and their desire for any female were reasons Dominique needed protection.

"But no one ever did anything in my presence. So I can't say who did or who didn't touch that child."

"Why didn't you tell me what you felt? When you felt it, didn't you think I would want to know?"

"You didn't seem like you were attached to the things that Zeke did. I mean really Brenda you knew what the Friday nights were like. You even agreed when I told you Dommi needed someone other than her father with her during the week. I thought you knew and just didn't want to discuss it openly. I don't push; you know that. I understood your silence and did what I thought a friend would do. I was there for you and Dominique and no one touched her while I was in this house."

"Hmmm…so what does that say?" Kendall asked. "Zeke had people here when you weren't here Viola? I have been here when you weren't here, so I know."

"What do you know Kendall?" Brenda raised the question with a bit of sarcasm.

"I… I… I listen there's no need to put me on trial. I definitely didn't touch Dominique if that's what you're thinking. But yeah, we'd get here sometimes before Viola would. And another thing, you never followed anyone upstairs. When they went to the bathroom. Maybe it happened then."

"What happened? Kendall! Please what happened! I don't know what happened to my child and she thinks she was touched! Molested, maybe even raped. What the hell is maybe it happened then? What is it?"

"Alright, calm down Brenda. We'll find out what it is. Maybe we need to include Dominique so she can tell us all. Maybe she can tell us who." Pastor Turner wanted to avoid the argument that was brewing.

Brenda looked at Kendall. He felt as though her eyes were laser points piercing his chest.

"Yeah, I agree with Pastor. Let's talk again with Dominique. She'll tell you it wasn't me."

"Maybe she will." Brenda watched him as he stood putting on his coat and offering to help Viola with hers. "Kendall, I really hope you've changed for your sake."

"Goodnight Pastor, thanks for the opportunity to be in the hot seat."

"C'mon Kendall. We all need to keep a level head about this. No one is accusing anyone here. If you can think of anything or remember anything I'm sure Brenda would be glad to hear from you." Jacob knew his comment fell upon deaf ears. Kendall went out the door without saying anything to Brenda.

"Pastor, Brenda, I'm sorry I couldn't be of any help to you. Talk to Dommi honey and let me know when you want to meet and where. Get some rest girl. Don't mind him, he wanted to find out who it was too. I don't think he had anything to do with it. Dean told him some mess about him being too high to remember."

"Viola, how would Dean know?"

"Girl, you know Dean and Zeke were competing with that after hour mess. Zeke started it here that's why I wanted to be with Dommi during the week. Well Dean was furious. Zeke was tapping into his business at the bar. They had a few young girls here. I couldn't say nothing or Zeke would have put me out. I was afraid if I mentioned it, you and Dommi would be in trouble. Anyway, there were a few romps in the other rooms but I stayed with Dommi in her room. It's true after she fell asleep I would try to keep the rest of your house in order. I didn't follow no one to the bathroom. I can't imagine who would open that child's door and violate her. I'll see if I can talk to Dean."

"He's in jail right?" Brenda was in shock. She tried not to show it as she continued to listen.

"Yeah, he's on Doremus for something else. He never did much time for that mess at the bar. I don't know something with a teenager. He'll never get enough of dealing with those fast ass girls. Oops sorry Pastor. Listen, let me go, Kendall's waiting at my car. Brenda really I don't think Kendall has the heart to do anything like that. But we'll get to the bottom of it. Do you think Dominique will come here to talk?"

Jacob helped Brenda into her coat. The trio stood on the porch as Viola locked the door.

"She wants to come here so maybe this will help her and me get a grasp on this ongoing nightmare. Thanks for coming, and thank Kendall too. Apologize for me, he wouldn't hear me if I did it."

"Alright goodnight to both of you."

Jacob waved as he walked ahead of Brenda opening the passenger door of his Buick Regal.

Fifty-five

Boat brought the pain medication and a glass of Ginger Ale to the couch for Dominique. They were watching television and talking when the pain in her foot became unbearable.

"I don't know Dommi, maybe you stayed on your feet too long. It looks swollen around your toes."

"How can you tell with this cast on?" She propped herself up to take the pills. "Besides I sat in Westlene's office and at my mother's. I wasn't standing."

"Yeah well, you'll be off it for the next few days. I'm glad you changed your mind about going over to Rose Terrace."

"I'm gonna call and get Viola's number. Maybe she'll come here. I can't wait on this thing to heal."

She turned her cast looking it over which brought on an instant frown. "Did you call Claudia? I'm sure she's got plenty of work. I really didn't mean to bail out on our project."

"She said she'd be here tomorrow to visit you. I'll go to my office while you guys work."

"Tomorrow is Saturday, who will be there then?"

"No one, I've got some reports due next week. I'll get them done while you ladies do that thing you call talking. I'll check out Eric too. Claudia will make sure you stay off your feet. The weather will be better next week if you still want to go to the house."

"I should call Westlene. I need some of that tea to help me forget this pain."

"Sounds like you're addicted. Are you sure that stuff isn't a narcotic."

"I don't care if it is. It serves the purpose."

Boat picked up the remote to surf the channels for another movie. "HBO or Showtime?"

"Either baby this medicine will kick in and I won't know the difference anyway."

"And you want Westlene's tea too? Yeah you've become an addict."

She smacked his arm teasingly, as he lifted her legs placing them on his lap. He put the remote down hoping his movie selection would hold his attention. Dominique moved the pillow he provided, adjusting her position for comfort.

Just as Dominique had predicted, it wasn't more than twenty minutes before she began to doze. Boat stopped talking to her about the mystery he found on HBO. Her answers didn't relate to the picture at all. She laughed a few times at his teasing her and then he heard her snore. He got the comforter she kept in the closet and covered both of them. He was glad her sectional was large enough for the two of them to lounge comfortably.

It was close to two in the morning when Dominique's dream took her to her past once again. The bedroom complete with Teddie sitting on the floor near her closet was more vivid. She knew where she was and she could hear familiar voices outside her bedroom door. Viola was arguing with her father. He was trying to whisper, not wanting his company to hear. He showed no concern that his seven-year-old daughter could be listening.

"This is my house. Why you here anyway? Dommi is sleep!"

"Zeke, you know Brenda wouldn't want these girls in her house. It ain't right Zeke. That little one down there can't be much older than fifteen. You getting them younger and younger. What are you thinking?"

"I'm thinking it ain't none of your business. Now you want to keep an eye on Dommi, then that's what you do. What I do in my house with my company is my business."

Frustrated Viola started down the staircase.

"Oh, and if you mention who my company is to my wife, you won't be here no more to watch that child in there. It's only a matter of time anyway. She's bound to be just as fast as those downstairs."

Then there was noise from the room next to Dominique's bedroom. From the guestroom she could hear the bed squeaking and a girl moaning. The sounds weren't distant like when her mother would whimper her father's name from their room. She couldn't identify the man who was grunting louder than the girl's cries.

She covered her head with the covers trying to muffle the cry she was sure were to follow. "Zeke, oh Zeke." Her father was in the next room with another woman. "Zeke, oooowww." She wanted to scream herself, but Viola wouldn't respond. She never did when they used the guestroom.

The noise faded and she could her them mumbling. The girl was begging for him again. Dominique didn't understand completely what she wanted but he promised her he wasn't finished. The guestroom door opened after they romped again. She heard her father tell her to freshen up and come downstairs when she was done.

Dommi waited until she was sure her father was at the bottom of the stairs before she got out of her bed. She opened her door and knocked on the bathroom door.

"Who is it?" The female sounded agitated.

"I got to pee." Dominique whispered her answer. She didn't care who the girl was. She could go to the bathroom and safely return to her bed if someone else was upstairs. He wouldn't dare come to her room knowing someone would see him.

"Oh, wait baby." The girl opened the door for the younger child and smiled. Dominique didn't know her. She looked like one of the teenagers from the big school next to the elementary school she attended. She attempted to leave, giving the child privacy.

"No, please don't leave me. I'll pee fast." Dommi pulled up her nightgown quickly. Her panties fell down to her ankles before the girl could answer. She shrugged her shoulder and turned her attention to the mirror. She pushed up her hair with her hand and put on more lipstick.

"You done sweetie. You're cute. What's your name?"

"Dominique, what's yours?" She questioned as she flushed the toilet. She stepped to the sink to wash her hands.

"Noani."

"Thank you Noani, I just don't like walking out with my gown on."

"You're welcome."

The two left the bathroom. Noani continued down the stairs. As the girl reached the bottom of the steps, Dominique heard her father arguing with Dean. It was obvious Dean didn't know that Noani and her sister were there. He was questioning, "What the hell was going on?" Dominique couldn't make out the rest of what was said. Between Viola telling them to calm down and others saying, "Take it outside", her fears were peaking. She heard Dean threatened to kill her father before the front door slammed. She felt the tears falling from her eyes. She wondered if Dean knew what her father and the young girl had done.

Fifty-six

Noani found Kendall sitting at the kitchen table when she got out of bed. It was where they ended their conversation the night before. Kendall told her about the meeting, his feelings, and his failed attempt in changing Brenda's mind. He knew she still thought he had something to do with her daughter being violated. She didn't want to disturb his thoughts, but she had to share her views with him.

"Do you feel any better about meeting her and Viola at the house?"

"Better than what?" He looked up from his coffee cup. Noani brought over the pot and refilled it for him.

"C'mon now. You know you didn't touch her right? So why feel down about her wanting to know who did? Listen, I lied about where Dean and Zeke had that argument. It was at his house. You wasn't around that night. Me and my sister went there to see what all the talk was about. A few of the girls would leave Dean's place and go over to Zeke's to really get what they wanted. Money and a better lay. You know, in a bed. It was easier there then convincing some of those cheap bastards to get a room. They'd pay Zeke, but you know all that. Anyway we went there. Got bored quick and got drunk, we lied about Dean knowing where we were. Zeke had it going on. He had been watching me and to tell you the truth. It was a toss-up between you and him for me. I loved older men and that night Zeke was it."

"So you telling me that you fucked Zeke is supposed to make me feel better?"

"Whew, baby, calm down, I'm trying to help you put the pieces together. My uncle showed up. Thank God we both were downstairs. At least Zeke was. I was coming down the stairs when they started arguing. Like I told you Dean threatened him; me and my sister never went back there again. Dean told us we'd find ourselves homeless if he heard we fucked with Zeke again."

"Okay, so how does that help me? I wasn't there, you and Zeke got together, and Dean threatened you both. What am I missing? That shit don't help me none. Did you see somebody messing with that child?"

"No, she came in the bathroom with me. She said she didn't like coming out in the hall with her nightgown on. That was it. Nobody went up there that night but me and Zeke. Everybody else stayed downstairs."

"She said she was scared?"

"No, but she acted like she was sneaking. You know, to the bathroom and back into her room. I just figured she didn't want her father to catch her out of bed. Dean was like that with us until we started our periods. After that he'd let us come and go to bed when we pleased."

"Yeah and then he turned you out at his bar. I wonder if that was what Zeke was doing."

"She wasn't old enough for that. Hell I don't think she was having no cycle. Nah, I don't think so."

"Your uncle would know right? I mean he kept on coming to the house after that night. I was there plenty of nights when Dean was there playing cards. He even took a few girls upstairs for his self."

"My uncle wouldn't give two shits about Zeke's daughter."

"Why you say that?"

"Cause he said Zeke didn't give two shits about us."

Fifty-seven

Viola called Brenda early Saturday morning. She knew she'd catch her as she was finishing her morning coffee. She wanted to talk with her alone. There were things she didn't remember from their past and she needed to know the missing pieces.

Kendall was right. Something just didn't sound right about the night Zeke was killed. Not to mention, she told Brenda about the company, the girls and the men that frequented her home. They both agreed not to tell Zeke that Viola had told her. He seemed to be annoyed that Viola would be around more.

Brenda told him his complaints about being stuck in the house night after night would be settled if Viola watched their daughter during the week. She didn't leave the house until ten. She worked the eleven to seven shift; getting home in time to get Dominique ready for school.

Viola thought hard about the nights she was there. Zeke didn't have company every night; Thursdays off and on, the weekend for sure. She would talk with Brenda and narrow the days down. Brenda preferred Viola being there whenever she had to work. Most nights she left after the house was clear of company. She made sure she was the last to leave with the exception of Kendall. If Kendall was a part of the problem she didn't want him to be there when they discovered it. Brenda seemed relieved that Viola wanted talk and agreed together they would be able to calm their fears.

She had been up an hour before making the call and waited until ten to put her coat on and leave. She grabbed her purse and the phone rang just as she retrieved her keys from the hook on the wall in her kitchen. Viola looked at the clock hoping the unexpected call wouldn't take long.

"Hello", she answered hurriedly as she put on her coat.

"Ms. Viola?" The caller paused. Viola knew even though she hadn't spoken to her in years, it was Dominique.

"Ms. Viola is this you?"

"Yes, yes. Dominique your voice hasn't changed much. How are you dear? Your mother told me so much about you, including your bad foot." Viola hoped her voice didn't reveal how nervous she was.

"I hoped you wouldn't forget who I was. I'm fine, well other than my bad foot. How have you been? My mother said she hadn't kept in touch with you over the years."

Viola wondered if what Dominique said had an underlying message about her mother. She took off her coat and continued the conversation sitting in the kitchen chair.

"She's right, we hadn't talked until recently. We've been catching up on old times; years have gone by. I mean, you're grown now. The last time I saw you was after your dad's funeral."

"Yeah, it's been some time. I guess that's why I'm calling."

"Really?" Viola hoped she didn't have the same questions Brenda wanted answered.

"Did your cousin tell you I called about the house on Rose Terrace?"

"No, she didn't mention it."

"Oh, I thought since she told my mother maybe she told you as well." Dominique didn't know where to start. She rehearsed the conversation before dialing Viola's number. Now she had become tongue-tied.

"What did you want to know about the house?"

"I've had nightmares, Ms. Viola. They began after my dad's death. My mother had me medicated, I went through therapy and we moved. I guess she thought they would end there. Over the years they've gotten worse and now they also have clarity. Recently I've been seeing a doctor who thought going to the house I might discover the root of the nightmares.

I told my mother about it and of course she thinks I'm crazy. I wanted to know what you think. Am I crazy Ms. Viola?"

"What makes you think you're crazy?"

"I don't think I'm crazy. I just think someone in that house raped me, molested me, or touched me. Which would mean someone covered for them; some adult let it happen to me. Ms. Viola that leaves three people and one is dead."

Fifty-eight

"What did you say?" Brenda poured a cup of coffee for her friend. Viola arrived after twelve. When she opened the door for her she could see she had been crying. Viola cried to herself while she took off her coat. She sat on the couch rocking. Brenda hadn't seen her that upset in years. It took her fifteen minutes to calm down and tell her about the call she received before leaving her home.

"What could I say? I don't know when it happened, and she doesn't remember who did it. She didn't accuse me. She feels we covered for whoever did this to her. Brenda it didn't happen while I was here."

Brenda was silent. She was sure it happened. Dominique was sure it happened. Now Viola was saying she wasn't there. It was obvious to her as it had been during her arguments with Zeke. He allowed it to happen.

"Viola, you warned me about the company Zeke kept. I didn't say anything to him and my child was violated. I need to find out who did this."

"Why?" Viola's comment brought an instant frown to Brenda's face. "I mean, if we find out. What can we do? Whoever it is, we may not know where they are or if they're alive. What can be done now?"

"Dominique can have peace of mind. She'll know that we didn't keep another secret from her."

"Another secret?"

Brenda hesitated before answering. "She doesn't know much about the night Zeke was killed. Pastor Turner took her out the side door. We kept her upstairs away from the commotion."

"So what does she think happened to her father? Didn't she hear the gunshot?"

"It was months later when she asked about Zeke's death. I told her an intruder came in to steal from us and shot her father, that's all she knows. I never asked her about the gunshot. She never said she heard or saw anything. I guess seeing her father and all that blood…she was in a trance. She just stared on those stairs and didn't make a sound."

"Strange, Kendall says he didn't hear anything either. He remembers coming down stairs to help you but he didn't hear any shots. This is all so weird."

"Viola, Kendall was upstairs. We told the police he came after a call was made to Pastor Turner. It didn't seem strange that Zeke's friend would stop by."

"So what were you hiding Brenda? If he was upstairs what was going on. Do you know who shot Zeke?"

"I don't know why Kendall didn't hear the shot. He went upstairs when he heard me coming in the front door. I asked Zeke what was going on. I went to the store and came back to him and Kendall drinking. We argued and then…"

Brenda started crying. Viola sat waiting; she wanted to hear the story that everyone wouldn't tell.

"I guess the door was open. I thought I saw a shadow in the hall then I heard the shot and Zeke fell on the floor in front of me."

Viola knew it was the short polished version of the lie Brenda had told over and over again. She looked at Brenda as she hung her head. It was then that Viola understood the truth would relieve more than Dominique.

"Brenda, what was going on? Do you know who touched Dominique? She wants us to meet her at the house Brenda. Me and Kendall, I think she knows. What do you know?"

"She can't know Viola, she can't." Brenda began crying and rocking. "This nightmare was over years ago. He's dead."

"Zeke was touching her? You knew it was your husband?"

"I don't know who it was but it ended when he died and that should have been it. She didn't remember, and now…why Viola why do we have to rehash this mess. I've prayed and prayed about it. It's over why…" Brenda fell back on the couch and closed her eyes.

"Brenda it won't go away until the truth is told. Dominique is looking for the truth. I'm going to call Kendall. She deserves to know the truth. We're going back to the house Brenda to answer her questions. I didn't help her when she was younger. If you feel the way I do, you'll be there too."

Fifty-nine

"I don't think you should walk on that foot Dommi. Boat said for you to stay off it."

"Are you going with me or not?" Dominique was determined to go with or without Claudia.

"Do I have a choice? When are you going?"

"Tomorrow, my mother will be at church. Viola will bring my dad's friend Kendall. I don't remember much about him, but she said he was there just about every night. Anyway, I was thinking about Westlene. What do you think? I mean if my memory doesn't kick in maybe she can help me."

"At the house? You want her to hypnotize you at the house?"

"Why not?"

"I don't know. You want to go through being raped again?"

"I go through the same shit every night."

Claudia picked up the tray that held their lunch. "Do you want something from the kitchen? You better call Boat too."

"Maybe she should hypnotize all of us." Dominique continued ignoring Claudia's reference to Boat. "Viola said Kendall can't remember anything, my mother acts like she can't remember. Yeah, I think we all need to go under."

Claudia laughed as she walked off. Dommi picked up the phone and dialed Westlene's number. She would talk to Boat later. She would call him after she had been to Rose Terrace. She had convinced Claudia to stay over. He'd be, mad but she couldn't wait much longer for answers.

"Dr. Adashay, please?"

"May I say who is calling?" Dommi knew right away it was the nurse who she and Boat talked about while at the office. She sighed before answering her question.

"Ms. Preston, is she available?"

"Aha," she replied, "Tis the little woman with the bad foot; the one who is not a patient." She said mockingly to the others who were listening and commenting in their native tongue.

"The phone ain't on hold, you dummy. Geeesh, I swear."

Claudia frowned as she returned to the couch. She shook Dominique's medication in front of her as a reminder. She handed her the pills and a glass of water.

"She will be right with you, uh Ms. Preston."

"Listen, you better change your attitude Missy. I'm sure I'm not the only one who complains about your non-professional manners."

"You are not, but they are patients. Your complaint won't go far. Aha, she is ready for you now. I transfer the call; you make your complaint. My name is Nadera Adashay."

Dominique rolled her eyes. Claudia tapped her leg and mouthed, "What?"

"She's related to Westlene, same damn last name."

Claudia giggled as Dominique rolled her eyes again before speaking.

"Westlene is she your sister?"

"Aha, Dominique, how are you? Who Nadera? Don't mind her, no, no she's my cousin. A pain, as you might say, at times. Don't give her the attention she seeks. How may I help you my dear? Have you and your mother come together?"

Stunned that Westlene wasn't concerned about her cousin's attitude, she paused before answering.

"Uh, we got together and she raised my suspicions. She does know something, I just don't know what. That's why I'm calling."

"I see, so you want to have a consultation arranged, yes?"

"No, my mother has said all she will, I'm sure. I'm going to the house, as I planned. Can you meet me there?"

Westlene took a deep breath, careful not to sound evasive she replied. "What good will this do Dominique? You and I know what has happened. I am sure if you discuss what you have come to know with your…"

"Doctor, I believe my mother was protecting them. Whoever it was, she had an idea what was going on. She had another woman take care of me each night. My father was home, why would she need someone else there?"

"You said yourself, your father and his friends drank and played cards. This would not be good for a child to see. Her friend, Ms. Viola kept you safe. Safe from the late night adult entertainment your father brought to your home."

"I don't want to discuss this with my mother. I told her about our session. She doesn't believe anyone would or could touch me. I don't know. Her mouth speaks about it not being possible. Her eyes tell me how sorry she is that it happened. I do believe the truth is buried within my hidden thoughts. As you said I've protected myself over the years by suppressing what happened. I want it in the open so I can move on."

"So what can I do for you to, as you say, to help you move on."

"I'm going to the house tomorrow morning while my mother is in church. I'm meeting Ms. Viola and Kendall, a friend of my father's at the house about eleven. I want to talk with them and then be hypnotized in the room that was my bedroom."

The line was silent. Westlene knew the possibilities could cause problems for Dominique.

"And if you find the answers, maybe who this man really is or was?"

"I believe I will have peace. I will be able to sleep."

"There are many 'what ifs' that I would like you to consider. I don't want you to rush to this decision about being hypnotized in the house. Dominique, suppose the man is someone close to you or your family? What if your mother did know? What if this had something to do with your father's death?"

"I'll just have to deal with it. My father's dead I can't change that and I sure as hell can't change what happened to me. I just want to close this repeating chapter of my life. Please, doctor, I don't need time to think. It's time for me to heal."

Dr. Adashay had no other comments. Her emotions were overwhelmed with Dominique's desperation. Although she knew, or thought she knew, the answer was with Brenda Preston. She agreed to meet her Sunday morning. She would rearrange her day and attend early worship services. The Preston's, the mother, daughter, and soul of the father, would be included in her prayers.

Sixty

Boat didn't question Dominique when she told him she and Claudia would be up all night. She explained how far behind she was in her work and they would be catching it up for a meeting on Monday. It was almost the end of the month and he understood how much time would be needed for the preparation of reports and monthly data updates. He had a few to complete himself. Pam called and offered her assistance, but he refused when she told him to bring the files and his body to her private office.

Now hours later and nowhere to go, his secretary crossed his mind again. He hadn't had sex with Dominique since her injury and wasn't sure it would be the same. He found it hard to approach her. He made attempts to put the possibility of her being raped out of his mind. He too was having nightmares about the man who may have ruined his pleasures.

Eric had become his sounding board although he hadn't told him the root of Dominique's dreams. He insisted Boat keep their friendship and end their intimacy. The thought of moving on crossed his mind before her injury to her foot. Now he was torn between love and what he hoped wasn't lust. The volume on the television had drowned the voice that continued saying, *"call her back"*, now it was speaking in stereo. Frustrated he picked up the phone to call Pam; promising himself he wouldn't take it any further than work. The voice that spoke before he could finish dialing Pam's number changed his evening plans.

"Lawrence, I don't want to worry you but I thought you should know dat dis has become very difficult for me, my friend."

For the first time in their five-year friendship Westlene sounded as though she was plagued. The silence between them indicated they understood the diagnosis was serious.

"Lawrence, Ms. Preston and her mother have not faced reality. Somehow Dominique's father was killed because of what was going on in that house. It has bothered me now since I first spoke with her mother. The killing released her mother but trapped Dominique. His spirit won't let go easy."

"Whoa, hold on Westlene, why you talking spirits? This is not some supernatural mess. I thought you didn't delve in those type readings."

"Because I don't delve, as you say, in it doesn't mean I don't know about it. There's a spirit there, in that house and Dominique will definitely find it if she goes there again."

The doctor wouldn't break patient confidentiality by telling him about the earlier conversation she had with Dominique. She wanted him to stop her from going to the house.

"She's not able to walk on that foot. She's with her girlfriend working this evening. I'll be there tomorrow and until the foot heals."

"And then…Boat, she wants answers and I can't blame her or help her. The dreams are clear to her now. It will only be a matter of time before she knows who it is, who touched her."

"So you think going to the house will answer her questions?"

"Yes I do. Especially if she falls to sleep or…"

"Why would she?…" Boat hesitated repeating what the doctor was implying. "She wants to fall asleep or be hypnotized there? Will you do that? It may put an end to the nightmares?"

"She may open her eyes to reality and pray for the dreams to return."

"You've got me wondering now. What could be worse? You said her father's murder. Do you think her father did this and her mother is covering for him?"

"Or maybe her mother ended the torment for her."

"Westlene, do you think her mother killed him?"

"Somebody did, Boat there was no intruder."

"Westlene, there was someone else there who came into her room at night; maybe not the night of the killing."

"Maybe not that night, but my feelings tell me that she may find more than she really wants to know. Do you and her mother speak? You need to tell her what is going on. Maybe she will listen to you. Try, Boat if you love her, try."

Sixty-one

Brenda was looking forward to the Sunday service. She was drained. She hadn't slept well since talking with Dominique. Pastor Turner had consoled her and now she needed to hear his sermon to carry her through the week. He suggested she should talk with her daughter. Although she promised she would, she prayed for strength to call Dominique. It was Sunday and she still didn't have the courage to confront her daughter with the truth.

Getting up early on Sundays was a habit. It gave her enough time to have breakfast and listen to the Gospel choirs on the radio. It gave her an uplifting as she hummed along preparing her outfit for worship. She was moving a little slow which she attributed to the lack of rest, but she was in good spirits. When the phone rang she wasn't prepared for the conversation that would change her Sunday routine.

"Good morning Mrs. Preston, it's Lawrence, Dominique's friend." She knew who he was but allowed him to continue his introduction.

"It must be something important, you calling me this morning using your real name Boat. Is everything okay, is Dommi alright?"

She sat in the kitchen chair preparing for what she assumed would be the worse.

"Mrs. Preston, I may be stepping across the line but I was hoping that you and Dominique could have another talk. She's determined to go to the house where you lived. For some reason she believes being there, she may uncover the reason for her dreams. I'm sure she'll go there with or without telling you or me. I thought maybe if you spoke to her and answered her questions, she wouldn't need to revisit the house."

Brenda didn't know what to say. Her heart sank. Her fears were now a reality. Dominique would stop at nothing.

"Boat digging up the past won't answer any questions about her dreams. She's been having those dreams since her childhood."

"Maybe if you tell her what you know."

"I don't know what you're talking about or what you want me to say to her. If she thinks a house is going to give her relief, maybe she should go and get it over with."

"I've been told that may not be a good idea."

"Told by who; that witch doctor she's been seeing? God will keep her and with prayer…"

"Mrs. Preston, this is not a question of her faith. Dr. Adashay is worried about her mental state. This trauma, the rape or molestation, is bothering her. It has been for years and for some reason you won't address it. Do you think you're protecting her or are you protecting yourself?"

"I haven't done anything to her. I've protected her through it all; her father's death, the aftermath, and the dreams. I've kept her from any questions, rumors or gossip. I don't want her to be scared but if she feels it's necessary to go to the house, Boat how can I tell her not to go there."

"Mrs. Preston someone will need to be there if this visit jars her memory. Someone will have to be there to explain, to help her through this."

Brenda had thought about explaining for years. What would she say now? Her excuse had always been, her child was too young. She couldn't do it there, not at that house.

"When is she going there?"

"I don't know. I'm hoping her foot will delay her actions, but you know Dommi. Maybe after you talk with her she won't see the need to go. Mrs. Preston, Dr. Adashay is a great doctor. I know how you feel about her. Her ways may be funny, and at times unorthodox, but she has saved many who have had mental blocks. She's been a colleague of mine for years. She sees things Mrs. Preston. I think she knows what no one will tell."

"What has she told you?" Brenda closed her eyes awaiting the dreaded answer.

"Nothing, as I said she's a great doctor and a professional. But she did express her concern and wanted me to call you. She knows, Mrs. Preston, I don't know what it is, but Dr. Adashay knows."

"I will call my daughter but as you well know, if she's made up her mind to go to that house, she's going."

The end of the conversation brought on tears. Brenda called the church hoping to catch Jacob before his first sermon. She left a message on his personal line. Not sure what to do, she fell back hopelessly on the couch. She wouldn't be able to control her emotions in church. She wouldn't be able to contain her fears. The clock read nine, too early to call Dominique or Viola. She wasn't sure what time they would be meeting. Pastor Turner wouldn't be available until after the eleven o'clock service.

Brenda went by the house often. She would sit outside reminiscing. She prayed for Zeke, his spirit, and forgiveness. She hoped he would find rest. His death brought relief, but didn't guarantee her peace of mind. His spirit had haunted not only her, but their daughter too. She moved hoping they left his spirit and the memories there.

She went into her bedroom and put up her church ensemble. A pair of jeans, her walking shoes and a sweater would be comfortable for the visit to Rose Terrace. She would stop there and then go and talk with her daughter. Maybe they both would welcome a few sessions with Dr. Adashay. Brenda would like that. She took her time preparing for the unknown. It was almost ten thirty; she was stalling. She drank three cups of coffee and was glad she had stopped smoking. No one would think she wasn't at church. She prayed knowing facing the truth would bring her and Dominique answers.

Sixty-two

Dominique pointed at the parking space that seemed to have been left for them in front of the house. She and Claudia waited until eleven thirty to leave. Claudia didn't ask any questions, but she wondered why they didn't leave earlier. She turned the key in the ignition and waited until Dominique made a move to exit the vehicle.

"Wait I'll help you. How's your foot?"

"Numb, I took my meds when we ate breakfast. I'm good for a couple of hours."

"I don't think they work well while you're moving around though."

Dominique began to laugh as Claudia bent into the car attempting to help her out of the passenger seat. The sports car was great on gas and did fairly well in the snow, but it was no help to Dominique and her bad foot.

"Girl you can't carry me. Here hold the crutch I can get out the car. Just give me a minute," she grunted.

"Oh, okay. I'm sorry."

"It's okay, I can balance myself. See I'm fine, give me the crutch." Dominique braced herself holding the hood of the car. She stood holding her foot in the air careful not to put it down on the cold cement.

Claudia followed her instructions and closed the passenger door. She walked behind Dominique looking at the house as they approached the stairs.

"Are you going to wait for the doctor before you go in?" Claudia stood at the base of the stairs watching Dominique's careful mount. She paused to look back briefly.

"Viola should be here, we can wait inside, c'mon."

Claudia hit the door lock on her key ring and waited for the beep. She looked up and down the block hoping no one would attempt to take her prized possession.

"C'mon girl, the hood ain't that bad, well at least not on this street. They'll see you going into this house and be scared for you."

"Why's that?" She followed Dominique's pace up the slightly iced stairs. "Woo, I didn't know there was ice out here. You be careful."

"The porch is okay; you be careful."

"Why would they be scared for me?"

Dominique rang the bell. "Oh, because my father was killed in the house; it's an ongoing rumor that his spirit is here. I never thought twice about it, but my mother moved hoping his spirit would rest. I never believed in spirits and stuff."

"You've got enough with your dreams."

Dominique wanted to comment but Viola opened the door distracting her thoughts. The women stepped into the house and gave their coats to Viola, who took no time putting them in the closet.

"I would imagine the children love this place." Claudia spoke as she gave herself a tour of the room. "They should have a place like this in every neighborhood."

She smiled at the walls that were decorated with the children's artistic version of the snowstorm. There were attempts of Styrofoam balls becoming "Frosty" and other winter projects on the large conference table.

"Claudia, this is Ms. Viola, my mother's friend and my favorite babysitter."

"Well, I'd hope to be considered your friend too. I sure can't be your babysitter now."

"You still were the best."

"I was your only. C'mon, I made tea and coffee in the kitchen."

Claudia was in awe, eyeing the children's talent she made it to the kitchen behind Dominique and Viola who had taken seats at the table.

"I love the wood trim. Most people ruin it by painting over it. Wood adds character to a home." She stated as she took her seat.

"My mother loved this home too. She was upset when we moved but she thought leaving it was the only choice she had. Viola, did she ever talk to you about moving, I mean how she felt?"

"No, not really, she wanted you and your father to have peace. At that time you were having such bad dreams, and well your father had died here. Your mother felt he never really was at peace, always watching over the two of you."

"I invited Dr. Adashay here, I hope you don't mind. I've asked her to hypnotize me."

Viola's expression changed. She wasn't expecting anyone other than Kendall. She thought they would talk and move on.

"What will that prove?"

"I'm not looking to prove anything. I want to know what went on in my bedroom. C'mon Ms. Viola, you of all people should want to know who may have violated me and your trust of them."

"My trust of them, what are you implying? I don't have any idea who violated you or if they did. Dominique if you were mistreated it was when your father was here. Not while I was here."

"I'm not trying to upset you or blame anyone. I want to put this behind me and being hypnotized here in this house may be the answer."

Viola looked at Claudia who seemed to be waiting for her to reply to Dominique's comment.

"Hmph, and what role does your friend here play in this? Is she a doctor of sorts as well?"

"No not at all Ms. Viola, I'm here to support Dominique. I work with her, that's all. She asked me to come along."

"Ms. Viola, what do you know about the men my father entertained here; were they friends or just men that paid to have a good time?"

"Your father knew each of them, so I guess they were all his friends. He didn't let strangers in the house. There would be times that his friends showed up with others and he didn't allow them in. He said it was his home and you were here. He'd stop them at the door."

"So it had to be someone he knew."

"Dominique, what happened? Your mother told me what you thought happened. Are you sure it's not just a dream? Maybe you've had problems with men and it's mixed with your childhood in some way."

"I don't have problems with men." She answered thinking that she never really had a relationship with any man for more than a few dates. She didn't feel close enough to anyone. Boat was different. She didn't have a relationship to compare him to and she didn't think about it until now. "No, I've had the same dream since my childhood. This man entered my room and got closer and closer."

"And he touches you? Does he penetrate you in the dream? We would have known if you had been molested. There would have been some evidence of a grown man violating you as a child. You would have cried out, I'm sure. How did he get you not to scream?"

Viola's bluntness caught her off guard. Yet, she felt answering may help. "I don't know, that's why I want to be hypnotized in that rom."

The doorbell rang startling the women. Viola got up to answer the door. Claudia took the time to whisper to Dominique.

"Do you detect a bit of guilt?"

"Yes, I do. My mother has that same defensive response to my comments and questions."

Their conversation ended as Westlene entered the room. She bent to hug Dominique and smiled hello as Claudia introduced herself.

"So, have you found out anything else?"

"No, I haven't. We were just talking about what Ms. Viola may have remembered."

Westlene took out her pen and pad. She was sure that she would be writing in her journal about the Preston's and her part in helping Dominique through her sleeping disorder. She had diagnosed it as emotional and psychological trauma, which would explain the transition from childhood to adulthood with no changes.

Nothing had been done to help Dominique through her traumatic event. The doctor was more than certain they would get answers to the problem being in the house where the trauma took place.

"Well, if you don't mind Viola, can I call you by your first name?" The doctor asked as she pulled out a chair. She placed her pad on the table and crossed her legs.

"No, I don't mind. I was just telling Dommi that I wouldn't know who would do such a thing. It certainly wasn't done while I was here. Dominique, you can't believe I would allow someone to do that."

"Viola, you must understand. No one is here to blame you or anyone else. Dominique wants these answers so her spirit will rest at night. She has held on to this fear of resting. It was then that an intruder stepped into her room. Maybe it was more than once, we don't know and it is that she can't remember. She needs this to move on."

"Her mother worked nights. On those nights I was here until five or six in the morning. Once I was sure her mother was leaving her job I would leave. The hospital is only blocks away. A fifteen minute ride at the most. Her father would have gone to bed most mornings. No one else would be here. Now there were times when Brenda wouldn't call for me and Zeke would watch her. Never when she worked, but maybe if she went to the store or to the church, Zeke didn't know she went to the church. It was our secret. She would tell him she was going to get doughnuts or cake for desert and go to the early service. Zeke didn't care too much for Pastor Turner. Her being in the church or around him caused plenty of arguments. Anyway, he'd watch Dominique if she said she had errands to run."

Westlene looked at Dominique who seemed to be taking it all in and weighing the odds of who would have been in the house at those times.

"Do you remember those times; times when your father was home with you and no one else?"

"No, I can't remember and I don't remember doughnuts or cake. My mother baked a lot. I don't remember her bringing in any. I remember my father being annoyed about the church but I don't quite remember why.

Strange, my mother never took me with her to the church until after my father died."

"Maybe Kendall can shed light on who may have been here. He and your father were close. No one was closer to Zeke than Kendall and Dean. If Kendall doesn't know then I don't know who would. He should be here shortly." Viola sat back in her chair. She had nothing else to say. "If your mother doesn't want to even talk about it, I don't see how we'll get any answers."

"Dean, he's the one in jail that owned the bar?" Dominique was trying to match names with faces she hadn't seen in years

"Yes, your father was a customer there, as we all were at one time. I even worked there." Viola watched Westlene out of the corner of her eyes.

Dominique looked from Viola to Westlene before she continued. "I remember my mother yelling at him about that bar. Not that I remember how that argument started but I remember his name. I don't remember what Kendall looks like. Isn't he Mr. Randall's brother?"

"I don't know why you don't remember him. He was here all the time. Like I said he and your father were close." Westlene had enough information to lead her client into her past.

"So, do you want to get started? Have you been upstairs at all?"

Dominique didn't answer. Claudia stood waiting to help her friend to her feet. Westlene gathered her belongings as Viola led the way.

Sixty-three

Viola showed them the three bedrooms that were converted for the use of the children in The Neighbor's House. Dominique deliberately lingered behind. She felt as though she was walking through a dream. Each room took her into the past.

As they stood in what had been her parent's bedroom she saw the room as it had been when she was a child. The smell of her mother's perfume took over her senses and brought a smile to her face.

The doorbell rang the three women turned toward the stairs. Viola excused herself saying it had to be Kendall. They would remain downstairs while Westlene and Dominique had the session. Claudia continued to look around the room ignoring her separation from the group. She walked into the room where Dominique's fears came to light and suddenly felt unwelcomed. She returned to the hall where Dominique and Westlene were standing.

"Uh, if you don't mind I'll wait in this room, I'll be just fine in here." She noticed Dominique's inquisitive stare.

"I'd just rather wait in this room. You two go on. Viola is downstairs if I need anything. I don't think I should be in the middle of the hypnosis, you know."

"I know you sound scared. It's okay, wait where you like." Dominique made light of Claudia's obvious fear.

Claudia didn't hesitate. She went into the room and began searching the shelves for a book. Westlene and Dominique went into what had been her old bedroom to get started.

Kendall entered the house and quickly closed the door. Viola took his coat and offered him a seat in the kitchen.

"I've got some coffee brewing, you want a cup?"

"Yes, it is getting cold out there. Did they show up?"

"They're upstairs. You were right, Dominique thinks she was raped and we knew about it." She poured his coffee and handed him the cup.

"So what is she doing with this doctor?" Kendall stirred the sugar and milk slowly. His question was more of a thought but he did want to hear what they told Viola they hoped to accomplish.

"She wanted to be hypnotized. I don't know Kendall but if that girl was really violated here in this house, where was I?"

"Hmm," he said as he sipped the hot coffee. "I don't know. I sure hope it wasn't a night I was here."

"What does that mean? Do you think it could have been while we were here?"

"Viola, you and I are saying it didn't happen when we were here right? Well when, when did it happen? Zeke wasn't the type to talk much about what went on. If you weren't there, he sure wouldn't tell you who was. I don't know, I stayed drunk, high and looking for more. Randall said that himself. I talked to him and my mother. They both said my story was vague. I'm here to find out if it was me."

"You, you think you could have touched that child? Aww… Kendall, no don't say that."

"Viola, I'm not saying I did it, but my mother and brother are right. I don't know what happened the night of the murder. I can't remember much about those times other than getting drunk and high. I did like young women and well you know Dean always had young girls. I don't want to live with the thought that I molested my friend's daughter. I also want Brenda to think better of me. I'm here for Dominique to tell me something."

"Well that's why she's here. She can't go on, or so she claims, without knowing." Viola passed the plate of pastries for Kendall to take his choice.

Westlene made herself comfortable in the rocking chair that sat near the closet. She suggested they get another chair from the room across the hall. Dominique sat on the large cedar toy chest that was sitting in front the only window in the room. She turned her body the length of the chest to rest her leg. She laid the crutch on the floor near her. There were large throw pillows assorted in color stacked in the corner.

"I think these pillows will give you some comfort. Let me help you." Westlene got a few of the pillows and put them behind Domique's back. She eased back and smiled. The make shift comfort was more than she expected when they entered the room.

"I guess they use these pillows for story time. They're comfortable; I'm good. Where do we start?"

"Dominique, I hope you will be comfortable. It looks like you are cramped. As I told you, you must be comfortable, relaxed."

"I understand. It's funny I keep remembering small things. The smell of my parent's room — that room across the hall was theirs. I didn't go in the bathroom, not much they could have changed there. This room is different"

Westlene let her ramble. She recognized Dominique's need to erase her fears. She talked about her room, pointing to spots where her possessions once sat. Westlene began to hum softly. Dominique recognized the tune and felt her tension fading.

"Sit back Dommi, close your eyes and relax. Tell me more about your room and Viola reading to you." The doctor seemed to be singing the words softly.

"I don't remember a lot of the stories. I loved Alice In Wonderland, you know the persistent Rabbit and the Queen of Hearts."

"What about your mother or father, what did they read to you?"

"My mother would read stories from the bible. I had a picture bible growing up. She would choose from it and read. My father," she hesitated as though she was lost in her thought, "My father didn't read to me."

"The nights Viola wasn't here, it was just you and your father. Did he tuck you in and—"

"He always had company. They played cards for hours."

"What do you hear from your room? Can you hear them talking, the music, can you hear the laughter?"

Dominique nodded her head and continued describing the sounds. "My father is bidding. They're playing the game they play every week. They're smoking; my mother doesn't like the smell it leaves. She'll be upset when she comes home. I can hear the chairs moving, a hand is over."

Dominique eyes began to tighten as though she was frightened to open them.

Westlene whispered, "What's wrong? What is it my child?"

A tear runs down her face. "The stairs are creaking. They're coming up the stairs. I heard them tell the others they were going to use the bathroom."

"Who is it? Do you see the faces?"

"No, my eyes are closed tight. I want them to think I am sleeping." She whispers back clenching her teeth. Dominique became still holding herself and crying softly. "He's standing in the doorway. I can smell him."

The doorbell rang causing Westlene to listen intently at the voices below. Dominique sat up and looked around the room as though she was lost. She took a deep breath as the tears ran down her face. She could hear her mother's voice coming from downstairs. Westlene watched her reaction. It was though she was still in a hypnotic state.

Dominique whispered with her eyes still closed tightly, "My mother is home he won't come in the room now he'll have to go downstairs."

Westlene listened to the voices coming from downstairs. She recognized Brenda and Viola's voice but wasn't familiar with the male voice. Brenda's agitated voice increased in volume as she questioned his reasons for being in the house. She could hear him trying to give Brenda an answer. Dominique appeared to be hearing a different conversation.

"I've got to stop him, he'll hit her again. No! No! Stop it!"

Westlene turned her attention to the screams of her client. Her eyes were still closed and the tears never stopped.

"I'll stop him. He'll hurt her."

Brenda's voice was now loud enough for Westlene to clearly hear the argument from the kitchen.

"Viola, you were right, I knew. I knew about the filth, the scum, the sluts and whores Zeke brought into my home when I was at work. I knew about the nights they played cards and wallowed in my bed, on my couch on the floor pleasing their lustful passions. Yeah, Kendall you loved me, you loved me enough to watch as they took turns at night with my child. He told it all that very night. What were you doing upstairs that night Kendall? Did you get tired of watching him touch my child? He told me how you sought the younger girls. I ought to have your ass locked up. All I want to know is did you touch my child? You have the nerve to show up asking questions? You perverted bastard! Did you touch my child?"

Westene looked at Dominique who was suddenly quiet, as though she too needed to hear the answer.

"Brenda, listen, listen to me. I didn't go in the room with Zeke and Dean. They never let me in the room. I tried to stop him many nights. They said the child wouldn't sleep. Zeke would go upstairs and read to her. I don't know what Dean did. They'd close the door. I'd knock on it 'cause they would be holding up the game and people was getting upset down here. They never opened the door." Kendall began to cry. "Brenda, believe me I didn't know"

"What the hell was you upstairs for on the night he was killed?"

"I went to the bathroom. There wasn't nobody here but me and Zeke. Dommi was sleeping in her room the door was opened as I passed. I heard you come in and I froze. I knew you wouldn't like it, you know, seeing me in your house after you warned us. That was the night after you told all of us never darken your door again. I guess I was scared cause after Dominique came out of your bedroom with the gun I couldn't move. She walked to the stairs with it like she didn't see me in the hall. I never heard the shot, Brenda I didn't remember all that happened. I wanted you to know I never touched your baby. I didn't want to believe Zeke or Dean did either." Kendall couldn't believe his memory of the night was finally clear.

"I shot him. I stopped him. He won't hurt us anymore." Dominique's anger was building as she broke down crying. "My father yelled at my mother cursing and bragging about what they did. He told my mother that he watched as that man touched me. He said couldn't bring himself to touch me. He wouldn't let them penetrate me 'cause I was so young. So he sat in the chair and masturbated as he watched. He'd talk softly to me afterward, promising he wouldn't let them hurt me. They'd put their penis on my leg, each time getting closer and closer. They'd leave me with my father after they ejaculated on me. He'd clean me up and tell me I was such a good girl."

Westlene had heard enough. She walked over to Dominique and embraced her as she cried loudly. The yelling from downstairs had turned into silence. The house was quiet.

Sixty-four

Claudia met them in the hall. The stairs squeaked as they helped Dominique, who was still crying down the stairs. Viola met them at the base of the stairway.

"Is she okay?" Viola asked as Brenda and Kendall came from the kitchen asking questions.

"Baby, are you alright?"

"Is there anything we can do?" Kendall was unsure what he would be able to do. Brenda cut her eyes in his direction, but he ignored her curt look.

"She needs water, please just a glass of water." Westlene sat her in a chair at the kitchen table and helped her prop the glass to her lips.

"Each of you need to talk, maybe a session of counseling to get you through this would be helpful. This has been a traumatic event in each of your lives. I know, I know Mrs. Preston you are not a believer in this but you must understand what your daughter has gone through. All her life she has had a fear of remembering this event. It must be talked about in its entirety. The two of you have been abused and until you talk about it, it will haunt you."

"Dominique killed her father?" Claudia heard the yelling from the kitchen. She had been in the hall listening as the voices increased in volume.

"Yes, she did. I lied and told the police it was an intruder. They didn't think anything of it and never pursued an investigation. I never told anyone the truth. Kendall never mentioned it and shortly after he moved. I didn't want the nightmares I had to become my daughter's. She told me many times about her nightmares, the shadows, and the man's voice. Kendall, for years I thought it was you. I hated you for it. I wanted to believe that my husband was drunk that night and lied about what he had done. He never mentioned Dean's name. I knew in my heart it was you. I prayed for you to die. Then when you returned, I prayed that I would have the strength not to kill you."

Dominique sat still, unable to speak or move. Westlene massaged her shoulder as she offered her another sip of water.

"Dominique, I am sorry. I didn't want you to go to jail, or whatever punishment they would give you. I thought not telling you would be best. I didn't know what the police would do." Brenda pulled a chair close to her daughter. She sat down and reached for her hands. "Please forgive me."

Her daughter didn't answer. She held her mother's hand in silence. The reality of it all was overwhelming. The tears rolled down her face as the thoughts of her tormenting dreams crossed her mind. For the first time she saw herself pulling the trigger. She could see it all. Her father laughing at her mother as she cursed him for all he had done. Zeke told his wife about the money he collected night after night for the nasty sex acts performed in her home.

Dominique held the heavy gun up and pointed it. Her mother screamed "no" as she pulled the trigger her father once told her would push the bullet out of the barrel. The scene repeated in her mind in slow motion. The bullet hit him in his chest after he turned to see who was in the doorway. The nightmares would finally come to an end. Her father was dead. She saw his body lying in a pool of blood. She dropped the gun. She turned without a word or a tear. She walked to the top of the stairs in a daze. There she sat as Kendall rushed by her and saw his friend in a pool of blood. Brenda never noticed him dart past them and out the front door. She was holding Zeke crying and rocking while she mumbled to God in prayer.

Brenda had her visions too. As they sat at the table she told what happened. She watched her husband fall. Her daughter had done what she didn't have the nerve to do. The gun was in their room. She warned Zeke about showing the weapon to their daughter. A warning he ignored. He had shown the child how to load the gun. Dominique was anxious to fire the weapon and he promised her she would know when the time was right. Brenda picked up the gun and hid it in the floor board where she kept a stash of money. She checked for his pulse and waited before calling 911. She wanted to be sure he was dead. A faint pulse meant they would revive him. She wanted the man she loved, the father of her child, the perverted molester, dead. She went to the front door and opened it. She would wait for the police to ask her why the door was opened.

"I just got home. I put the key in the door and was pushed forcefully by an intruder. He put the gun to my head and walked me into the dining room where my husband was sitting. They argued and the intruder pushed me to the floor and shot my husband." The officer's listened and took notes. "No, I don't know who he was or what he wanted. No, after he shot him he ran. No, I don't know if my husband owed him anything."

Pastor Turner arrived. Brenda called him or thought she had after she made the call to 911. She asked him if he would check on her daughter. Kendall came in with the police and the EMT's as the Pastor went upstairs to get Dominique. He brought her down and went out the side entrance.

When everyone left, Kendall joined Brenda where she stood staring at the bloodstained floor. He secured the front door and helped her scrub away the scene of the murder. Brenda retrieved the gun and gave it to Kendall. He nodded and told her not to worry about a thing. Kendall shook his head as his memory painted the picture as she spoke. He didn't know how close he was to his own death that night.

Viola gave both Brenda and Dominique tissues to dry their tears. Kendall walked out of the kitchen as he realized he had been tormented with the murder as well. Westlene was right they needed to talk; counseling would help them get over the trauma.

Westlene sat with them, listening as she was trained to do. She explained her services were available if they felt it would do them any good. Brenda could only smile. She didn't want to admit the Voodoo doctor had been right. Westlene nodded towards her returning the gesture. They understood they would need each other to put the past to rest. There would be no cause for the police to re-open the case. Zeke was dead and so were the nightmares his death caused.

They all agreed to the counseling sessions. Westlene told them to call her office and she would set an appointment time and date. Kendall and Brenda went into the conference room to speak alone after the doctor left.

"Kendall I am so sorry. I've held this anger for years and I was so sure that you stayed with me and cleaned that night because you were guilty."

Kendall didn't reply. The tears welled in his eyes as she continued.

"I guess I was blessed to have Viola and you in my life. There's no telling what may have happened if you weren't there."

"I wasn't. Look what did happen. Look at the damage it has done to all of us. Brenda, I know it has been years but Dean violated your daughter. He's looking to be released. I don't know what they've got on him this time but it involves young girls too. I may be wrong but I think you and I should talk with the authorities. He shouldn't be let out."

"But then we'd have to tell the truth about the murder. Dominique would be in some kind of trouble I'm sure. If not, I would be for lying. No, no Kendall I don't want that."

"I don't want him to get away with what he did. One way or another he's gonna have to pay."

"Well God has a way of making things right. I truly believe that. Are you really going to attend the sessions?"

"Yes, I am." Kendall tapped her on her hand and she held his tightly.

"Then God is already working it out."

They returned to the kitchen to say their goodbyes and promises to keep in touch. They hugged; thanked each other and Brenda said a prayer asking forgiveness for them all. Kendall responded with a heartfelt amen but the thought about Dean's actions lingered. He wasn't sure the sessions or prayer would rid his thoughts of revenge. He would need both.

Other Novels by Nanette M. Buchanan

Family Secrets Lies and Alibi's

A Different Kind of Love

Bruised Love

Skeletons Beyond The Closed Door

Gossip Line

Bonded Betrayal

Scattered Pieces

The Perfect Side Piece

The Hustler's Touch

Duplicity

The Corner Pew

Purchase Your Copy Today

www.NanetteMBuchanan.com

Books are available in Kindle, Nook and other ebook formats